DEADLY DISCOVERIES:

A DR. WALLER FORENSIC

THRILLER

By

R. NOBLE

DEDICATION

This is dedicated to my mother for lending me her strength, my sister for lending me her fearlessness, and my dog for lending me his companionship. In no particular order of course.

TABLE OF CONTENTS

CHAPTER 1

Crickets chanted, begging for rain in the sprawling wilderness, as the lights from the rooms at the secluded Adirondack Resort and Spa slowly blinked out of existence one by one. Besides the hum of nature, the valley lay eerily quiet as the guests settled in for the night. The night desk clerk, a college kid filling in for the summer, watched from his station as the guests made their way back to their rooms, all the outdoor activities for the day having concluded as well as the dinner services. This was *the* resort that many from New York City would come to visit, especially during the summer months, if they wanted a "wilderness" getaway. With 5-star accommodations and an all-inclusive menu of culinary delights and rustic outdoor activities they were not really roughing it but working here paid the bills, so he kept his judgment to a minimum and to himself.

The job did have some perks, however. Celebrities wanting a private getaway or a wealthy husband who wanted a fling with their mistresses graced the secluded location quite often. Tonight, for instance, he watched as one particularly leggy blond sashayed by on the arm of an older man whispering into his ear causing the grown man to giggle as they stopped to look at the listing of tomorrow's activities mounted in the lobby display case. Man, how did he get to be like that guy? Obviously, he didn't have the money to attract that kind of female companionship but he could aspire to it. Maybe the gentleman would be willing to give him some tips if he asked politely. Heck, maybe the guy would give him a large monetary tip if he actively helped in protecting his anonymity.

Distracted, he didn't notice the angry-looking elderly woman in a housecoat who had sidled up to the front desk and was currently staring daggers at him and ringing the front desk bell aggressively.

He sighed deeply and addressed the woman with as much

professionalism as he could muster so late at night. She went on and on complaining that she had called the front desk ten times, which was false because the phone hadn't rung once, and that she required extra pillows due to sciatica or some other ailment he was not really paying attention to. He assured her he would have housekeeping bring her an extra pillow which she seemed to accept and watched as she waddled away without so much as a thank you revealing the next guest in line.

It was a sharply dressed man wishing to check out. He was wearing gloves, which was weird because it was the middle of summer, but rich people were often eccentric. Checking out at such a late hour was odd as well, but not completely uncommon. They got all types that came through the resort's doors, so he did his job and obliged him. He inquired if the man needed any assistance with his luggage but noticing he only had a small briefcase with him assumed that wouldn't be the case. The man paid in cash, which was odd but again not out of place for the eccentric people who frequented the resort, and left briskly entering what looked like a car service that had been waiting at the lobby entrance and drove away.

Having dealt with all the customers, the desk clerk scanned around the lobby to see if the man and the blond bombshell were still around and upon not seeing them allowed himself a sigh lamenting that he had missed watching the blond walk away down the hall. He glanced back at his computer screen to see if there were any other outstanding tasks he would begrudgingly have to complete when he found that the screen had gotten fuzzy.

After cursing the general manager's refusal to update the computer since the stone age, he clicked furiously trying to clear the screen, and even went so far as to give it a few good hits to see if that righted it. As he went to bend down to do the tried and true unplug-it-and-plug-it-back-in method, he felt a little light-headed and noticed his surroundings had become a bit blurry as well. The late shift must

2

be getting to him. Too many hours awake and not enough energy drinks. He rubbed his eyes to wipe away the fatigue but found his vision was still fuzzy. It was then that he noticed a raised red sore the size of a dime on his hand. When did he get that? Did that ornery older lady literally give him hives? His musing was abruptly interrupted by a scream echoing down one of the halls to his left causing him to hit his head on the desk as he tried to stand. This was quickly followed by another screech from the hallway to his right. He went to investigate the occurrence but only made it a few steps from his station. Suddenly, air was evading him, and his breath stalled as he slowly sank to the floor gasping like a fish out of water which was quickly followed by an enveloping darkness and then nothingness.

**

I awoke with a start. It was that same nightmare again. Faceless forms surrounded me. Pointing at me. Accusing me. I would scream 'I'm sorry' and 'I didn't know' repeatedly until one amorphous blob would ungulate and form into a face I was intimately familiar with. He would briefly grace me with a charmingly disarming smile before strangling me with cold bony figures as I did nothing to fend him off. Luckily for me, the alarm had interrupted my restless slumber dragging me back to the land of the living.

"Get yourself together Elizabeth" I stated for no one's benefit but my own while wiping the sweat that had formed on my brow. One notable side effect of living by oneself for as long as I have is that you start talking to yourself more and more.

"There's a fine line between insanity and genius" I yawned, stretching and reluctantly rolling over onto my elbow to grab my phone to see what time it was. I groaned my displeasure into my pillow. Another first day of work. Hooray for me. You would think that after going through this so many times it would become second nature but here I was dreading yet another one. There were lots of perks to being a forensic science consultant for the FBI. You got to travel, take on interesting cases, and pick up some new tools and techniques, but there was a downside. It meant meeting new people, my least favorite thing in the world. New coworkers always had an onslaught of questions and I was an introvert by birth and by design. They started out innocent enough along the lines of 'How do you like the town' or 'how was your last assignment'. But then they slowly get personal like 'why don't you have a boyfriend 'or 'why don't you ever talk about your family or friends'.

I *loathed* personal questions with a passion. I liked my solitude and keeping my personal life, well, personal. It's one of the reasons why I chose the profession that I did. I wanted to assist in solving crimes so that innocent people didn't have to suffer and those who did bad things were punished. It helped ease the guilt but never quite washed it away. I had my reasons, and they were my own. Personal attachments were diametrically opposed to my goals and if I could prevent another tragedy from starting in the first place even better.

"No attachments," I said aloud, again, for no one's ears but my own. "Maybe I should get a dog or something." At least I wouldn't seem so crazy if I was talking to another living thing. I surveyed the apartment and determined it was too small for a pet, I would be moving on eventually anyways, and pets are literally attachment given life. Although the apartment was small, it had character. It was on the third floor and came fully furnished as I had requested. The entrance was welcoming with a warm ambiance, furnished with a vintage rug and a small console table.

The living area was compact but inviting, with a well-worn sofa that begged you to sink into its cushions. Soft, muted colors on the walls create a serene atmosphere, and strategically placed art added a nice touch. In the corner there was a small bookshelf which I planned on filling up as soon as I made it through the first week or so and a soft reading chair, creating a perfect nook for quiet moments of

4

relaxation. Honestly, it was one of the selling points for me when I had decided on the apartment.

The kitchen, though small, was efficient and organized. Open shelving displayed a collection of mismatched vintage dishes and glassware which I thought added character to the space. A small dining table would serve nicely as a multifunctional area for meals and as a makeshift workspace if needed.

The bedroom was a tranquil retreat with a comfortable bed dressed in soft linens and a few carefully chosen accent pillows. Limited floor space encourages simplicity, with just enough room for a nightstand and a small dresser. The only thing that ruined the charming apartment at the moment were all my moving boxes laying stacked in the living room untouched. It was a nice find, but the real reason I chose it was its location. It was close enough to the new Field Office I would call home for the next few months. A quick search confirmed it was in a location that had a decent number of restaurants which would deliver. I always found cooking for one a chore, so takeout was my go-to for weeknights.

I stretched again, finally gaining the motivation to get out of bed, and decided a bit of caffeine was needed to get me going. I put the kettle on the stove and examined my hiring papers. The position was straight forward enough. I would be running the Albany, NY FBI Field Offices Forensic Lab while the current Forensic Scientist was on maternity leave. It was a smaller field office than I was used to, and the complexity of the cases seemed low, meaning I could finally catch up on some recent publications on forensic techniques that I had been eying. I was looking forward to a change of pace. It appeared I would also have an intern which meant I could have them assist in some of the work which could be very useful, especially for the menial tasks.

My thoughts drifted back to my own days as a graduate student.

The excitement of finally getting into the labs, the pressure of testing my hypothesis, bouncing theories and ideas off colleagues, *and* the thrill of being proven correct. Slowly, my happy thoughts were invaded by what came shortly after some of the happiest times of my life. The lies, the betrayal, the death. The kettle whistled loudly, causing me to jump and pulling me from my musings as I hurried over to take it off the stove.

After drinking the tea faster than I should have, burning my tongue in the process, I quickly got dressed and finished getting ready in the bathroom. I looked into the mirror. For being in my 30s, I still managed to somehow retain a youthful glow only needing to apply some tinted moisturizer and some mascara before heading out into public. I smoothed my long brown naturally wavy hair into a bun. Having long hair in a lab was risky business so I always opted to keep it out of the way. I took another look in the mirror thinking that was as good as it was going to get, grabbed my bag, and made my way to the door.

"Here we go again," I said audibly, cursing the increase of my talking to myself, shutting the door to my apartment behind me, and making my way to the newest chapter of my life.

CHAPTER 2

"Are you Dr. Elizabeth Waller?" I heard a masculine voice call from behind me just as I had signed in and got my badge.

"That's me," I answered, turning around to find a specimen of a man looking none too pleased to see me. Curious, I thought, considering I was sure we had never met, and I would have remembered if we had.

"I'm Sam Han, special agent in charge of this field office."

"I'm Elizabeth Waller," I said politely, putting my hand out to engage with the social customs of introductions when he interrupted me.

"Your resume is incomplete," he said in an accusatory tone.

"Pardon me?" I responded, putting my unreciprocated handshake away. Obviously not a gentleman to leave a lady hanging like that.

"Your resume" he continued, stepping forward to close the distance between us, his tone suggesting I was an inconvenience that had to be dealt with "only covers the last few years and only lists your most recent education and nothing more."

Frustratingly enough he had a point. One that most people didn't care about or didn't look hard enough to notice. He obviously got to the rank he had based his attention to detail, but this wasn't my first rodeo and I was getting scarily good at deflecting a question I couldn't or didn't want to answer.

I took a closer look at my new nemesis. He stood about six feet tall with a well-defined, athletic build. His posture was impeccable, radiating confidence and an air of authority. His facial features were chiseled, with sharp cheekbones, a strong jawline, and expressive, almond-shaped eyes that revealed a depth of intelligence and determination. His jet black hair was meticulously styled, adding to his polished appearance, and he maintained a clean-shaven look that accentuated his handsome features. Despite his stern exterior, his lips held a subtle curve that hinted at a reserved charm, leaving an air of mystery about him.

So he was handsome, the literal definition of tall, dark, and handsome, if you're into that kind of thing. His face looked as if it was chiseled out of stone and at this moment the steadfast and unmovable expression of displeasure he was emoting seemed to verify this. Glancing downward from his unyielding face I saw his arms were crossed, further indicating he was not in the slightest bit happy to see me, which had a secondary effect of displaying his toned arms and chest. His closeness and his obvious examination of me stirred something inside of me that hadn't been awakened in some time. I immediately decided I didn't like it. On the other hand, it might be nice to have some eye candy around, and nothing more, for this assignment. I nicknamed him Special Agent Eye Candy, part of my personal no attachments protocol, and moved on. It was time to put my carefully honed deflection skills to work.

"Do you interrogate all new employees that walk through the door or is it just my lucky day?"

"Only the suspicious ones." He answered in a low tone. I could feel him assessing me but knew that my body language would give nothing away as he continued his inquisition. "You were appointed to this position by Executive Assistant Director Keene were you not?"

"I *applied* and interviewed for this position and had a recommendation from the Executive Assistant Director so no I was not *given* the position as you seem to be implying."

He shuffled, obviously not liking that I had called him out on his line of questioning. It was my first day and I was probably not making a very good impression or any friends for that matter, but he seemed to have already formed an opinion of me which I didn't think I could further tarnish by not fitting into the mold he was trying to press me into.

"What is your relationship with the Executive Assistant Director?" Special Agent Eye Candy continued. This is exactly what I don't like about personal questions.

"I'm pretty sure I don't have to answer and that HR would agree with me, but I have worked for him in my previous assignments for the FBI." This guy was starting to get on my nerves so I kept it polite but short. "Am I free to go, Special Agent?" This was fun and all, but I had a job to do, a lab to assess and I was done with the line of questioning.

He glared, which I translated from Alpha Male to mean yes for now, and I went on my way to find the labs. I could tell he was following me down the hall, so I turned around to confront him.

"Are you tailing me now Special Agent Han?" He seemed surprised that I had once again called him out on his lackluster behavior, his eyebrows furrowing, but he quickly recovered. His face morphed into what I assumed was his most disarming smile, but it felt unnatural and put me even more on edge. He was obviously trying to switch tactics, attempting charm instead of intimidation.

"How did you find the move from California? Are you and your husband settling in?"

I smiled. It was a good try and I had to give him credit. He was persistent and attempted to be sneaky at concealing his line of questioning while subtly indicating he had done his research on me. He was skilled, but I had obviously had more practice.

"Why, Special Agent Han," I responded coyly. "If you wanted to know if I was seeing anyone you could have just asked. Very bold of you, this only being my first day and our first-time meeting. I'm flattered." Without looking to see his reaction I continued to make my way down the hall with a smile on my face. The lack of footsteps behind me indicated I had won this round. After that awkward welcoming party of one, I was looking forward to the quiet solitude of the lab.

***

"OMG, Dr. Waller, I am so excited to meet you! I'm Nina!" The young woman who I assumed was my new intern squealed as I entered the lab, taking my hand and shaking it more forcefully than I thought her tiny arms could muster. She was a petite thing with platinum blond hair and wore an outfit that looked more suited for clubbing than for lab work.

"The other manager wouldn't let me touch anything!" she lamented with a pout. "She was all, 'Don't touch this, don't smell that, you can't put food in that fridge, it's for samples,' but you look cool."

Little did she know how uncool I was. Of all the words in the dictionary, cool was definitely not one you would use to describe me. There went my hopes of finding respite in the lab. I nodded politely indicating that the very one-sided conversation was over, and made my way over to my desk. I put down my things and logged onto the new laptop and ensured I had access to the relevant programs.

Having been accosted by the intern I hadn't yet taken the time to take in my new workspace. The equipment was more advanced than in the previous lab where I had been stationed which was a pleasant surprise. The shelves seemed stocked, all the glassware and solutions put in their proper place, which made me respect the forensic scientist on leave. The lab space was enclosed in all glass making me feel as if I was some exotic sea creature on exhibition at an aquarium. Even the walls facing the outside of the building were mostly glass putting the finely manicured lawn on full display.

I was not a fan of feeling like I was on display, but I was confident in my work and it meant I could keep an eye on the ever-changing New York weather and an even closer eye on Nina. The facility was a bit from the main gate of the field office so any cases of wandering eyes from the public were minimal and worth getting some natural sunlight during work hours for once. Lab work had the unfortunate repercussion of causing you to lose touch with the outside world when a lack of windows was involved, your eyes staring down a microscope for hours on end.

As I continued to scan the room, I made the mistake of looking over at my new energetic intern. Apparently, my dismissal was far too subtle for her, and she was desperately trying to make eye contact to continue the conversation. I tried my best to ignore her, but I could feel the off-putting sensation of her staring at me, so I obliged her.

"Yes, Nina. How can I help you?"

"So, you must be really smart to be a consultant, right?" She asked, biting her lip and looking unsure of herself.

"You have to be versed in the various aspects of forensic sciences to be a consultant and demonstrate a high level of proficiency in the field," I hoped that would be the end of the conversation.

"So that's a yes?" she answered with far too much optimism so early in the day. Obviously, the conversation would not be ending anytime soon. I made a note to pick up some Tylenol on the way back to my apartment, I could feel a tension headache starting to form.

"Correct," I answered with a stern tone hoping that the conversation was over. I glanced back down to the computer noting that my session had timed out. I had just made it past the login screen of the program homepage when I noticed Nina had silently crept closer to my desk.

"Can I help you, Nina?" I was trying to keep the annoyance out of my tone and failing miserably.

"It's just that"- she started while looking down at the floor and fidgeting with the hem on her skirt "-most consultants have doctorates like yourself which means they went through a Ph D. program and when I Googled you, I found some publications from the last couple of years, like the Donovan Case, epic by the way, but I couldn't find your Ph D. thesis."

Well, crap. She had me there. She wasn't as much of a bubblehead as I had originally thought. Maybe this assignment wasn't going to be as easy as I had initially thought it was going to be with Special Agent Eye Candy and now Detective Barbie digging into my past. She must have detected my unease as she began to backpedal.

"You don't have to answer. I've been told I ask too many personal questions. I mean, I was just curious and thought that maybe you published and then got married and changed your last name and that's why? Are you married? I don't see a ring. Oh, sorry that was another personal question, I'm sorry." The second time I was asked about my relationship status in the span of a few hours. New record. She stopped her tirade and then sheepishly made her way back to her desk muttering and chastising herself all the way. I remembered when I was like her. Wide-eyed, innocent, curious, thinking the world would open and share its secrets with me just because I asked. I sighed, realizing that I would probably regret my next actions, but I continued against my better judgment.

"How about this Nina, you can ask as many questions as you want, but that doesn't necessarily mean I'm going to answer them, so if I don't you will drop the topic. Deal?"

"Deal!" she squealed, opening her mouth to no doubt begin her barrage of questioning at this very moment.

"Starting tomorrow, Nina." She smiled, miming that her lips were zipped shut, and went back to her own work. It was evident I was going to need something stronger than Tylenol if I was going to get through these next couple of months.

***

"Something's off about her," I muttered, not realizing I had said it out loud.

I was Samuel Han for fuck's sake. When I asked people questions, they normally had enough sense to answer them. Nothing about me gave off the air of accepting a dismissal.

"What's off about her?" Benny muttered with half a donut lodged in his mouth. "Does she have a weird mole or something on her face 'cause that can be removed so I can work with that."

"What? No."

I shook my head at my comrade. Of course Benny would focus on her looks. He'd chase anything that was female and had a heartbeat. He really shouldn't be judging anyone's looks as right after agent training he had let himself go a bit. He was shorter than me and had short brown hair that seemed to always look greasy, I'm hoping from the massive amounts of hair gel he used. As to *her* looks, they weren't anything remarkable on the surface. Her features were unassuming but created a soft and approachable profile. Her eyes, though not enhanced with striking colors, conveyed a depth of emotion and wisdom. In terms of style, she opted for simplicity over extravagance almost like she was trying to downplay her figure. She didn't wear elaborate makeup or a fancy hairstyle, but her understated elegance shined through. Honestly, in a world often dazzled by the superficial, her simple but beautiful presence was a breath of fresh air.

Her looks were not what I should be focusing on at the moment

13

and I cursed Benny under my breath for making me mentally go off course. I couldn't get distracted. Something was definitely off about this woman based on my gut feelings and they had never let me down before.

"So what's got your panties in a bunch then?" Benny asked, staring at the box of donuts scoping out his options for round two.

"Well, her resume has some pretty glaring gaps of time in it. I couldn't find anything in any of the FBI databases until 5 years ago, she was evasive when I asked her about her work history and her personal life. Also, Executive Assistant Director Keene personally hired her. Something about her just seems off."

"So you think she's banging Director Keene? I mean she doesn't sound like the homewrecker type." Benny answered unhelpfully.

"I don't have any proof but..."

"I call dibs then!" Benny yelled, cutting me off, shoving an additional donut in his mouth, and sprinting off to accost his new prey.

I replayed my interactions with our new Forensic Scientist. She deftly dodged every personal question I asked and didn't seem flustered by my line of questioning at all. She even managed to catch me off balance.

"Like I would hit on her," I said with a huff to anyone who would care to listen. Women usually hit on me and not the other way around. I had a career to focus on and anything beyond a one-night stand would only serve as a distraction. Bruised ego aside, maybe I was slipping. One thing I was sure of though was that the newly appointed Dr. Waller was hiding something, and I'd be damned if I didn't get to the bottom of it.

CHAPTER 3

I had barely scratched the surface of looking through the catalog of supplies and equipment in the lab when there was a knock on the glass wall right next to my desk causing me to launch into the air.

"You're a jumpy one" a man I had yet to be introduced to affirmed in the most monotone voice I had ever heard. Oh, the joys of your first day in a new job. The gift that kept on giving.

"Hello, I'm Elizabeth Waller," I said, standing and turning to muster up my most cordial introduction.

"Dominic Ortiz," he grunted and gave me a once over like he was scanning a scene for possible threats. This one at least shook the hand that I offered, giving me an opportunity to appraise him. He was the muscle of the team that much was evident and looked like he would be more at home in a ring at the WWE then at an office. His tall, broad build gave me Dwayne Johnson vibes, shaved head, and tight t-shirt included. After a moment of uncomfortable silence, the mountain that was supposedly a man began to speak. "Yeah. I know. Sam sent me to get you. We have a new case, so we need to debrief everyone before we head out to the crime scene."

"Why? Because here at the Albany Field Office, we're family." I laughed waiting for a response from my new colleague. Nothing.

"Because your name is Dominic, like Dom Toretto from the Fast and Furious? Get it?" Either he did indeed not get it or he was choosing to ignore my attempt to ingratiate myself into his favor.

"Okay-," I answered, going back to his original request. It was becoming painfully clear that the males in this office were the strong silent type and their communication skills were severely lacking. "- And what does that case briefing have to do with me?"

Usually, in these situations the Forensic Technicians go and collect the samples and bring them back to the lab, meaning I should be able to stay put. My specialty was forensic microbiology which meant I got to stay in the lab and rarely saw any field work, just like I liked it. I could already tell this Field Office was not running things the way I had become accustomed to, and I wasn't pleased about it. On the other hand, maybe they were short-staffed and needed someone who knew how to not trample all over a crime scene. Either way, I wasn't too keen on leaving the relative solitude that the lab provided me.

"Look lady," He responded, his eyes furrowing and jaw clenching. "I was told to tell you to come to the meeting so are you coming or what?"

"Well with such an eloquent invitation, how could I refuse?" I replied sweetly, earning a glare from Dominic who continued to stare at me impatiently.

"Yeah sure, Of course," I answered quickly, gathering up my laptop to jot down notes. Would I need to take notes? Did they just invite everyone to the debriefings around here? This was unlike all my other consultant jobs before. I felt unprepared, which was a sensation I was not used to feeling and was not in any way relishing. Dominic was already halfway down the hall when I gathered my things, so I hurried, attempting to catch up to him and not wanting to get lost in the maze of hallways.

I entered the conference room and noticed various members of the field office chatting and taking their seats. Not one for the spotlight, I found a chair in the back and settled in. One man in the front row turned around, obviously looking for someone, he scanned the room and once he locked eyes with me, he began to smile broadly. He proceeded to do a little "yoo-hoo" wave. All he needed was a handkerchief and he'd fit right in on a production of Oklahoma. Nope.

I was not dealing with this right now, so I pretended not to notice and glared down as if I was intensely reading something on my computer screen.

My new biggest fan, Special Agent Han, entered the room and took his place at the front podium and I watched in admiration as everyone quickly dashed to take a seat and instantly halted all conversation. He was either greatly respected or greatly feared, I thought to myself, as he brought up his first slide on the projector.

"10 hours ago, local PD received a 911 call from a woman staying at the Adirondack Resort and Spa, indicating that her partner had suddenly collapsed and was unresponsive. An additional 911 call came in shortly after from another patron from the same establishment reporting that a woman had collapsed in the hallway and seemed to be unresponsive and not breathing. When the local PD arrived, they were told of a third potential crime scene in the lobby where a hotel staff member was found dead near his station. Local PD secured the crime scenes and then due to the nature of the incident and the number of victims contacted us.

"It should be noted that all three victims were found in different areas of the hotel, one in the East Wing, one in the West Wing, and one in the main Lobby as shown on this map of the resort. Local PD interviewed witnesses at the site. According to these witness interviews, all three victims seemed to have been in good health and were not acting out of the ordinary. At this time Resort Management is cooperating with the investigation and has closed the resort down. Yes, Dominic, you have a question."

"How were the victims related?" Dominic inquired obviously not quite grasping why this case was escalated and passed on to the FBI and not the local PD.

"That's the thing. None of the witnesses recall seeing any of the victims interacting and upon the initial background check, there is no

17

obvious proof that these victims were related at all. Socioeconomic status, careers, common social circles, nothing matches up. One victim was a male having a weekend away with his mistress, the other victim was an old lady who won the weekend away at her Bridge Club, and the final victim was a male in his 20s working the night shift at the front desk."

I leaned forward in my chair. Now *this* was interesting. My interest continued to peak as I began to theorize about the case. Maybe there was something connecting the three that was missing and would be discovered with some good old-fashioned detective work. Gambling debts unpaid? Underground sex trafficking? All interesting theories but again nothing that required my particular set of skills. I once again wondered why I was here.

"Cause of death?" Dominic inquired, seemingly bored by what must be an out-of-the-ordinary case even for them. For someone who seemed like the strong silent type, he sure asked a lot of questions.

"I'm glad you asked Dominic." Sam grimaced like it was physically painful for him to say whatever it was he was about to tell the group. "The answer is *causes* of death."

"As in more than one cause of death." my new-found admirer in the front interrupted, "So you're telling me that three different people, who wouldn't be caught dead at a dinner party together, died the same night by different means."

"They died within 15 to 30 minutes of each other from causes ranging from heart failure to hemorrhaging to suffocation. It should be noted that these findings have yet to be confirmed by an autopsy and should be noted as possible and not definite causes of death. " Sam continued with more details, but I had stopped listening. This was pretty fascinating. I mean, what could cause three deaths with different symptoms almost simultaneously? Was it three different accomplices all carefully coordinating a near perfectly timed execution of their attacks? Could it be a naturally occurring virus or bacterium that thrives in that specific biodiverse area? What about a zoonotic disease that passed to a human from a deer or a fox? Was it merely just a coincidence all three had a medical emergency at the same time? No, the scientific method left no room for anything remotely close to coincidences. I was deep into my own thoughts when I heard someone calling my name.

"Dr. Waller."

"Yes, pardon?" I responded trying to pull myself back together and attempting to recenter myself back to the presentation.

"I'm not boring you, am I?" Agent Han continued, displeased by what I was sure appeared like my ambivalence.

"Oh, no, my apologies. Please continue." I slid down slightly in my chair, silently chastising myself for allowing myself to lose focus on the briefing.

"As I was saying," Sam continued, obviously annoyed that he had to repeat himself "Dominic, Benny, Dr. Waller, and myself will be traveling to the crime scene to see if we can ascertain a better idea of what happened and determine if this is murder case or simply a series of coincidences."

"No such thing," I mumbled to myself under my breath. I had literally just had that conversation with myself.

"Something you'd like to share with the rest of the room, Dr. Waller?" How the heck did Agent Han hear me? He must have the hearing of a Labrador retriever.

"I said sure thing" replying in the most counterfeit enthusiasm I could muster, giving an awkward thumbs up, which upon realizing how stupid I looked, I put away immediately. "And how far away is

19

the crime scene?" If it was close enough, we could wrap it up in a few hours and I could be home in time to finish the last chapter in the book I was currently using for some much-needed escapism.

"About an hour and a half. Is that going to be a problem?" I could tell he was losing his patience with me. The attitude dripping from his words was palpable. Oh no, how could that possibly ever be a problem? Stuck at a remote resort with my new not-so-secret admirer, Grumpy Pants, and Special Agent Eye Candy. Why would I possibly have a problem with that? It seemed as if my book was going to have to wait which was unfortunate because it was at a really exciting part.

Agent Han dismissed us from the briefing and after gathering up all the supplies I could possibly need for the scene and letting the over-excited Nina know she was to look after the lab until I returned, I made my way to the small parking garage the field office owned as I readied myself to make the trek to the crime scene which I was told was located on a mountain in the middle of the wilderness. I was looking forward to the long solo drive. I had a podcast I had been wanting to listen to, and I needed some time to center myself. I had my hand on the door handle of my car when I noticed a shadow of a man blocking the shiny visage of the vehicle. I gripped my keys between my knuckles and tensed.

"Where are you going?" I recognized that voice as the man from the front row at the debriefing. I loosened the grip on my keys and relaxed slightly as I saw him coming towards me from the other side of the garage.

"Excuse me?" I replied, arching my eyebrow to indicate I was not pleased by the line of questioning. He rubbed his neck sheepishly, realizing his approach was not being well received, and tried again.

"I mean the van that is transporting us to the crime scene is in the other parking lot. I'm Benny by the way. Benny Dowley." He stuck out his hand for a handshake which I reciprocated and went on for a little bit too long for my comfort level. After finally retrieving my appendage, I figured some clarification was due.

"I have my own form of transportation and I was given the location, so I don't need to carpool. Thanks for checking in though." I thought that would be the end of the conversation and again tried to reenter the car hoping to revel in some peace and quiet when I was interrupted yet again.

"What I mean is- "Benny continued shifting his weight from one foot to another "- is that Sam likes us all to drive together to scenes so that we can discuss the case on the way there and review any findings on the way back, hence the van. Here, let me get your pack for you, looks heavy."

I went to retort that I could very well carry my own bag when he scooped it up and started carrying it in the direction that I assumed the van was. All I could remember was all the videos I was forced to watch when I was younger from law enforcement about not getting into vans with strange people yet here I was.

"Better get a move on. Sam hates waiting." Benny called out a few feet ahead of me, not even bothering to see if I was following. Of course, he does, I thought to myself. Could this day seriously get any worse?

CHAPTER 4

Thirty minutes into the drive things, just like a self-fulfilling prophecy, had indeed gotten worse. Between Benny's pathetic excuse for pickup lines that were being slung in my direction every few minutes or so and the wave of suspicion emanating from Special Agent Han, it was officially the longest van ride I had ever experienced in my entire life. The only respite I had was Dominic who broodingly stared out the window in silence for the entirety of the ride.

Looking out my own window, I had to admit that I could see why people came out to the Adirondacks. My last assignment was in California; any sort of topography, let alone mountains covered in trees, was not to be found in the cities, making me realize how much I had missed the comfort of the wilderness.

Upon turning off the main road to the resort's expansive private drive, tree after tree zipped past the window, the canopy blocking out the sun in some locations with only stray beams of light managing to break through to the forest floor. Suddenly, the forest receded and the main building of the resort came into view. You could tell from the structure that it had been built at a time before buildings were mass-produced. Its charm emanated from every deliberately ornate carving and from the supporting beams to the shingles. It sat nestled into the side of the mountain by a crystal-clear lake that seemed to reflect back the resort's stunning image.

What was most likely a serene location on a normal day crackled with nervous energy as hotel guests and staff were ushered out of the building. Local police and the CDC were buzzing around like a hive of bees with the police seeming like they were gathering statements while the CDC seemed to be checking over individuals in a makeshift medical tent.

We were first greeted by the CDC staff who informed us that based on some initial rapid testing and the fact that no additional individuals had presented with any symptoms, that we were cleared to enter the crime scene if we donned the appropriate PPE which in this case was full gowning, mask, and shoe booties.

After we secured and donned our PPE, local PD took us around to the three different crime scene locations which were shockingly spread out across the resort. The bodies had thankfully already been removed by this time so that was at least some good news for me. Agent Han, however, was none too pleased that they were already on their way to the morgue and was giving some poor local police officer a talking-to.

While the boys, as I determined to call them, continued to speak with the local police, I unpacked some swabs and various-sized collection tubes and bags from my kit that would be needed to start taking samples and set off to get down to work. I did the traditional spots, potable water samples from the kitchen and bathroom, the rooms the victims were staying in, the rug in the hallway where the one female victim had been found, and the marble from the lobby where one of the male victims was found. The location was quite expansive, and I was beginning to regret my choice in footwear, a simple pair of loafers, as even though they were not kitten heels, they were not the running shoes I wished them to be. Running around was also causing me to sweat more than I was comfortable with. It was in the older male victims' room where I was taking samples that at last, I felt a slight cooling breeze on my neck from the air conditioning. It was a refreshing break from the sweltering summer weather, so I decided to bask in the frigid air stream just a little while longer.

Wanting to get a little closer to the delightfully cold air, I went about searching for its source but there was no obvious unit in sight. The resort seemed to be far too sophisticated for individual room units that rattled and shook during the night and most likely sprung for central air instead. Looking toward the ceiling I found a vent. Upon second glance, I realized this would make an excellent testing spot capturing any airborne causes for the deaths plaguing this location and ensuring it hadn't been contaminated. There was no way I was going to reach the vent unassisted and as the myriad array of symptoms the victims displayed before death didn't rule out an airborne cause I figured I might as well take a sample from there as well. Looking around for something to stand on I pulled over a chair from the in-room business center under the vent.

I was happily swabbing away when a voice boomed, "What are you doing?" almost causing me to lose my balance and topple to the floor.

"Jesus!" I screeched very unbecomingly, grasping the tube in one hand and the swab in the other. I turned around to face the person who almost caused death number four at this resort and found Special Agent Han, arms crossed and leaning on the door frame, once again staring at me. "I'm taking samples, what does it look like I'm doing?"

"Well finish up, we're heading out," he mumbled rubbing the back of his neck, before turning around and leaving the room. There was no mention of if I was actually finished or if I needed any assistance. Just a judging once-over and then marching away with an air of annoyance without even acknowledging almost causing my near-death experience. Chivalry was apparently the resort's fourth victim. I carefully but quickly packed up my samples and technical gear and walked back into the hallway of the resort. I visually scanned up and down the hallway, noticing a few staff being questioned by local PD. One woman, her uniform indicating she worked at the front desk, appeared particularly upset as she blotted the tears away from her face with the back of her sleeve.

As I passed the woman, head down to try and be respectful, she grabbed my arm forcing my gaze up with the jarring move. She was petite, with her blond hair in a bun, and showed signs of being properly frightened.

"Am I going to get sick? Am I going to die to like Martin, the night shift guy they found in the lobby? I saw you with all those test tubes and stuff."

She forcefully grabbed my hand and placed it on her forehand. "I feel warm, don't I feel warm?" Man, her grip was surprisingly strong.

"Ma'am" I answered, attempting to be polite as I wrenched my hand from her forehead, "I'm not *that* kind of a doctor, and the CDC indicates there is no cause for alarm".

"Oh thank God" she exclaimed with relief, the tears drying up and a smile gracing her face. "That is such a relief to hear."

"Ah, I see," I muttered under my breath as I walked toward the lobby. She wasn't upset about her colleague's death, she was worried that the same fate would befall her. People really are the worst sometimes.

I made my way out through the opulent lobby, giving the architecture once last admiring gaze, before heading out to the parking lot and locating the deathtrap of a van that transported me here.

I had just situated myself in my designated back of the van seat when Dominic and Benny filed in, shortly followed by Sam.

I was writing up notes, happily being left alone in the back seat, while Dominic and Benny's conversation slowly shifted from the investigation to that of idle chit-chat. There was a lull in the conversation when Benny turned around and beamed at me with what I believed he thought was a charming smile and made small talk about the scene. I was polite but was only mildly participating in the conversation when I heard him cackle "Am I right Lizzy?"

"Do not call me Lizzy," I said a little too loudly and a little too forcefully, lifting my eyes from my work, causing all the occupants in the van to turn around and look at me. I could even see Special Agent Han glaring at me in the rearview mirror reacting to my outburst. "I apologize," I coughed, trying to regain my composure and a little professionalism. "Please just refer to me as Elizabeth or Dr. Waller."

"Yeah. Sure Doc," Benny said tentatively like he was a child who had just been scolded and was obviously confused about my outburst before he turned back around. I leaned my head against the window silently chiding myself. Today was officially the worst day ever.

When we got back to the Field Office, Agent Eye Candy led another briefing in which he filled in the team with what the local PD and CDC had shared at the scene. It was nothing revolutionary, the only new information that we got was that the CDC has confirmed there was not any sort of active outbreak or risk to the general populace. I could see the relief wash over the teams as I'm sure they were worried about friends and family. Anyone with half a PhD would know that you'd have a lot more deaths if it was indeed an outbreak but I couldn't fault them for not having a scientific education.

Back at the lab, Nina began helping me catalog and store the samples until we could analyze them the following day.

"So..." Nina started in a singsong voice. "How was your first day?"

"It was definitely memorable," I answered as I applied barcoding to the sample labels.

"God I would kill to be in the field," Nina answered while

following behind me with the barcode scanner and computer to catalog the labeling. "Plus, you got to spend time with Special Agent Han, he's super-hot. Like there is hot and then there is like 5,772 kelvins surface of the sun hot. I'm talking magma hot, like …."

"I get it" I chuckled, cutting Nina off, impressed with her use of the Kelvin scale to describe someone, "you think Agent Eye Candy is hot." I stopped stockstill noticing my error.

"OMG," Nina exclaimed dramatically, turning towards me. "You call Special Agent Han, Agent Eye Candy! That is so good. Like really good. Why didn't I think of that? Can I use that one? It fits his hit it and quit it reputation so well."

"This conversation does not leave this room." I countered in a more serious tone.

"Aye aye, captain!" Nina answered with a salute. "What happens in the lab, stays in the lab." She added a little wink at the end like we had suddenly become co-conspirators in some sort of espionage plot.

I sighed deeply and returned back to my work. What had I gotten myself into with this assignment?

CHAPTER 5

As night came and I was still deep in the work generated from today's field trip to the crime scene I yawned and stretched noticing Nina had stayed as well. She was currently doing a terrible job of keeping her eyes open and looked to have sorted the same paperwork three times in a row. Even though Nina nearly begged me to stay longer I sent her home for the day pointing out that she was becoming more of a liability then an asset at this point, and continued to catalog on my own. At least I now knew that she would listen to reason. Thank goodness for small miracles.

It didn't take long to finish up the cataloging and once all the samples were away, I was finally able to sit down at my desk and take a breather. It was an eventful first day, that was for sure. I didn't think I would find myself getting bored anytime soon. Nina would make sure of that. I had never had an intern or an assistant before and I was going to have to read some articles or papers on delegation and leadership. If I was being honest it was not one of my strong suits. I tended to keep to myself in my past assignments. I would be friendly and cordial, kindly turning down offers for happy hours and after work get togethers until they stopped asking. It was the safest move, for everyone involved. I shook my head to clear my thoughts and moved on to the next task.

Catching up on paperwork, I watched as staff member after staff member walked past in the hall heading home for the evening, some waving politely and some just continuing on. I went to grab a coffee from the break room and realized how much the office had emptied out. Due to the lights remaining on at all times for security purposes, it was hard to tell who was there and who wasn't. I'm sure once I was here for a bit longer I would figure out people's schedules. Today was atypical for me as well, having gone to an actual crime scene. That was a first and I made a mental note to ask Agent Han if this was an expectation of his that I be present at crime scenes. If that was the case, I would have to brush up on my proper scene documentation and procedures. The walk back to my office was eerily quiet, the hum of the fluorescent bulbs and the clack of my shoes on the linoleum creating a muted symphony that echoed down the halls back to the lab.

I took a sip of my coffee and reflected on the day while finishing up my report. "At least the coffee is half decent," I said aloud, enjoying the silence. I was used to solitary work and being around so many people today was exhausting.

I leaned back in the computer chair, which had some give, and was stretching my arm back for a nice big stretch for some lower back relief when suddenly a large force out of nowhere propelled me backward and I found myself sprawled on my back on the floor behind my desk.

Pain radiated through my body, the piercing sound of the fire alarm accompanied by a ringing in my ears causing a cacophony of agony. Dazed and vision blurred from what I was self-diagnosing as a slight concussion, I righted myself, scanning around the room. It looked like a literal explosion had gone off in the lab. Glass shards lay everywhere, bits of paper lay scattered, and edges burnt. I peeked around the desk to find that what was once the glass wall that faced the exterior of the building was now a jagged portal to the darkness outside, the damp summer night air rushing in. It was then that I heard the sound of glass crunching under foot.

I painfully rolled over onto my elbows and scooted under the desk. I shook my head trying to regain some clarity and shake the debris from my hair. My ears rang as I tried to discern muffled voices. They entered the room stealthily indicating they were not here by invitation, and I instinctively covered my mouth afraid to even breathe. One figure was coming dangerously close to my desk and

29

rounded the corner, allowing me to take in their head-to-toe black tactical gear, masking any distinguishing characteristics. Suddenly I saw two feet in front of me and I slowly forced myself to look up. I quickly wished I hadn't as I took in the true image of a bringer of death, a gun with a silencer on it pointed straight at me. I caught a glimpse of a man's wrist with a tattoo of a snake coiled around it.

Was this the last thing I was ever going to see? I had figured I was on borrowed time, but I had wanted to pay my penance a bit more before I died. I closed my eyes, resigned to my fate when there was nothing. I slowly opened one eye and found the masked intruder looking at me, head cocked to the side. Then, as quickly as he had appeared before me, he glanced at the hallway, made some sort of hand gesture to the rest of the intruders, and ran out the hole in the glass into the dark cover of the night. I remained huddled under the desk for what felt like an eternity until I heard Sam's voice.

***

I mulled over the case details trying to make some sense out of it. I thought it might be interesting at first. A nice case study for the new hires but now it was just getting frustrating.

"Three deaths and not linked at all," I said angrily out loud. It was getting late and mostly everyone had left for the day, Dominic and Benny abandoned me hours ago which left me here stuck in my own head. "They don't have any connections. They don't even go to the same fast food restaurants." It didn't help that the new Dr. Waller was starting to become a bit of a distraction. There was something about her that was pissing me off and instead of focusing on this case, I found my thoughts drifting to her. I was pulled out of my musing by what sounded like an explosion.

"What the hell!" I yelled out and dashed into the hallway, the fire alarm already kicking on and smoke billowing out from the direction of the labs. I ran back into my office and called for backup, then grabbed my gun and cautiously made my way to the lab wing.

"Anyone in here?" I yelled, looking over the scene to see if it was safe to enter, the sound of fire sirens getting louder as they approached indicating that help was on the way.

"Over here," I heard a female voice call tentatively from what sounded like one of the desks. I walked over, crouching down to see a disheveled Dr. Waller under the desk.

"Are you alright?" I asked more politely than out of concern as she seemed fine and only slightly rattled. It was then that I noticed her arm had a scarlet trail of blood running down it.

"I think so?" she replied, more of a question than a statement. "I think I got a little concussed with whatever explosive they used to blow in the glass wall but other than that-" I interrupted her, pointing to her arm as she had obviously not noticed it had been sliced by a stray piece of glass. "Oh, and apparently my arm is bleeding. It doesn't look like it's deep enough to require any stitches. This seriously is the worst first day I have ever had on a job."

"Was anyone else in here when the explosion went off?" I asked while surveying the scene once more, ensuring it was still relatively safe and we didn't need to relocate.

"No, I sent Nina home a while ago, so it's just me. How did you get here so fast? I didn't think there was anyone left in the building." She appeared slightly dazed as she examined the damage.

I ignored her question as the answer was evident and went to look around the scene. "What were you doing in here that caused an explosion?"

Her face scrunched in indignation. "*I* didn't cause the explosion thank you very much! I was packing up to leave when the wall was

31

blown in, three goons wearing tactical gear came in, did I don't know what, and then left after sticking a gun in my face." She attempted to hoist herself to her feet but made the mistake of using her injured arm, causing her to wince and flop back down to the floor,

"They left you alive?" I asked, offering her a hand to help her up. It would have taken a very sophisticated criminal to get through our defenses to get close enough to the lab so why would they take the risk of leaving any witnesses?

"Yes, they left me alive, were they supposed to kill me?" she answered angrily, swatting away my offered hand and using her good arm and the desk to help herself up to her feet. She brushed herself off angrily and then paused.

"Well now that I think about it..." She continued, her voice returning to its normal intonation as she peered around the lab. "That wasn't a very smart thing to do. I mean they wore tactical gear and didn't speak so I wouldn't be able to identify them if I tried or if you put them in a line-up or something. One did have an identifying marker though, a snake tattoo on his wrist." She walked away towards the back of the lab muttering to herself as she did.

"What else can you tell me about what happened during and after the attack?" I yelled after her as she continued surveying the lab. I heard her gasp and ran over to where she was standing seeing the look of confusion in her eyes.

"Sam." She said looking me straight in the eyes with a mixture of bewilderment and dread. "They're all gone. All the crime scene samples are gone."

***

I wearily entered my apartment completely spent after the long eventful day I had endured.

32

"I know I have said this multiple times but it bears repeating. Officially the worst first day on the job in history" I said to myself flopping onto my bed instantly regretting it knowing I would probably have to change the sheets with all the soot and blood that was now most likely transferred onto them. Laundry was most definitely not on my list of things I felt like doing tonight but I knew for a fact I didn't have any other sheets as I travel light. After being seen by the EMTs and being fussed over, convincing them I did not need to go to the hospital, catching everyone up to speed on what happened during the incident, *and* confirming that the crime scene samples were the only things missing, I was finally able to go back to the peace and quiet of my apartment.

The first order of business, once I convinced my weary bones to remove themselves from the bed, was a nice long hot shower. I heard my phone buzzing and wearily glanced over to see I had five missed calls from the same person and buried my face into my pillow.

"Ugh."

I knew I was being like a petulant child but I couldn't deal with his nagging right now. I'm sure he'd understand and could get a full report from Agent Han or someone else at the Bureau. I was still alive and fairly uninjured so I would deal with the lecture tomorrow.

I slunk off the bed and headed to the shower letting the hot water roll over my head and shoulders in soothing waves, my thoughts drifting to the criminal who let me go. *Why* he had let me live was still bothering me. Not that I wasn't grateful to be alive and everything, but I had resigned myself at the moment the gun was pointed at me that it was karma. Comeuppance for my past transgressions and that this was where my story ended. When he simply walked away I was horrified to find that instead of relief to still be alive, I felt disappointment. Attempting to break myself from those intrusive thoughts I scrubbed the filth off my body even harder.

Breathing in the steam from the shower I realized a call to my therapist was probably in order. We hadn't touched base in a while and today's events were definitely in the call me if you need an emergency session bucket. I'm sure there was a logical reason for letting me live. Logic was a safe place for me to think right now and I always did my best problem-solving in the shower. If then hypothesis statements were simple, logical, and safe. I'm sure I didn't look like a threat huddled under my desk and wearing a lab coat and the intruder could obviously see I was not in a position to be carrying a gun or weapon of any kind. If I was not a threat, then he didn't need to eliminate me. It was a strong hypothesis for the situation I had found myself in.

My thoughts then went to the fact that nothing was missing from the lab except the samples from storage. If the only items taken were samples from crime scenes, then the intruders were looking to cover up a crime from where the samples were recently collected. I felt some of my anxiety start to slip away, the tension leaving my shoulders and neck, finding solace in my rational thought processes.

Due to the fact that all the samples were stolen, they could have been covering up any of the crimes that were currently being investigated but my money was on the Resort case. All the other samples had already been processed or were in process.

Anyone sophisticated enough to get as far as the labs at an FBI Field office would have known retrieving the samples this late wouldn't do any good. It had to be from the most recent case. It was only a short amount of time from when the samples were collected and brought back here to the lab to when the break-in occurred. I hadn't even begun cataloging them into any of the online databases so it's not as if those systems could have been hacked. Someone must have been there physically monitoring the scene to see that the samples were taken. It also meant that something in those samples could have broken the case wide open. I quickly dashed out of the

34

shower, threw on a towel, and peeked through my paperwork to find Agent Han's phone number.

"Special Agent Han." He answered the sleep evident in his voice. "This better be God damn good."

"Special Agent, it's Dr. Waller."

"What? What the hell are you still doing up? I thought you'd be passed out by now."

"Normally I would have but I thought of something in the shower?"

"You were thinking about me in the shower?" I could hear the smugness rolling off of him, the sleep in his voice vanishing all together causing me to become flustered and aggravated all at the same time.

"What. No." Typical male to jump to that conclusion when I had pertinent information on a case to discuss "I called because I had a realization about the break-in and about the Resort case."

"Oh, and what is that?" I heard him rustling about sounding like he was reluctantly pulling himself out of bed.

"How did they know we had taken samples so quickly unless -"

"Unless –" he interrupted, finally figuring out where I was going with the conversation "unless they were monitoring the crime scene somehow." There was silence and then what sounded like him grabbing his keys. "I'm going to the office to see if we can reevaluate any of the Resort surveillance footage." I was starting to feel like I was actually contributing something to the team.

"Do you need me to come in and assist with the review or anything pertaining to the lab …?" The only response to my question was the sound of a dial tone. I tossed my phone onto my bed frustrated. If that was the way he wanted to play it then he could have fun all by himself going through the footage till his eyes bled. I, on the other hand, was going to attempt to get some sleep having done my job by passing my little realization on.

CHAPTER 6

The office was a flurry of activity when I got there the next day, everyone bustling around with a hectic energy that was previously unmatched. Sleep did indeed evade me the previous night and the whirlwind of commotion was leaving me feeling out of sorts. I decided the break room would be a nice place of solace and the caffeine it held couldn't hurt my current sleep-deprived situation either.

"What's going on?" I asked Benny who was currently hovering around a donut box like a vulture.

"Oh hey, Elizabeth. They went through the resort surveillance and it looks like it was hacked. Whoever was behind the incident has been pirating the stream from the day before the deaths up until now. Sam's going to hold a debriefing soon."

It was impressive how he was able to answer without even looking up, his face showing fierce determination as he tried to figure out which exact donut he wanted. He finally managed to tear himself away from the donuts and realization dawned on him that I was the one who was talking to him.

"I heard you were a badass last night." He said with a smirk and a sweeping appraisal that left me feeling a bit uncomfortable.

"I can assure you I was no badass. Sam found me huddled under my desk." I rolled down my sleeve concealing the bandages that were covering the cut I had gotten. It was interesting that he thought that was a badass activity, getting sliced by an errand shard of glass. Maybe just being around an explosion, having a shifty intruder point a gun at you, and being alive to tell the tale made you a badass around these parts.

"That's not what Sam said," Benny mumbled out, almost unintelligible, somehow managing to get almost an entire donut in his mouth. "He said you had some pretty quick thinking considering you were concussed, and you didn't even realize you were bleeding. He said they had to convince you to get medical treatment and once they were done you got right to pinpointing that they had taken all the crime scene samples."

I stood there with my mouth open, completely astonished. Partly because Benny had somehow managed to get a second donut jammed into his face like a snake unhinging its jaws but mostly because the great Sam Han had actually paid me a compliment. An indirect compliment of course, but still it wasn't something I thought would be possible.

"Come on, the briefings are starting," Benny exclaimed, pulling me from my swirling thoughts and I followed the cloud of powdered sugar that seemed to be emanating from him to the conference room. As we were walking down the hall, I noticed that Benny's work attire seemed like an interesting choice.

"Save the Tatas? Is that really work-appropriate?" I asked Benny and he came to a complete stop.

"My mother had breast cancer." He said in a serious tone turning to address me.

"Oh I'm so sorry- "

"Nah my mom's tits are fine now." Benny's voice returned to its jovial playful tone. "She got a nice upgrade and has been cancer-free for 2 years now. But could you imagine a world without any tatas? They must be saved!" He shook his head in disgust at the thought of a dystopian world where apparently breasts did not exist and continued walking down the hall. I shook my head and reprimanded myself as I should have known better than to ask.

"Everyone take a seat, we have a lot of work to do today." Sam directed from the front of the room. I watched as everyone immediately quieted and took a seat. I had to admit that his ability to command a room was a trait to be admired.

"As all of you know, last night we had a breach here at our home office. Our labs were compromised and samples from our most recent crime scenes were taken. Upon reviewing our own surveillance feeds, we found that the footage from the time of the incident has been corrupted indicating that they had somehow penetrated our firewall and got into our surveillance feed. At this time the only information we have on the event is from Dr. Waller who was in the lab when the incident occurred." I could feel all the eyes in the room slowly turning in my direction. I did not enjoy being the center of attention, making this into my own personal nightmare. I would have almost preferred the guy sticking the gun in my face. Sam briefly glanced at me and then breezed on to another topic.

"Steps forward are as follows: Security will be increased at the site now extending to a 24-hour watch. Our cyber security team will be looking into exactly how they were able to interrupt our video and audio feeds remotely in such a way that they were invisible to our cameras. The cameras in the lab were targeted with the explosion. Additionally, they will be working to trace the IP of who was pirating the feed from the resort and if it is ongoing. Construction teams will be on hand to repair structural damage to the exterior of the building and perimeter fencing. Lastly, Dr. Waller will conduct a thorough search of her lab after the crime scene unit has cleared out to ensure nothing else is missing. Get moving people, we have a lot of work to do."

After recognizing Sam's words as a dismissal everyone began clearing out of the conference.

I had multiple questions after the debriefing. What about the bodies? Has anyone gone to the morgue to collect samples? Did the CDC have some samples already on test? Could I go back to the resort to take additional samples?

"Dr. Waller." I heard Sam call as I was formulating my list of questions.

"Yes, Agent Han?"

"The CSI team should be cleared out in about an hour." I nodded indicating I had heard him and went to launch into my questions as he spoke again.

"How's the arm?" He asked, pointing towards me.

"Oh. It's fine, thanks for asking." Well that was unexpected.

"So, you will not have any issues today resuming your work in the labs?" Oh, so there it was. He wanted to make sure I could still fulfill my duties. How kind of him.

"Yes. You don't have anything to worry about in your plan moving forward to investigating the break-in."

"Well, that is good to hear," he coughed, looking back down at his notes. Was it just me or was this conversation getting more and more awkward as it progressed? To save us both from whatever the heck was happening I thought now might be a good time to bring up my concerns.

"Has anyone taken samples from the bodies at the morgue?" I inquired, pulling out my notepad to take notes just in case.

"We haven't but I can let them know we want samples collected. I can give you the contact information of the coroner." He answered, pulling out his phone so I could jot down the contact information.

"What about the samples the CDC collected?" I inquired as he started to walk away.

"The CDC only collected samples from those not presenting any symptoms." He sighed like I was taking up his precious time. Well excuse me for trying to assist in solving a multiple casualty murder case.

"Can I go back to the resort to take more samples?" I asked, following behind as he tried to retreat.

"Yes, Dr. Waller, go back. See if you can get any more samples. Go nuts. I'll let them know you're coming. Can I go do my job now?" Sam huffed, looking aggravated.

When I didn't utter another question, he turned and went in the direction of his office muttering what I think were curse words on the way.

As Agent Han had stated, the lab was opened to me about an hour later on the dot. After the CSI team vacated the lab I was able to go in and have another look around with fresh eyes. Most of the lab was eerily intact. The window had been boarded up, the stray glass swept away, and the furniture returned to its upright position. All the lab equipment would have to be recalibrated, of course, some I could easily do but others require a service professional or outside vendor but other than that not as much damage as I had previously thought. I guess it is hard to do an impact assessment on your blown-up lab from hiding under a desk and being concussed.

"OMG, Dr. Waller!" I heard Nina wail as she barreled toward me, almost knocking me over when she hugged me, caging my arms to my side in the process. "You almost died!" she cried, squeezing tighter tears forming in her eyes.

"I'm still in one piece." I tried to reassure her tentatively with a few quick taps on the part of her arm I could reach. "But you are pushing on the bandages on my arm so if you wouldn't mind."

"I'm so sorry!" she gasped backing away from me like I was on fire or something. "What do you need? A cup of tea? A chocolate bar? I always want some Chicken Noodle soup when I've gone through something horrible like a breakup or a bad haircut."

Oh, youth. I can't remember when something like a bad haircut made it seem like the world was ending. Actually, I don't think I ever had that luxury even when I was Nina's age.

"I'm fine Nina." I tried to reassure her once more. "What I *do* need from you is a list of all the samples that were in storage, a catalog of all the equipment manuals, and maintenance contracts for said equipment. I'll also need a list of locally approved and qualified labs that we could potentially redirect samples to as we are not going to be in a position to accept any new samples anytime soon."

"On it Boss!" Nina saluted with the ferocity of a soldier on their way to the battle field and hurried off in a cloud of pixie dust and determination.

The remainder of the day was spent running calibrations and assuring Nina I was fine and didn't need a break. I could see her watching me out of the corner of her eye while she worked like she assumed I was going to have a mental breakdown at any moment. I had seen as she had slyly, or what she thought was stealthy, placed a box of tissues on my desk. It made me smile, but I had been through something far more soul-shaking than last night and if I could survive *that*, a simple break-in was nothing to cry over.

With the lab finally back in the best shape it could be, I pulled up the coroner's office number and gave them a call.

"Albany County Coroner's Office." A gruff voice answered.

"Hello. This is Dr. Elizabeth Waller, a forensic scientist consultant for the Albany FBI Field Office. I was wondering if I would be able to come down and procure some samples from the adirondack resort case if you haven't already?"

"What's the case number and your credentials?" The staff member asked in a monotone voice like it was an inconvenience to be doing their job.

After providing all the pertinent information, I was put on hold. Not that I wasn't enjoying the smooth jazz that emanated from the line but after being on hold for about 20 minutes I was starting to get worried.

" Uh, I got good news and I got bad news" The staff member replied sheepishly after finally taking me off hold.

"Okay." I responded not knowing how to take that statement.

"Well, your credentials cleared and I can talk to you about the case."

"That's good. So when can I come down and secure samples or when should I expect them to arrive at my lab?"

"That's the bad part." He hesitated before continuing. "We don't have the bodies."

"Excuse me?" I paused trying to wrap my head around the situation. "The bodies are still on route to the morgue and that's why they are currently not in your possession?"

He cleared his throat. "No doctor. I mean we never got the bodies. Looks like they were supposed to show up hours ago but they never got here."

Well, this was going to complicate things and I didn't want to be

43

the one to tell Special Agent Eye Candy. We were already on rocky terms. Besides, sending the disgruntled morgue employee on the other end of the line to inform Special Agent Han felt like exactly the right amount of retaliation for the attitude and absurdly long hold.

"Could you please let Special Agent Han know of this development. I have some pressing matters to attend to based on this information."

"Ah, yeah sure." The morgue staff member responded tentatively and hung up.

With that deadend, I packed a kit to take some samples at the resort and let Nina know I would be at the scene for the next few hours if she needed me. After telling her multiple times that she could not come with me and listening to the slew of reasons why she should, I was finally able to make my way back to the resort.

This time, the drive to the resort was much more pleasant. No one glaring at me, no one hitting on me, and an audio book to calm my nerves. I was hoping the lack of bodies at the morgue was just some sort of mix up, but that was Special Agent Eye Candy's problem and not mine.

When I reached the resort, all the CDC staff had cleared out and only a few local PD. They confirmed that Special Agent Han had called ahead to have the areas cleared so I could take the additional samples. Good to see he was a man of his word. After donning all the appropriate PPE once more that the CDC kindly left behind, I went to the three crime scenes and began taking samples. It was when I began to start sampling the second crime scene that something began to nag at me.

The rooms were almost too clean. Not a speck of dust in the vents and I could smell that distinct cleaning product smell. The room seemed spotless. To test my theory, I went to one of the rooms next door. The vents were filthy when I swabbed. No smell of cleaning products to be had. I had a feeling my samples were going to come back with nothing but I did my due diligence and sampled anyways.

I packed up, thanked the local PD, and made my way back to the lab so I could test my new samples immediately. I was halfway back when a call from Special Agent Han came across my car console.

"Dr. Waller speaking." I answered, accepting the call.

"The fucking bodies were cremated." Agent Han practically yelled through the phone.

"Can you start from the beginning please?" Man he had anger issues.

"The bodies." He responded slowly like I was a small child. "Were cremated."

"How did that happen?" I asked sincerely curious.

"I don't fucking know! We went to question the morgue transport and when we showed up he nearly pissed his pants. He said he was about to leave the site with the bodies when someone dressed up in PPE and identifying themselves as someone from the CDC gave him an official report that said the bodies needed to be sent for cremation instead of to the morgue because they could be contaminated."

"Okay." I said in a voice I was hoping was calming. "I collected some samples from the resort but I'm not optimistic as the crime scenes were scrubbed clean."

"So are you saying we're fucked?"

"Not entirely?"

"I expect a report on my desk by the end of the day." And with that final demand, he hung up before I could utter another word. I guess I had a report to write. Not that I knew what I was going to put in it. Most of the tests I could run in my recently exploded lab wouldn't finish until tomorrow, anyway.

The next few days fell into a comfortable monotony. There were still no additional leads on the case, the IP address of the pirated feed led to dead ends and the description of the tattoo and clothing I gave of the intruders went nowhere. The samples I collected came back clean as a whistle as I had anticipated. Not even the normal mold or bacteria that was commonly found in air vents was present indicating someone had gone in after and cleaned up the spot. I submitted this in my report to which Special Han remarked with some colorful language. It seemed like all we had were deadends and no leads in sight.

Nina glanced at me from the corner of her eye trying to make small talk in what I believe was an attempt to fill the silence in the lab. I finally let her turn on some music which seemed to alleviate that but added a new headache when she began to sing aloud. It was the lesser evil so with a shake of my head I allowed it to continue, grabbing ear plugs. I had to admit that Nina had good taste when it came to music and I found myself wanting to bop along to the tunes. As that would be highly unprofessional and just encourage Nina more, ear plugs it was. I worked to redirect samples to other labs that had capacity and worked to get the last pieces of equipment back in running order.

"Soooo. Whatcha doing tomorrow night?" Nina inquired as she slowly stalked towards my desk on what had been a quiet afternoon in the lab. I needed a new pair of earplugs if I was still able to hear her. I should have known she was plotting something. Today she was sporting a chic ensemble featuring a bright pink top, and a short, flirty skirt with leggings paired with stylish heels. If she didn't have the lab coat on I would have had an issue for safety reasons but altogether it

46

was a playful yet polished look.

"Reading a book and researching online to see if there are any plants I can purchase that are hard to kill because I need to liven up my apartment, but I'm like the grim reaper when it comes to plants. Why do you ask?"

"Oh good so you're not doing anything." She gleefully smiled as she plopped herself on the corner of my desk.

"Nina" I scolded and she bounced off the desk like it was on fire.

"Sorry, sorry I keep forgetting how much you hate that." She came around the desk and stared at me with a very determined look in her eyes and took a deep breath.

"So, there is this new club that opened up and I have an in with the bouncer. Don't ask. Okay you can ask but I'll tell you later. Anyways, you need a girl's night out because I mean all you do is work and you were literally, I mean literally, blown up and you're new to the area and your only friend is me which makes me sad which probably means you are sad which makes me even sadder so I need you to not be sad."

"Nina take a breath." I laughed as she was finishing up her rant. I hadn't quite realized Nina had gotten so attached to me and maybe she was right. Maybe I needed to let my hair down a bit. I couldn't remember the last time I had gone out. Maybe this would get her off my back for at least a few days and perhaps the personal questions would stop as well. I needed to keep a low profile but a club would be anonymous enough. Right?

"Okay," I answered and watched as she began to wind up for another tirade on why I needed a night out.

"Wait really? OMG, we are going to have so much fun! I can get us free drinks and maybe I can snag the VIP section. What are you going to wear? Do you have anything to wear because I have like 2 closets worth of stuff you could borrow. No wait I have a better idea, I'll bring in some stuff tomorrow and we can change here and just Uber or whatever to work the next day. This is going to be amazing!"

With that, she raced back to her desk and seemed to be intently working on something until it was time to leave, at which time she dashed out the door murmuring something about what color palette goes with pale skin. What had I gotten myself into?

CHAPTER 7

The next day Nina was basically bouncing off the walls of the lab. I could see her checking the clock multiple times waiting for the hours to count down.

"Nina, did you redirect Lot 256 samples to the County Lab?" I asked, trying to get her back on the task at hand. I was met with silence. "Nina," I said again a bit more assertively, and finally her head whipped up from her cell phone.

"Huh? Oh Lot 256 yes. Totes sent them to County on dry ice as directed by my fearless leader." She smiled brightly. What was she up to?

"Thank you Nina, and as a reminder, no personal cell phones in the lab please."

Her posture slumped in an exaggerated show of disapproval. "I hate that rule." Nina pouted. "Who came up with that anyways?"

"The US Government under Good Laboratory Practices," I answered nonchalantly, having gone back to my own work.

I could feel her staring at me from across the room. "Geez you're so smart. How did you learn all this stuff?"

I smiled and peered up "From books."

Nina smiled and waved away my comment. "See, this is why we are friends, we can have playful banter while we work."

"I'm the only one currently working Nina..." I started before she cut me off.

"Yeah, yeah, back to work or no clubbing for you I get it." and she finally went back to her tasks.

I was deep into my reports when I heard a loud yelp coming from Nina.

"It's time! That was the longest day in the history of all days!" She popped up from her desk and pulled out the most neon pink duffle bag I had ever seen.

"Here you go. You're outfit for the evening my lady carefully curated by yours truly. You're going to look so hot!" With that, she bounced off to most likely don her own attire.

I made my way to the restroom and unzipped the duffle bag pulling out the contents inside. It was an emerald green dress embellished with sparkles that caught the light from the fluorescent bulbs above. Dear lord, there was not that much material to it. Was Nina trying to kill me? I slipped into the dress and with slight dread came out of the bathroom stall to see what the damage was. The dress was sleek, accentuating my silhouette while the shimmering embellishments added a glamorous and vibrant touch.

"Not half bad," I said out loud as I allowed myself to admire my reflection in the mirror.

"I knew you would look killer in that!" A voice yelled as the bathroom stall door next to mine flew open.

"Girl are you trying to give me a heart attack!" I gasped putting my hand to my chest and only then realizing how exposed my chest was in this ensemble.

"You're the one who's going to be handing out heart attacks, lady. You look hot! What are you going to do for your hair and makeup, 'cause I have ideas." She scurried over and started examining my face, one hand on her chin like she was trying to figure out how to paint a masterpiece.

"No hair, no makeup. You've done enough with the dress thank you."

"Okie, dokey pokey." She sang as she shrugged her shoulders and touched up her own makeup.

Her phone dinged and she lit up. "Ride's here. Let's go shake our booties and make bad decisions!" She grabbed my hand and dragged me out of the building. I fear the making of bad decisions has already started sometime yesterday when I agreed to go clubbing with Intern Barbie.

Da club, as Nina so eloquently called it, was indeed the spectacle she had promised. The facade of the club was unassuming. The only way I knew we were going to a club and not just down some alley way to get murdered was the long line of scantily clad patrons that was snaking down the block. Nina grabbed my hand, I was thinking because she thought I might escape, and walked confidently to the front of the line. To my surprise, and chagrin, they let us in right away and I heard the moans of frustration and jealousy of those who had yet to make it inside.

The inside of the club was a complete contrast to its outside. The club exuded opulence with its sleek, modern design, decorated with plush furnishings and state-of-the-art lighting. The pulsating beats from a world-class sound system reverberated through the stylish space, where an eclectic mix of music sets the rhythm for the night. High-end bars serve exotic cocktails, and the dance floor was a magnet for the fashionable crowd, creating an immersive experience that blended elegance with vibrant energy. A VIP section could be seen off to the side of the dance floor offering exclusive seating which added an extra layer of indulgence to the upscale atmosphere.

"Let's go!" Nina shouted over the pulsing music and dragged me

51

over to the bar. After a round or two, or three, Nina pulled me over to the dance floor.

"Come on!" Nina leaned over as she observed me shuffling my feet in a feeble attempt to dance. "I know you got some moves! Shake that ass. Move what your mama gave you."

In order to get her to stop talking about my assets so to speak, I began to sway my hips and let go. I slowly relaxed, the alcohol I consumed I'm assuming helped and I began to actually enjoy the music and get into the rhythm.

"I knew you were a good dancer! I'm going to get us some more drinks." Nina yelled in my ear and danced her way towards the nearest bar.

I continued to enjoy the music allowing my body to sway along with the beat while the liquid courage flowed through me. I was enjoying my own little private dance when someone came behind me and slowly slid their hand on my waist. I peered down at the hand and noticed it was large and well-defined as he confidently gripped my hip. Normally, I would have kicked whomever it was in the shin and bailed but I was feeling the song and the alcohol was clouding my judgment so I went along with it allowing him to pull me closer pressing myself to him.

We started to move in sync as we sensually swayed. We moved well together and I allowed myself to relax against the mystery man, enjoying that he didn't try to make idle small talk and ruin the mood. His hands began to explore, roaming over my hips and stomach. I lifted my arms and looped them around the back of his neck allowing him access to wherever he wanted to explore, and my goodness did he *explore*. It felt like I was uncharted territory and he wanted to map every mountain and valley I possessed. God, it felt so good to just *feel* and not worry about the consequences. I determined I had to at least get a look at this enigmatic stranger before I left the dance floor,

52

perhaps with him, to find a dark corner where we could be alone, and spun around my hands still looped around his neck to get a look. My gaze went up admiring his broad chest on my route to his face, my goodness he was tall, and to my utter dread saw the last person I wanted to see at this moment, Special Agent Eye Candy.

We made eye contact and Agent Han removed his hands from my waist like I was on fire and I removed my hands looped around his neck like they were on springs. They shot back so quickly to my own body as I attempted to cover myself up for reasons unknown to me.

"I didn't know it was you!" I yelled over the thumping rhythm as we continued to look at each other in utter shocked horror.

"I didn't know either!" He yelled back. "I just saw an attractive woman dancing alone and shit. Shit I didn't know it was *you*."

"What the hell is that supposed to mean?" I bellowed back. I knew there was a compliment or an insult in there somewhere and I needed to know which one he intended.

"Oh, so you guys found each other," Nina smirked as she saddled up to us, handing me another drink as she took a sly sip of her own. What the heck was going on?

"Did you know he'd be here?" I accused Nina, narrowing my eyes to show my displeasure.

"I mean I know he frequents here because he's totally a player but I didn't know for sure he was going to be here tonight." Obviously, my death stare was losing its touch as she was being very nonplussed about the whole situation. "I saw you guys dancing, it was pretty hot." She remarked, continuing to sip on her drink.

"I'm leaving." I needed to make my exit before I died of

mortification. I turned back around to say, well I hadn't quite formulated what to say, but I was saved as Agent Han was missing having already slipped back into the mass of people. Thank heaven for small miracles.

***

I slipped back into the crowded dance floor finding Benny bopping his head to the music on the edge of the dance floor.

"Benny!" I growled as I approached.

"Woah woah woah buddy. You're coming in pretty hot. What's up, my dude?"

"What's up, is that Dr. Waller is here. You wouldn't happen to know anything about that would you?" I snarled.

"Me? Nah, man. But damn you guys looked like you were feeling it, if you know what I mean." He waggled his eyebrows as if I missed his innuendo.

I replied by grabbing his shirt and pulling him towards me. "Benny. What. The. Fuck."

"Okay. Okay!" He answered, trying to remove my hands from his shirt. "Watch the fit man. This is Prada. Well, Prado which is a knockoff but they still do a really good job."

I continued to glower at him waiting for an explanation.

"Fine. So Nina casually mentioned in the breakroom that they were coming here tonight and I might have seen that as an invitation and I may have thought you needed to blow off some steam cause you seem hella stressed."

I released him and focused back towards the dancefloor seeing

54

that Dr. Waller and Nina were nowhere to be found. At least that saved me the embarrassment of addressing what happened tonight. Hopefully, we could just pretend this never happened and I wouldn't dwell on how good she felt pressed up against me and how she felt in my arms.

I grabbed Benny's drink and downed it in one go. "I'm going home," I announced and made my way towards the door.

"Wait for me. You're my ride!" I heard a frantic Benny yell as I made a beeline for the exit hoping Dr. Waller's and mine confrontation on the dancefloor didn't haunt me in more ways than one.

CHAPTER 8

My alarm clock went off and I groaned, a light headache gracing me. I ran my hands over my face in distress. I was not looking forward to going to work today. I could call in sick. Would Agent Han think me a coward if I called out? Why did I care about his opinion anyway?

I threw off my sheets and went to get ready for the work day. I aggressively brushed my teeth and gave myself a pep talk as I stared in the mirror.

"You have nothing to be ashamed of. It was just a dance. A slightly spicy dance. You didn't even know it was him. You're not embarrassed in the slightest. If he's embarrassed then *he* can ignore *you*. I'll just walk up to him and say listen, mister, if you have a problem, get over it because I am a professional." I nodded, my pep-talk well done, and proceeded on with my daily routine.

I walked into the office head held high and retrieved my interoffice mail. I turned to head toward the breakroom and saw Agent Han exiting his office, us both making eye contact. Like a deer in headlights, we both stared at each other from across the hall for what seemed like an eternity, only for both of us to abruptly dart in opposite directions cursing myself as I scurried towards the safety of my lab.

"Good morning Dr. Waller." Nina singsonged from her desk. "Did you run into..."

"Nope." I cut her off. "We are not doing this."

"But..." Nina pouted and I raised a hand to silence her.

"We are never speaking of last night again." She made like she was going to say something else. "*Never* again."

I walked to my desk, turned on my laptop, and put in some ear plugs, delving into my work and avoiding Nina's gaze. Sometime in the late afternoon of what felt like the longest day on record (which is saying something given my week to date), I saw a whirl of activity in the hallway. I looked to Nina to see if she knew what was going on and she simply shrugged her shoulders. I saw Dominic walking past so I quickly went into the hallway as he passed the lab pulling out my earplugs.

"What's going on?" I asked Dominic as he was looking down at some paperwork and making his way down the hall.

"We got a lead on the IP address the cybercrime division was tracking." He answered not even looking up from his paperwork or stopping, causing me to follow him as he walked. "We're casing out the location as we speak and getting a strike unit together." He entered the conference room and I got a brief glimpse of Sam dictating from the front of the room before the door was literally shut in my face.

***

I stood in front of my team priming them for the mission ahead.

"Cybercrimes has tracked the IP address as originating from this location displayed on the map in front of you. The IP address is still active meaning that the perpetrators may still be in the building. Here's the plan for the mission. We have an entry team stationed here and here." I gestured at the map being projected.

"We'll have snipers on these surrounding buildings here and here and backup stationed on these roads blocking all exit routes. This building is an older abandoned factory space so be mindful when moving around of perpetrators hiding behind shipping crates or pieces of machinery. We are also intimately aware that these guys are professionals, may be armed, and know how to use explosives as evident by the break-in here at our own labs. The cause of death of the three victims from the resort case is still unknown at this time so

57

be on the lookout for anything potentially hazardous as we are operating under the assumption that the break-in here and the resort case are linked. Keep your communications devices on at all times and be safe out there. Let's get rolling."

I had an uneasy feeling about this raid. For some criminal organization to have enough insight to steal samples from right under our noses but not be smart enough to cover their digital tracks had me on edge. The team hadn't participated in this kind of operation in a while but I wasn't worried they were rusty. My concern was that they might be a little zealous considering they had infiltrated our own home base.

Benny appeared to be bouncing off the sides of the tactical vehicle we were currently in and I thought I saw a quick flash of a smile on Dominic's face which was more than frightening even for me. I felt the vehicle stop and we hopped out and I watched as my people poured out racing to their positions. Right as we were about to get in position I saw three unmarked vehicles peel out from the building all going in three different directions.

"Can I get a confirmation that those roadblocks are in position?" I called over the communication line.

"That is a negative sir." Someone answered and I swore under my breath kicking the wheels of our tactical van knowing that meant that the outbound vehicles had escaped and with it potentially our only lead. The idiots probably drove right past them.

"Alright everyone move in now go, go, go," I commanded over the line hoping that we could still salvage something from this mission. It had been a few minutes after the team entered the abandoned building and I hadn't heard a word over the line either indicating we had nothing or that maybe we had something useful.

"Report," I demanded impatiently over the line as I scanned over a map at our makeshift command station trying to determine the direction the three vehicles had gone in hoping to correlate with known hot spots of criminal activity.

"Sir the building seems to have been swept clean, but we do have one suspect in custody. They are currently inbound to the Field Office for holding."

"Good work team." I congratulated them over the line. Well, at least that was something with one suspect being better than none.

I went into the building to look around the scene and swept clean was an understatement. Looking around the space you could have eaten off the floors. For an old abandoned building the space was squeaky clean. There was not a speck on any of the table surfaces and not a sign of a fingerprint or even a stray dust ball. It was evident that they had enough time to do a thorough wipe-down before we arrived. There were no traces of weapons of any kind but judging by the drag marks that were in the concrete flooring it appeared as if something on the larger end had been moved out recently. Everywhere I turned were dead ends. I cleared out letting the crime scene investigation team in to see if they could pick up on anything. The only lead we had now was sitting in a holding room back at the office.

Once I finished up at the scene I headed back to the office with the rest of the team leaving the CSI team to finish up. I had just settled back at my desk with a cup of coffee going over the report from the raid when Dominic came into my office and took a seat. He seemed aggravated, running his hand through his hair before he spoke which was a rare sight.

"The suspect is not talking" Dominic grunted before leaning back in the chair in a signal of utter defeat. "She acts like she doesn't even care if we put her away for life and we threatened to throw the book at her."

I hadn't realized the suspect was a female but that didn't really change anything. Any human was capable of a crime and I didn't discriminate based on gender.

"And you are telling me this because ..." I asked Dominic as he continued to stare at me like I could read his mind. "You want moral support?"

He continued to stare and I tried again. "You want me to order takeout because this might take a while and it's my turn?" The mountainous man continued to stare.

"You want me to take a crack at her?"

He nodded slightly.

"Well, let's have a go." Alex didn't ask for help often and I wasn't going to make him spell it out. He only came into my office when he recognized he was over his head which was two-three times a year tops.

I entered the interrogation room to find a slimly built woman sitting in a chair, legs crossed, and staring uninterested at her well-manicured blood-red nails that look more like talons than fingernails. She had blond hair and a red skintight dress on. Her makeup was meticulously and expertly applied, and the scent of a strong expensive perfume permeated the room. I wasn't up on women's fashion but that didn't seem like a functional outfit for running a criminal enterprise. As I continued to assess the suspect, I noticed that her features were similar to Dr. Waller's. Change the hair color and tone down the makeup, and they would be remarkably similar. I personally preferred Dr. Waller's more natural look but that line of thinking was not helping the case. As I sat down across the table from her she gave me a long once over and leaned back in her chair when she was finished with her appraisal, obviously pleased by what she was seeing which she indicated with a sly smirk. At least that was something I could use.

"I was wondering when they were going to bring in the big guns. My what big guns you have at that. I was starting to think I didn't rate enough. My name's Delilah. Charmed, I'm sure. " she said in a bored but seductive tone.

"Well then my apologies for keeping you waiting" I answered flirting back a little. Sometimes you catch more flies with honey than vinegar. "Let me spell it out for you. You were found at an address we have linked to a break-in at a federal building which is a federal offense so if you don't give me something soon I'm afraid to say I'll have to ship you out to accommodations that I can assure you are not as nice as this." Hearing no response and not wanting to waste my time any further I went to get up.

"Wait. You win. I don't know why I'm being so closed-lipped about the whole situation when those jerks left me behind." She answered matter-of-factly. "How much do you know about black market weapons dealing?"

"You better be careful throwing around that term. We could go after you for terrorism." I added trying to incentivize her into giving up more information. "Are we talking guns here?"

"I don't know." She answered while flipping back her hair and staring at me with bedroom eyes.

"Bombs?" I tried again.

"I don't know," she answered, more strained this time.

"Rocket launchers, sniper rifles? Were those killed at the resort a cover-up so they didn't expose the underground black market?"

"I don't know. Jesus" she answered putting her hands up in mock compliance. "I only sell the stuff, they make the stuff, whatever it is exactly. I work for a third-party broker whom I'm not going to tell you anything about because I like my pretty little head on my shoulders so don't bother asking. Anyway, I went to go check on the progress of the goods, which again I'm not going into details about so don't even try because my buyer was getting antsy, so I decided to pay an unannounced visit to start the ball rolling. They had wanted to wait until some masquerade ball or something to do the deal. It was a little dramatic even for me." She paused, rolling her eyes in disgust.

"So anyways I show up and I'm about to get out of my car and enter the warehouse when you guys come in guns blazing and everything spooking my driver who left me high and dry."

"When and where is the buy supposed to happen?" I asked, finally getting somewhere.

She laughs and then turns to look me in the eyes, taking the whole meeting seriously for the first time.

"Before I tell you anything I'm going to need to hear what kind of deal you can get me." She demands leaning across the table and attempting to put her chest on display.

"Well before *I* can do that" I counter leaning across the table as well "You'll have to give me something to bring to the table to get you a deal."

"Fine." She pouted, leaning back and crossing her arms. "How about this? The warehouse was rigged with cameras, so your whole team had been made so they would see you coming a mile away. I know they have some fancy facial recognition at the drop and you guys will be public enemy number one. I was warned that there'd be no hiding if they were double crossed. Apparently they got their software from a government agency, one of the ones with a three letter name. Your people stopped me before I was fully in range of the cameras so I'm in the clear as we've never met face to face before, but they know to expect a woman in a red dress. And-" She concluded, looking me up and down "I don't think my dress would fit you." She smirked, clearly proud of herself that in the end the bad guys would win.

I got up to leave the room and tasked Dominic with seeing what kind of deal the team could put together. After the suspect got her plea deal she gave us the location and the date for the buy. The good news was that the deal was going down here in Albany at the fanciest venue in town with the wealthiest clientele.

The bad news was that it was tomorrow night and there wasn't enough time to get a female agent in town and briefed in time. We also didn't know if the facial recognition software the criminals had could tap into the FBI agent's database meaning all our female agents could be compromised as well. Plus, we didn't even know who the suspect was supposed to meet with let alone what they were supposed to be buying. I stared at the red dress that we had confiscated from the suspect's car. It really wouldn't fit me.

Shit, I thought, raking my hands down my face in defeat as I got my things ready for the debriefing of the rest of the team. I really messed this one up. I had called all the active agents to the raid and if what the suspect said was true they would all be made. All active FBI agents could be picked up with the facial recognition program and I couldn't risk that local or state police wouldn't be recognizable as well. The one thing we had on our side was that we could take advantage of the theme for the event which was a masquerade and could wear masks to conceal our identity, but she was right. If we didn't at least look similar to the suspect, we were not making it even close enough to get a description of the seller. I gathered myself together as I had to debrief the team on the status of the case which was currently fucked.

CHAPTER 9

I made my way to the debriefing room when Benny caught up to me.

"Hi, Doc- I mean Elizabeth," Benny said, catching himself expertly. At least someone was not avoiding me after last night's disaster on the dance floor.

"Hi, Benny."

"You've had a heck of a start here at the Field Office. You know-" he continued, lowering his voice like I was a co-conspirator in some sort of spy movie. "- if you need a shoulder to cry on or want someone to come over and keep you company."

"I'm going to stop you right there." I interrupted in a firm tone. "I'm a big girl and can take care of myself. Okay."

"Had to try" Benny shrugged as we continued down the hall passing a few agents escorting a beautifully dressed woman in handcuffs. I wonder what she was here for? As she walked past she bumped into me hard, sending me sprawling to the ground, my notepad and papers scattering on the floor.

"Oopsie. Didn't see you there." She said in a sickly-sweet voice that covered malicious intent.

"What the hell is her problem?" Benny said as he bent down to help me pick up my items as the agents continued to lead the women down the hall. "I'm all for some woman-on-woman action but that was uncalled for. She totally looks like you too! I mean if you, you know, wore some makeup and did your hair and stuff. Spooky."

I shook my head at Benny's comment and peered down the hall at the woman they were carting away, her face now looking over her shoulder to give me a proper scowl for some unknown reason. I could see what Benny was talking about. We did look eerily similar. We entered the conference room with Special Agent Han already in the process of updating the group. I tried to get my traditional seat in the back, but I could feel Sam's displeasure at me being late, so I grabbed the closest seat I could and attempted to slink down further into the floor melting under his gaze.

"As I was saying." He continued, finally turning his judgment-filled gaze away. "We have the manifest of all the guests that were staying at the resort as well as the ones that checked out on the date of the murders as well. We are currently seeing if any of the guests have any ties to the victims, would have a reason to do them harm, or are in any way connected to the underground arms dealing black market."

Looking at the list of names there was one that stood out and I let out a quick chuckle quietly to myself.

"Yes, Dr Waller. Do you find something funny about the list of potential suspects?" Oh no he heard me. Did he have bionic hearing or something?

"Oh, no Special Agent Han, it's just one of the guests checked in under the name of Gerry Lane."

"And what's so earth-shattering and funny to you about that?" Sam answered questioningly. Oh so now he was speaking to me. If he could keep it professional, so could I.

"Gerry Lane, that's Brad Pitt's character's name in the movie World War Z, the zombie movie. So-"

"So, it's most likely an alias." Sam continued cutting me off. Well, I'm glad the awkwardness from last night was officially over. "Dominic, look into the billing information this Mr. Lane gave to the resort." Dominic immediately got up and left to do Sam's bidding as Sam continued with his debriefing.

"You're welcome," I muttered under my breath as I heard a quick snort come out of Benny meaning he had heard me. At least my love of movies was coming in handy. I preferred the book to the movie but that was a discussion for another day.

"Moving on to the second topic, by the time we had formed a team to raid the potential site of the culprits of the break-in all traces of them and what they could have potentially been working on had been cleaned out."

"Have we concluded that the break-in here at the office and the incident at the resort are linked at this time?" an agent I was unfamiliar with asked.

"Due to the samples from the crime scene being taken during the break-in, the IP address leading to a warehouse, the sophistication of the break-in, and the high-end fixers obviously used on both crime scenes we are moving forward with investigating them both in this case." Oh, so he doesn't get mad when other people interrupt him. Good to know I thought and began doodling angrily on my notepad.

"The raid was not unsuccessful, however." Sam continued. "We were able to capture one suspect who has informed us they were there to check in on some merchandise for an arms trafficking ring. We don't know exactly what type of guns or weapons they were trying to produce and move so we have to be vigilant. It is our current belief that at least one of the murders at the Adirondack Resort was due to this weapons production and the other deaths might have served as a cover."

I scrunched my face. Arms dealing? Then why did they go to such lengths to take all the samples I collected from the crime scene? I was about to raise my hand to bring it up but decided they were the crime experts so I should stay in my lane. That was a good point. Why was I in this briefing anyway?

"The hurdle we face however is that the raid site was rigged with cameras and all those that participated in the raid were made, making it more difficult to go undercover at the buy location. Luckily, the buy is going down at a masquerade event, so we can conceal our faces. The problem lies in that the potential buyer and suspect we now have in custody is female and all the nearest female agents were either called in for the raid or may be able to be identified through a pirated facial recognition program that may be used at the venue, and the buy is going down tomorrow night."

"Well, that sucks," I whispered to myself, instantly regretting it, earning Sam's laser-like gaze once more. To top it all off my phone unfortunately went off. I thought I had put the dang thing on vibrate.

"I'm sorry!" I exclaimed to the room as I fumbled to silence it but mostly for Sam's benefit as he was probably livid now. When I finally looked up to see what level of anger Sam was currently at, instead of a glare of disappointment he was looking at me with a weird smile on his face. I wasn't quite sure which one disturbed me more but I knew one way or another I was in trouble.

CHAPTER 10

"No freaking way," I yelled, not caring if anyone heard me out in the hallway. After the meeting had concluded Sam had asked Dominic, Benny, and myself to meet him in his office. I felt like I was being sent to the principal's office and dragged my feet the whole way there filled with dread. He then proceeded to drop a bombshell of a request.

"Do I look like an international black-market dealer to any of you?" I asked the room waiting for either Benny or Dominic to agree with me, but they never did.

"Obviously not." Sam countered. "But you have the same build and general looks as the suspect, so you are going to have to do."

"But I'm a scientist. I belong in the lab not out on a mission. If they asked me anything about the field of weaponry or tried to negotiate on prices or whatever I'll be screwed! Additionally, as stated in my contract, if you had taken the time to read it, my employment is in the capacity of laboratory contract work and not a field role, and as such I do not have the authority to take on this task, nor do you have the authority to make me. "

"You seem pretty smart to me," Benny added, jumping into the conversation. "I'm sure we could catch you up to speed pretty quick. Plus I've seen you in a dress before and you looked ..." He was abruptly stopped with a sharp elbow to his side from Agent Han.

I desperately deferred to Dominic to talk some sense into these people, but he just grunted in approval.

"Actually Dr Waller," Special Agent Han continued with a smirk I wanted to slap right off his face. " If you had fully read *your* contract, you would have seen the clause that allows for field work in special circumstances with approval from higher ups which I am currently waiting on confirmation for."

"Okay. Well maybe I can pick up on enough information to pass conversationally but I don't know how to use a gun or anything like that." That was a pretty good excuse. They would have to let this stupid idea go now, right?

"Considering it is a buy." Dominic added unhelpfully "You wouldn't be allowed to enter the venue armed let alone get near the target with a weapon." Well, this was infuriating. I was running out of excuses.

"I don't know how to use your complicated communication equipment?" I answered hesitantly figuring I'd give it one more shot to get out of this.

"Nice try but we set it all up and you literally just have to stick it in your ear," Benny answered.

"Look." Sam interrupted. "We don't like this any more than you do but we're out of options. Plus, if we are dealing with some kind of biological agent you would be the best person to identify it in this situation." The sound of ringing came from Sam's pocket. He answered it like he had already won the conversation.

"Understood. Thank you." He turned to the group looking pleased with himself. " And that would be the call confirming you can take on field work."

I glanced at Dominic and Benny who were looking back at me eager to see what my decision would be.

"Fine," I said exasperatedly, rubbing my temples. "I'll do it." Benny did a little "yes" like a football touchdown dance and Dominic simply nodded in approval. It wasn't like I really had a choice at this point.

"Okay." Sam finally said acknowledging my acquiescence. "We have a lot of work to do."

That was an understatement. The rest of the day was spent in training bouncing around from agent to agent. Learning the layout of the building, what code words to use for the coms if there was trouble or if indeed they were trading bioweapons, what to look for to determine if someone was concealing a weapon, and so forth. I felt like I had undergone Quantico Boot Camp all in a few short hours. I was just finishing up with an agent who was rerunning the plan with me when Sam came in.

"How's it going?" Sam asked the agent instead of me which miffed me a little causing me to shift in my chair uncomfortably.

"She's doing great!" the male Special Agent whose name I had already forgotten beamed at me. "Just like you said she picks up things pretty quickly."

Sam cleared his throat. "If that's the case then Dr. Waller please run me through the scenario."

Great. Getting put on the spot was not my favorite thing in the world but if I knocked that smug look off Sam's face it would be worth it.

"At nineteen hundred hours a private car will drop me off at the entrance of the venue. Undercover agents including yourself will be mingled in with the guests for additional support should I need it. Thanks, by the way. Once I have passed through the security checkpoint set up by the venue I will make my way over to the bar located in the back right of the ballroom where according to the suspect I will be approached by a man who will address me as Miss Scarlet to whom I will address as Mr. Green. Kind of tacky with the Clue references. I love the movie, it's a classic but- "

"Focus Dr. Waller." Sam interrupts impatiently.

"Of course," I say through cleaned teeth. I babble when I get nervous, but he doesn't need to know that little factoid.

"Mr. Green will escort me to the side room where we will conduct the buy and I will meet with the seller. I will say as little as possible letting the culprit take the lead in the conversation. The suspect, or the role I will be playing, was basically to be sent as a mouthpiece for the buyer with me only knowing the bare minimum of what the deal includes. Therefore, the cover for the earpiece will be that it is the method I will be using to communicate to the supposed buyer and thus shouldn't draw any attention or suspicion from the seller. You will have an expert in black market deals onsite to walk me through acting as the buyer and directing me on what to say. Once we have enough information you will give me the signal to which I will excuse myself as having to use the ladies' room. Once I exit through the rear entrance you will give the go for the tactical team to enter and conduct the arrests."

"I don't think I've heard anyone use thus in a mission briefing," Sam answered looking slightly more at ease and not as impressed as I thought he would have been. He went to walk away when I stopped him by placing my hand on his arm.

"I did have one question though."

"Yes, Dr. Waller." He answered looking aggravated, staring at my hand on his arm with an unreadable expression on his face. I quickly removed it and continued on with my question.

"Aren't we putting a lot of people in danger? I mean, the event is sold out and we know there are going to be some dangerous people there, it just seems risky."

71

"That is my risk to mitigate Dr. Waller." He answered obviously not liking that I was questioning his plan.

"If you must know, the venue has metal detectors at the entrance, most likely why the seller chose the location to ensure the buyer doesn't come armed and most of the buy will be happening in the back of the venue. As the tactical team will be entering from the rear of the building the public will have minimal disruption. Any other questions?" he ended with an annoyed tone that I was not super fond of.

Deciding it was better not to aggravate him any further for everyone's sake I simply nodded my head and he walked away thanking the agent for his work.

After being released from what Nina had deemed Secret Agent Training, I decided I needed to blow off some steam. I changed and went to a local kickboxing class I found in the weeks prior to officially starting work. At the beginning of class, the instructor said that if we needed a little extra motivation to imagine the bag as someone. I could tell she was joking but Special Agent Han instantly came to mind. After the "warmup" consisting of a hellish combination of jogging, mountain climbers, planks, and the ever-dreaded burpees I was ready to go with the bag work. Every hook, jab, cross, and roundhouse that connected with the bag I had projected Sam onto made me feel a little bit better.

"Nice form today Elizabeth" the instructor commented as she surveyed the class moving on to correct someone else's stance. It had been a while since someone had gotten under my skin like Sam had managed to and I needed to refocus. My next front kick landed a little too hard and the bag went over.

"What do we do when someone knocks over the bag in this class?" the instructor asked the class turning to me.

"Burpees!" they yelled in a traitorous union. Just what I needed more burpees as my penalty for kicking the bag over. This day was just getting better and better.

I was staring at the ceiling when my alarm went off the next morning. I couldn't seem to find sleep, the fear and anticipation churning within my mind. I still don't know what they were thinking putting me into a situation like this. I consoled myself with the fact that everyone seemed to think I could handle the assignment, even Special Agent Cranky Pants to some extent. I rolled out of bed, sore from yesterday's kickboxing class, and made my way to the kitchen to make some coffee. Today was definitely a coffee day. Tea was for relaxing and I was in no way going to be relaxed for the foreseeable future.

Sipping the dark liquid pick-me-up, I re-reviewed the case file, the plan, and the reading materials that the other agents thought might be pertinent to my assignment. I could tell they were anxiously loading me with as much knowledge as possible while knowing they will have missed something with the time restraints we were dealing with. I stood in my closet and went to pick out an outfit. I was pretty much going to have to change when I got there so I figured a more casual outfit wouldn't be beyond the realm of acceptable considering most of the agents came to work in jeans. I sighed to myself and said to no one in particular "Here we go."

CHAPTER 11

I glared at my alarm clock, daring it to go off. I hadn't slept a wink last night. This was a major operation and it hung on the performance of an obviously out of her league Dr. Waller. I was slightly impressed at how quickly she caught onto the way things work with a tactical team involved and how she had easily memorized her part in the plan, but I still felt like I was sending a lamb to the slaughter. If things went sideways, I didn't trust her not to get herself killed. The only reasons I even considered her to play a part in this operation is that she oddly looked very similar to the suspect who was supposed to do the drop, everyone qualified for the mission was compromised, and the higher ups gave me the green light. She also seemed to have handled herself fine with the explosion at the lab. She only appeared a bit disorientated but had enough quick thinking to hide under the desk. I also was not a fan of how only a slight touch from Dr. Waller threw me off balance. That was not something I could let interfere with a mission so critical to closing this case.

"Shit," I said to the empty apartment. I got dressed and made my way to the Field Office aiming to get there before everyone else. I needed to project confidence in this plan and the only way I was going to do that was if I had some time to re-review the plan in my office with a large cup of coffee before the office became a buzzing beehive of activity. It felt like I had just arrived when a slow trickle of knocks could be heard on my door and various field agents popped in and out with last-minute questions and loose ends that needed to be tied up.

I heard a light tap on my door and had to do a double take at Dr. Waller standing in my door frame. She had forgone her normal buttoned-up professional business attire and instead wore a pair of skinny jeans and a form-fitting t-shirt. It was apparent that she had been hiding her slim figure under business slacks and a lab coat. She looked like she had gotten just about as much sleep as I had and her hair, normally pulled back into a bun, was left to lay tousled on her shoulders. I mentally forced myself to focus on anything but Elizabeth and pulled my eyes away to stare at some paperwork on my desk.

"What can I do for you, Dr. Waller?"

"I have just some quick *logistical* questions to go over." The way she said logistical made it sound like it was a matter of something different altogether.

"And what might that be?" Whatever it was she was already supposed to be getting ready and I didn't need her being the cause of us missing the drop window.

"I have the dress which I already tried on yesterday and it fits fine so that's good, but I don't, how do I say this, do we have a hair and makeup team coming?"

If the situation wasn't so dire I would have laughed, hard, but this was not the time to be joking around. "This is not Miss Congeniality Dr. Waller. The FBI does not have a hair and makeup team on standby for situations like this."

"I love Miss Congeniality!" an overexcited Nina exclaimed bounding into my office with a multitude of bags in her hands from who knows where. "Mr. Special Agent in Charge Sir!" she saluted and then turned to a bewildered Elizabeth.

"Nina, what are you doing out of the lab? I asked you to call the vendors about the equipment recalibrations this afternoon." Elizabeth chided as Nina huffed and puffed like she was trying to catch her breath.

"Yeah. I know." Nina got out between breaths. "But that sounded super boring, so I ran home and got some of my hair and makeup stuff because I *so* knew you would be way out of your league."

Elizabeth turned to me for some sort of support to escape her assistant, but I merely shrugged my shoulders, not willing to touch the topic with a ten-foot pole. The horror that entered her eyes was a bit amusing I have to admit as Nina, oblivious to her distress, began to try to pull her out of my office.

"Come on." Nina pouted oblivious to the insult she had just laid on Elizabeth as well. "It'll be fun!"

"It's not supposed to be fun." Elizabeth chided slowly backing away from the overzealous woman.

"Agent Han, don't you think she needs my help," Nina asks, turning to me.

"Apparently, Dr. Waller, I stand corrected. The FBI does have the hair and makeup team you were looking for and it looks like she found you."

Elizabeth stared daggers at me as Nina grabbed her hand. "We better get started now Elizabeth because we have a lot of work to do. Those eyebrows alone yikes!"

I allowed myself a chuckle as Nina dragged Elizabeth out of the office with a look of pure terror on her face.

***

"I'm almost done," Nina said to me for the tenth time that afternoon. She had managed to turn an empty office into a makeshift hair and beauty salon. The problem was that there were no mirrors, so I had to wait to see the finished product as Nina worked away on me. After being poked and prodded for what felt like hours I was ready to get out of the room. There was no ventilation in the room either that I could tell as I choked on what felt like cans of hairspray that Nina had used. It was worse than the dust that had settled after the explosion in the lab.

76

"Seriously Nina," I said, trying to swat away her incoming hand. "I'm sure whatever it is good enough. I just need to look presentable."

"I just need to finish your eye makeup and you're done. Close your eyes" Nina said. I stared at her. "Close. Them." Who knew Nina had this bossy side to her? I relented and closed my eyes waiting for the onslaught to continue.

"Do we have to do so much makeup?" A simple bit of bronzer and some blush should have had everything covered, not that I knew how to apply any of those things, but Nina didn't seem content with just making me look presentable. It was like some unknown reputation she had was on the line.

"I saw that bad guy or bad lady I should say when I was dropping off some paperwork at the central desk and they were taking her to holding," Nina said as I felt her applying something to my eyelids. "Her makeup was supermodel good and she was wearing Loui Viton shoes, so you know she makes bank. Also, she seriously looked like she could be your evil twin. Spooky. Anyways, if you show up all plain you might tip off the other baddies." Unexpectedly Nina again made a valid point.

"My masterpiece is complete!" Nina squealed. "Just a bit of setting spray and you are good to go. Oh man, I wish I could go." I heard Nina pout as something misted my face surprising me.

I arched an eyebrow at Nina in disbelief. "You want to go to a party where you know there are going to be criminals that might be trading weapons of some sort?"

"Well, when you put it that way it doesn't sound as fun. You can open your eyes now. Oh, here I brought this standing mirror from my place. You are going to freak out when you see yourself! No peeking I want this to be a totally dramatic reveal."

She turned me around and I heard her shuffling to grab what I assumed was the mirror. "Is that freak out in a good way or a bad way?" I asked hesitantly.

"You tell me." She answered excitedly. "Oh my gosh, I feel like I am on one of those makeover shows. This is so cool. Okay, turn around."

I turned around and the image I saw left me utterly speechless. The red dress was floor length with a slit that was a bit higher than I was comfortable with, and it showed a bit more cleavage than I normally would have worn but it was stunning. Thank goodness it had sheer sleeves which worked to cover the injury to my arm from the explosion. The beading glistened in the fluorescent glow of the office lights which only accentuated my figure. My hair was up off my shoulders braided to the side with wispy strands that framed my face and exposing my shoulders and neck.

The makeup was expertly executed with a smoky eye that brought out a sparkle in my eyes and a highlight that made me appear as if I glowed from within. The lipstick was a deep burgundy making me feel like I was in a noir movie. I hadn't been this dolled up in a while. Not since he... I stopped that train of thought right there. I had a potentially lethal night ahead of me and I couldn't let the past distract me.

"So, what do you think?" Nina asked tentatively from behind the mirror breaking me out of my contemplative state. "Oh, you hate it." Nina continued before I could respond. "I know I have a makeup remover around here somewhere. I'm such an idiot." She continued mumbling.

"Nina." I tried to interrupt as she continued to mumble to herself. "Nina!" I said a bit louder, grabbing her arm to stop her from continuing to charge around the room. "You did great. I could have never done this on my own."

78

"Really?" Nina sniffled looking like she was on the edge of tears. "Like really really?"

"Really really," I answered, shaking my head at how absurd the situation was. We'd have to work on Nina's confidence a bit later but now it was on to the mission.

As Nina and I walked the hallway to the final briefing before we rolled out for the sting I couldn't help but feel people staring at me as we walked. Some guy even almost walked into a water cooler.

"Do I look that weird?" I whispered to Nina as we made our way down the hallway.

"No girl, you look hot!" she confirmed putting her hand up for a high-five which I returned to her delight.

"You're late." Special Agent Han said disinterestedly. He was leaning against the wall in front of the conference room and had commented without even looking up from his papers. It seemed like he had changed to play his part in the sting and was now wearing a black three-piece suit. It was a slim cut and showed off his broad chest and muscular arms. He looked a bit like James Bond and I had the urge to hear him say the phrase shaken, not stirred. I had to quickly look away to stop myself from staring.

"My apologies but Nina had her work cut out for her," I answered hoping he didn't see that I was affected by his change in clothing.

He glanced up, his face poised like he was about to reprimand me but instead, he stared at me, blinked a few times, and then coughed.

"Well." He started to speak but then seemed as if he was at a loss for words. I knew I looked like a kid playing dress up having deluded myself that I look good. I had no right to have any part in this mission. He went to continue but a few other agents trickled into the conference room including Benny.

"Damn, Elizabeth!" Benny said as he walked past giving Nina a thumbs up who blushed, wished me good luck, and ran off to parts unknown leaving me awkwardly alone in the hallway with Sam.

"Here," Sam said, offering out his coat jacket.

"Oh, I'm not cold," I answered, trying to push the aforementioned jacket away.

"Your outfit is-." He paused looking like he was searching for the right words "-distracting. I need my men focused on the mission."

Distracting? I couldn't tell if that was a compliment or an insult, but I decided it was wise to take the jacket anyway and place it over my shoulders.

"Better?" I asked knowing it was not wise to be antagonizing him at a time like this, but it came out before I could stop myself. I noticed I was doing that more than I should since I accepted this position which I would have to reevaluate at another time.

"After you." He responded by gesturing that I enter the conference room indicating that it was time to get down to business and for once I couldn't agree with him more.

The briefing was interesting, to say the least. I could feel some of the agent's eyes drifting my way from time to time and I thought I even caught Sam looking once or twice. The whole meeting my nerves started to catch up with me and self-doubt crept in. I consoled myself that backup was just a codeword away and took a deep breath.

"All right everyone," Sam commanded from the front of the room. "Be safe out there, stick to the plan, and let's catch these guys."

Sam came up to me after the meeting. "Do you have any last-minute questions?" he asked in an authoritative manner, obviously in mission lead mode.

"I'm good. I got this." I answered, trying to sound confident.

"Are you saying that for your benefit or for mine?" he teased with a slight smirk on his face.

"Both?" I squeaked honestly not really knowing if I was trying to convince him or myself.

"Special Agent Sanders here will get you wired up and the car is already up front." He went to walk away but then stopped a few steps away.

"Thank you for agreeing to do this." Sam coughed out, seeming like it inflicted physical pain to thank me in any capacity.

"You're welcome. Didn't really seem like I had a choice in the matter".

"Dominic followed up on the billing information for Gerry Lane by the way. It led to a dead-end indicating it was most likely an alias. Was that movie a favorite of yours or something?" Be still my beating heart it seemed like Sam was trying to have a civil conversation.

"Not particularly," I replied shortly, not wanting to get into any more details about my personal life. Realizing I was being rude I continued. "An ex-boyfriend of mine really liked it. He liked to pick out all the scientifically inaccurate bits and laughed when the scientist character didn't even make it five minutes into the grand mission without getting himself killed. I always closed my eyes at that part, so it wasn't a favorite of mine or anything." I peeked away, smoothing an invisible wrinkle out of my dress.

He nodded and proceeded to walk a few steps further away and then paused once more. "Oh, and Elizabeth."

"Yes?" I answered hoping he was going to provide me with some last-minute words of advice.

"I'm going to need my jacket back."

"Ah yes of course." I handed it over surprisingly missing its warmth immediately even in the June heat. He silently took it walking away and I suddenly realized I probably wouldn't be seeing him again until this whole thing was over.

After I got my earpiece all set, and we tested the lines of communication I made my way over to the car waiting to take me to the event and stopped to take a deep breath. I knew once I entered this car I was no longer Dr. Elizabeth Waller. I was a black-market broker feme fatale, at least for the next few hours.

"Here we go," I said to the cool night air and slipped into the car.

CHAPTER 12

I surveyed the splendor that was the Masquerade Ball. Even the outside had been decorated with spotlights and banners, a steady flow of people in beautiful gowns and dashing suits all in masks making their way up the stairs of the venue prepared for their grand entrances. Ribbon climbed up the columns outside the venue while opulent lighting beckoned guests to come and step into a fairytale.

"If this was any other situation, I would have actually been really excited to come to this," I said to the agent who was tasked with driving me to the event. A slight nod was the only response I received for my statement and I was almost happy to not have to hold a full-on conversation or I might start panic talking.

"We are a go." I heard Sam update over the communication line and recognized that was my signal to get out of the car and enter the venue. The driver opened the door offering me a hand as I exited the car trying not to trip on the dress with the stiletto heels Nina had lent me. I took a deep breath hoping it would calm my nerves, but the sheer grandeur of the event was enough to raise my anxiety meter let alone the hidden dangers I knew were inside. I nodded to the agent, projecting confidence I didn't really have, and made my way up the steps into the event.

Whoever put on the event was a creative genius and needed an award. It was a stunning venue with a mixture of classical and new-age design with the choice of decorations only seeming to further accentuate the architecture. Flowing banners lined the walls while aerial dancers spun and flew on ribbons throughout the venue. Twinkling vines intertwined with twinkle lights gave the space a Midsummer Night's Dream vibe and I had to admit I was entranced. Living statues circulated the room posing and allowing guests to take pictures with them. Hor d'oeuvres tables circled a large dance floor currently occupied by what appeared to be professional dancers. Masked guests looked on and cheered for the dancers as a half-moon decoration smiled down from above. Every once in a while a shooting star would stream across the walls of the venue or twinkling stars would fall most likely generated by some mapping projector. The room even smelled magical with a mixture of sugar and spice wafting through the air originating from a delicious dessert bar somewhere. Gently played music flowed through the room emanating from a string quartet seated on a decorated platform in the center of the venue.

I didn't think these kinds of events existed beyond the movies and I had to admit I was in awe even with my current mission. I quickly sobered, realizing that the character I was playing most likely wouldn't be all that impressed, so I sauntered around looking for the bar not knowing if the eyes on me belonged to simple party guests or mercenaries in disguise. I sidled up to the bar as directed, ordered a drink so I wouldn't look suspicious, and attempted to look like I was uninterested and impatient. I stared at my freshly painted nails to further portray boredom and swirled my drink around not wanting to drink it and dull any of my faculties.

"Alright, we're in position." I heard Sam over the earpiece. "Benny, Dominic, do you have eyes on Elizabeth."

"Heck yeah, I do!" I heard Benny's voice volunteer. "She looks hot."

I heard Sam groan "Could you try to be a little professional Benny?"

"Uh yes sir," Benny answered, sounding like a wounded puppy. "I have eyes on Elizabeth."

I tried to suppress a smile so as to not destroy my thin façade when I made eye contact with someone from across the room and he started to make his way towards me.

"Guys there's someone coming my way," I whispered into my drink trying to block my lip movements. "He's not wearing green, so I don't think he's the contact."

"He's probably going to try and hit on you. Just send him on his way. The suspect will not make contact unless you are alone." Sam answered unhelpfully.

"And how am I supposed to do that?" I turned around and hissed, startling the bartender. I mouthed an apologetic sorry and turned the other way.

"You must do it all the time just pretend you're at a bar and reject him," Sam answered, obviously annoyed that he had to explain to me how a female rejects a male.

"Only one problem with that. I don't go to bars and get hit on a regular basis so I'm a little out of practice. Oh no, here he comes."

"Um hello." I heard a male voice say behind him and I hoped that simply ignoring him would work. He cleared his throat and tapped my shoulder.

I turned around sighing that it wasn't going to be that easy. "Yes," I replied, acting bored, pulling inspiration from Sam.

"I saw you were here all alone, so I thought you might like some company?"

I heard Benny snort obviously amused by the horrible pickup line.

"Not from you," I said with an attitude wondering internally where the confidence in my voice came from, and watched the man sadly walk away making me feel like a complete and utter jerk.

85

"Well, that was harsh." I heard Benny over the line.

"It was effective." I heard Sam jump in. "Good work. Now keep an eye out for the contact."

After rebuffing three more attempts to either buy me a drink or share a dance I finally saw a masked man in a green suit come towards me. This was what we had been waiting for. I wished I could partake in the liquid courage in front of me but it was Showtime.

"Miss Scarlet?" He addressed me, and I nodded slightly trying to portray the cool confidence of the woman I was supposed to be.

"Mr. Green, I presume" I answered, projecting boredom and disinterest.

"May I escort you to the room which we have reserved?" He offered out his elbow.

"I thought you'd never ask," I answered only to kick myself as it sounded so juvenile.

He chuckled as he walked me toward the back of the grand room where I assumed the deal was supposed to go down. "I wasn't under the impression you were a woman known for her sense of humor."

Sugar cookies! I was blowing it. I needed a smooth recovery.

"I'm a woman of many talents," I answered smugly. "You'll keep my secret, won't you?" I whispered into his ear conspiratorially.

He coughed and sputtered "Oh, of course!"

"Nice recovery Elizabeth." I heard Sam over the earpiece. "Everyone get ready. Elizabeth is entering the room for the buy. Elizabeth, try to position yourself near one of the openings in the wall, so we can keep eyes on you."

86

The room was set up in a way I hadn't quite seen before. It had what seemed like the main door off to the side which acted as the entrance, but the wall consisted of individual panels suspended from a track above that seemed like it could be opened or closed depending on the needs of the venue. Tonight, they were slotted so that whoever was in the room would have a full, albeit slightly obstructed, view of all the activities going on for the event. It was smart for their surveillance, but it was also an ideal situation for me as well knowing the team would be able to see me at all times.

I walked into the room and upon closer inspection, I realized it looked almost like another miniature ballroom complete with a dance floor surrounded by chaise lounges and high-back chairs. Even though it lacked all the regalia used in the main area It was still an elegant space and seemed wasted on a black-market deal. I saw several what I would call goons standing near the rear exit which might pose an issue for a speedy exit. I filed that away to deal with later. I was led over to whom I assumed was the seller in one of the high-back chairs.

"Welcome Miss Scarlet " a robotic voice resonated from the man in front of me. He was using a voice modulator. I could tell that much. It was a smart idea to not give him away to the fictional buyer who was at the other end of my earpiece. He rose and walked towards me, giving me the opportunity to take him in. He was a specimen of a man I could tell just from the way he strolled toward me. He was fit and toned from the way his suit fit him, but his face was obscured with the most beautifully adorned mask I had ever seen. The intertwining of gold and silver paint as it swirled away from the eyes to the rest of the mask was accentuated by jewels and sequins. He had to have been in his 30s based on his gait and posture. At least we had more information now than we did before. I was told by the agents to look for any distinguishing marks but between the mask and his suit which also covered every bit of skin, I couldn't ascertain any.

"Let's have a drink before we begin negotiations, shall we?" the robotic voice asked, calling over a waiter who suddenly appeared and grabbed two flutes of champagne over his ornate serving tray. "Please indulge me in a little pleasure before business."

"I am pretty sure it's business before pleasure," I responded hesitantly, taking the champagne not wanting to look prudish.

"Easy Elizabeth." I heard Sam chastise me through the earpiece.

"Not the way I do it." I could hear the smugness in his voice even with the modular. "A toast to our future endeavors."

That was a bit presumptuous, but I clinked glasses anyway and saw him watching to see if I was drinking so I took a sip. It was the best champagne I had ever tasted so I took a couple more sips until someone came and took the glasses away from us. I heard the music in the venue change into a slow waltz.

"Honor me with a quick dance will you." He asked, offering out a hand with a flourish.

"My buyer is eager to get the proceedings rolling," I answered shortly, not wanting to enrage the possible arms dealer but wanting to get things moving.

"Oh, I know your boss and he wouldn't mind a little light conversation and a dance before moving on." This guy was a smooth talker. I'd give him that. Figuring he knew this 'boss' better than I did I nodded.

He was a good dancer, taking my frame perfectly for a waltz. It felt oddly familiar and I tried not to relax too much into position, but I couldn't help it. I hadn't danced like this since graduate school. I shook my head trying to clear those thoughts from my mind. Now wasn't the time for that.

"I must confess," he remarked as we continued to what felt like floating across the dance floor. "I find it a bit blasé for your boss to send you instead of coming in person. Hiding behind a woman is not very chivalrous."

"I'm an employee. Nothing more, nothing less. Why would he risk it? And by the way, what does my gender have to do with it? If a man came in my place, are you saying the business proceedings would go any differently?"

"Careful Elizabeth." Sam's voice hissed into my ear. Great. Just what I needed another man telling me what to do. I breathed in deeply to regain my composure wondering what had come over me.

I could feel the masked man smiling at me as he cocked his head to the side. "Well if you were a man conducting this business call, I'm quite sure we would not be waltzing so gracefully at this moment and he would definitely not look so beguiling as you do in that dress."

Okay so he was a very smooth talker, but I needed to remember why I was here in the first place and get back to the task at hand. Why had I forgotten about that? Had to get him to talk about the deal. My thoughts were becoming disjointed which wasn't like me at all. Was all the pressure and anxiety catching up with me?

I cleared my throat trying to reset and collect my thoughts. "Well, we aren't here to dance we are here to deal so if you don't mind I'd like to"

"We need to at least finish this song." He interrupted. I couldn't think of a reasonable response, so I simply nodded.

"See that wasn't so hard, was it? You dance marvelously." He said as we dipped and continued across the floor.

"I had a good teacher," I replied honestly. I shook my head once more trying to clear away the growing haze. Get it together girl. I couldn't believe a few sips of champagne were getting me this loose-lipped, but I had to rally.

"Oh really." He chuckled in a voice that sounded oddly familiar. When had he stopped using the voice modulator? He spun me again and then stopped moving, pulling me in close and leaning in to whisper in my ear. "I'm so glad you think I was a great teacher, *Lizzy*."

I froze feeling a sickening wave of dizziness and nauseous crash down on me.

"No. No. No." I repeated like a mantra trying to pull away, but I suddenly felt weak. He must have put something in the champagne. I didn't know what it was, but I knew I had to get away. Fight or flight was kicking in and I was going with flight. This couldn't be happening. It wasn't possible. All the running, lying, moving, isolation, and preparations. Was it for nothing? I had been so careful and purposeful in my actions and behavior. I saw all my best-laid plans spiraling down an invisible drain that led directly to him, my past in corporeal form.

"Shit, she's been compromised!" I vaguely heard Sam yell in my earpiece. "All units move in. I said to move in damn it."

That's right, I reminded myself. I wasn't alone. Sam and the team were right outside poised for action. I was going to be saved, I would be okay, I could get away from him this time and no one would get hurt.

It was then the fire alarm went off and although my vision had become slightly blurry, I saw Sam rushing through the panicked crowd. His face standing alone in a swarm of people going in the opposite direction as he fought against the surging crowd. Everything seemed to move in slow motion as I watched in horror as the panels that made up the wall began to shut the seconds ticking by tortuously, allowing me one final look into Sam's eyes which I hope conveyed that whatever happened from this point on was not his fault, and with that the panels slammed shut locking in place and sealing my fate.

"Elizabeth, can you hear me? Just hang on." I faintly heard Sam's voice call out.

"It really is rude to listen in on others' conversations, don't you think Lizzy." He whispered into my earpiece before removing it and casting it aside, the voice modulator completely gone at this point ensuring I knew whose arms I was currently caged in.

"Much better." He cooed as he reset our dancing frame and continued to have us sway across the dance floor. The drugs he had slipped me were in full effect now my limbs feeling weak with him mostly holding me up at this point as we continued our macabre waltz.

"How?" I croaked out trying to maintain consciousness, but I felt myself fading a tear falling from my eye as I knew how dire my situation was. Was I dying? Had he poisoned me? The woman in the red dress, her confession that brought me here, the IP address we found because it was meant to be found. Was this all orchestrated by him? My thoughts raced as I spiraled, emotions and thoughts converging like waves on the coast during a violent storm churning up all the bits of debris and wreckage I had banished to the deep dark depths of my mind. Maybe this was just a dream? A horrible vivid nightmare that I was going to wake up from any moment now.

"Oh, Lizzy." He soothed me, whipping a tear away and snapping me back to reality realizing how foolish I was to have hoped for just one second that this situation wasn't happening to me. "You know how I hate it when you cry."

He led me over to one of the chaise lounges and placed my head on his shoulder and I was unable to do anything about it whatever substance he had given me causing me to be completely helpless.

91

"When my associates said they had met someone with your description on a little late-night work for me I had to come and see for myself. You are *very* good at hiding your tracks. I'm impressed." He soothed caressing my face with the back of his hand like an old lover would.

I tried to speak, a million unformed questions swirling in my mind but only a pathetic rasp came out.

"Shh." He crooned, stroking my hair. "We'll have time to catch up later, but your new friends are almost here and I'm afraid I must leave."

He leaned me against the arm of the chaise gently and with great care much to my confusion, going as far as to adjust the pillows to cradle my neck.

"See you soon" he whispered as he placed a kiss on my forehead while sliding something in my hands, and then he was gone. I heard Sam's voice in the distance and what sounded like someone trying to break down a door before I relented and slipped into nothingness.

CHAPTER 13

I attempted to push my way through the crowd to the room that Elizabeth was now trapped in.

"We need the tactical unit in here now. Move it!" I commanded through my com.

I felt like I was swimming against the current as people pushed past me rushing to the exit. They were smart to vacate the venue but I grew frustrated as they slowed my attempt to get to Elizabeth. Was she dead? Taken hostage? I was so sure that this would work but was I being reckless with someone's life because my pride had been hurt that *my* office was broken into and damaged on my watch? Shit. I couldn't let those intrusive thoughts get to me. There would be time for that later. Right now, I had to get to Dr. Waller and salvage what I could from this mission.

I finally made it to the main door and found it securely locked. I backed up a few paces and tried kicking the door in but it didn't budge. I tried ramming the door with my shoulders. It didn't move an inch. I rubbed my shoulder where it had impacted the wall. I was going to need to bring in the big guns if that door was going to get opened in the next few minutes and every minute counted at this point.

"We have a door here that needs to be mechanically breached. Get someone over here now!" I ordered through the coms. I had a team on standby just in case for situations like this.

I moved on from the door, leaving that to the rest of the team and tried to pull on the wall panels, but they were locked in place solidly. What kind of entertainment venue had a lockdown like Fort Knox? These safety measures didn't show up anywhere in the research we did on the site prior to the operation. With the panels being a bust my next stop was the main door. I didn't have my gun, so shooting out the hinges wasn't a viable solution. I was running out of options and out of time. Every minute that passed meant dwindling hope for Elizabeth's safety and the chances of catching the assholes we came here for in the first place. I heard multiple voices responding confirming my orders, but I couldn't get the look in Elizabeth's eyes before the panels slammed shut out of my mind. They shifted from a look of absolute horror and panic to one of complete and utter resignation right before it closed.

"Dominic, do we have eyes in that room? Anything hotel security has a feed on." I asked, not used to feeling useless.

"Already on it sir." Dominic responded "It seems as if the feed to that room has been cut. We'll be going in blind."

"What about getting this door open?" I growled out not liking my limited options and getting impatient kicking the door to show my anger.

"It should have been immediately released when the fire safety systems were activated," Dominic answered matter-of-factly.

"What about the remote release of the doors?" I tried throwing my shoulder into the door again to see if it would budge. I painfully bounced off the door like a rubber ball. That was going to hurt in the morning.

"Tried that as well from the security booth here but it was no use. Looks like some extra locks have been added without the security team or staff knowledge. The whole system has been tampered with." Dominic replied.

"Have the secondary team on standby and secure the surrounding area. No one in or out." If the action spilled into the streets I wanted to make sure we were ready, and any civilians were out of the crosshairs. The suspect's comment about hiding behind a woman was also getting under my skin. I don't hide behind anyone, especially not women. When had he figured out that we had planned a raid? Was this whole thing a setup or did I somehow miss something and give us away? I was never going to hear the end of this from my father.

It felt like an eternity and a day before reinforcements came to knock down the door. Once the door came down agents swarmed into the room and I followed close behind. I scanned the room and saw Elizabeth located on the side of the room motionless. Her hands were neatly arranged on her chest holding a rose while her dress was neatly laid out around her. I could see a glass of champagne spilled on the floor next to her. It was like a macabre Sleeping Beauty. What the hell was going on?

"We need a medic in here now. Team fan out and sweep the area." I yelled and dashed my way over to her. She looked frail and her pallor was even more off-putting. Fearing the worst I put two fingers to her neck. I let out the breath I didn't realize I had been holding.

"I have a pulse! Elizabeth, can you hear me?" I shook her shoulders a bit to see if I could get a response but she remained eerily still.

"All clear." An agent yelled from the other side of the room.

"All clear here as well Sir." Another agent echoed. "Looks like they went out this back alley."

As the scene was secure, the EMTs rushed in, loaded Elizabeth onto a stretcher, and started to take her out to the ambulance.

"Dominic," I commanded as I followed the team out. "Finish up here. Find out what you can about the seller that was here and secure the scene. I'm riding to the hospital with Elizabeth, so I can find out

95

what went down once she wakes up."

"You got it, Sam." Dominic came through the communication line just as I loaded into the ambulance right behind Elizabeth.

The ride to the hospital felt like it was the longest ride of my life. The EMTs worked to try to figure out what had happened. They tried calling her name, tapping, to see if she had simply fainted, but they couldn't bring her around. They studied her for any signs of trauma or if she was injected with something and found none, her porcelain skin had not a bruise or puncture wound to be found. When we got to the hospital, they rushed her away to run some toxicology tests and indicated that I should call her emergency contact just in case. I went to the waiting room and called the Field Office to get the emergency contact number. I almost snapped my phone in two when they read me the phone number for her contact, the only contact number she had listed in fact. It was a number I knew very well. My father's.

"I fucking knew it," I said loudly under my breath earning me a disapproving glare from the nurse at the desk.

When I was living at home a few years ago my father would get phone calls in the middle of the night and would move to a room where my mother and I couldn't hear him.

Even when my mother was undergoing her cancer treatments and when she was in the hospital he would step out of the room when *she* called. I could hear it was a woman's voice at least. I brought it up to my mom once before she passed, and she just patted my arm and would change the subject. I couldn't stand to see my mother look at the man who was cheating on her with such affection even as she lay dying. I moved out soon after, but I knew he was probably continuing his affair and now I had proof. It all made sense now how Dr. Waller was able to get all those FBI consult positions. He fucking gave them to her. Her resume having more holes than swiss cheese was the first indication. I bet she didn't even have her doctorate degree. Well, she

96

had me fooled with her mousy looks and her shy demeanor. Bravo Elizabeth. I'd call my father, have him come down to the hospital, and then we'd see how they could hide the truth, and Elizabeth, if she woke up, would be out of a job and out of my life before the day was done.

I was sitting in Elizabeth's room impatiently waiting for my father when the man of the hour rushed in.

"Elizabeth?" he exclaimed breathlessly, looking like he had run all the way to the hospital ignoring me completely and sprinting over to the bed and grabbing her hand.

She started to rouse and then suddenly sat up abruptly startling both my father and me. "No!" she screamed looking panicked around the room trying to get off the bed until she saw my father and realized it was him holding her hand.

"Robert?" she asked, her voice meek sounding like a small child. He nodded, and she grasped for him crying into his shoulder. Well, if this wasn't confirmation I didn't know what was. He even showed no shame in front of his own son. I wonder if he was like this in front of my mother before she died too. Fucking asshole.

"Elizabeth." He said sternly and seriously, turning her so that she was facing him. "Was it him?"

She nodded slowly clutching at her bed sheets and drawing them close to her as if they would shield her from harm. There would be no hiding from my wrath. And who the heck were they talking about?

"Nice to see you *dad*," I said with animosity dripping from my voice getting up from the chair and walking towards him.

"Robert's your father?" she asked cocking her head to the side like a cockatoo which made her look ridiculous but did indicate she might not have known our relationship. One look at the two of us side by side and there was no denying the similarities in our features. He was tall, but not as tall as me which was always a sense of pride on my part. He was Caucasian and had once had jet black hair but was now mostly gray with the black peppered in. He still appeared stout for a man of his age and I hated to admit I hoped I had his physique when I was his age. Maybe that was why he was still able to attract the ladies.

"I use my *late* mother's last name," I responded by accentuating the word late. "Glad to see you ran over her to check on your girlfriend."

Elizabeth scrunched her face in what appeared to be sincere confusion and my father rose to meet me in the middle of the room.

"Get your head out of your ass son." He reprimanded me as he poked my chest. "Elizabeth's in the Witness Security Program and she's my charge."

I stood not moving for a minute or two. I stared over at Elizabeth who almost seemed to be shaking from fear like a puppy that had been scolded. It wasn't fear of my father or myself but something that went down at the masquerade. I suddenly felt like an asshole for accusing this woman of something she obviously would never think of doing. Now, I strangely felt like I needed to protect her from whatever she was so terrified of. I was obviously left out of some loop and I was not happy about it.

"Does someone want to explain to me what the hell is going on? What happened during the sting operation?" I asked, falling back to anger and not liking that I didn't know what the hell was going on and that I didn't have all the information that could have potentially impacted the operation.

"Jesus Son, do you see what state she's in?" My father responded by reclaiming the seat next to her hospital bed.

"It's okay Robert." Elizabeth replied, giving my father a brief attempt at a smile "he needs to know. It's relevant to the case."

"My name is not Elizabeth Waller." She said, turning to look me right in my eyes. "My name is Elisabeth Mallory."

CHAPTER 14

I took a deep breath, squirming uncomfortably under the gazes of the men currently waiting for her next words.

"Why does that last name sound familiar?" I asked, taking the seat across from the hospital bed.

"Before I can go into that," I continued, "I need to tell you the *whole* story." I watched Sam settle in and Robert gave me a supporting parental look, standing to peer out in the hallway before closing the door to the room and returning to my bedside. I took a deep breath and began.

"When I was born, I was put up for adoption and eventually ended up at an orphanage run by the state. As part of an effort by the state to improve its image, they started sending some of the orphans to private schools for education. The other students from affluent families did not look kindly on the poor girl without a mother or a father, so I spent most of my time holed up in the library where I found solace reading any book I could get my hands on. It turned out, I was advanced for my age group and soon a family on the board of the school took notice and adopted me. It wasn't an act of love or kindness, but one of convenience. They were making their way into the political scene and 'saving' the smart gifted kid got them good publicity. They would bring me out like a show pony during dinner parties and political events, having the guests ask me questions that I almost always knew the answers to. We were never a real family and I accepted that. I was grateful to have a roof over my head and access to all the learning material I could ever want."

"I'm sorry you had to go through that, Elizabeth," Sam interrupted awkwardly rubbing the back of his neck with his hands, "but I'm not quite sure what that has to do with what happened tonight."

"I'm getting there," I sighed and continued with my tale. This wasn't easy for me and an impatient Sam was not helping. "When I was old enough I went to college, finally free from my surrogate family. I was on my own without their judging and watchful eyes for the first time. As you can imagine, I was awkward and didn't make friends easily. That's when I met *him*."

I glanced at Robert, who squeezed my hand comfortingly, knowing how hard it was to talk about this part of my life. I plowed forward, trying to stamp down my rising anxiety.

"His name is Alex. Dr. Alexander Beal. I met him during one of our chemistry labs he was TAing in graduate school and I was quickly smitten. He was suave, handsome, and almost if not actually smarter than me at the time. It was refreshing. Instead of being intimidated by me like most of the boys in my classes were, he challenged me and talked with me, listening intently as I gushed over any interesting topic I had just learned about. Eventually, we started dating, and both got accepted into a prestigious microbiology PhD research program. We were two years into the program when he proposed. I accepted, of course, completely devoted and head over heels in love with him. Those were the happiest years of my entire life."

I let the emotions roll over me wave after wave giving myself permission to remember the good times.

"We even went dancing a few times," I continued. "We had watched a classic with Fred Astair, I can't recall which one, but I remember jokingly remarking on how men that could dance were sexy. A few weeks later, he enrolled us in some dance classes at a studio. He was always good at romance." I was stalling and I knew it.

I peered over at Sam, seeing him arch an eyebrow, discernibly wondering where I was going with all this. I took a deep breath in preparing for the painful part I didn't talk about often, if ever.

101

"It was around this time that I noticed Alex was getting an increase in phone calls, especially at night. The gifts he bought me also became increasingly lavish. The engagement ring alone was far outside of a post doctor's earnings meaning he was supplementing his income from somewhere. You see, one of the things that bonded Alex and me was that he was also orphaned. Instead of being adopted by a rich family, however, he was left to languish in the system until he was old enough to leave on his own. He never begrudged me for getting adopted by a wealthy family, or at least that's what he told me, and always joked that he'd much prefer his childhood over mine, locked away like a glass animal in a menagerie.

"What he did hold animosity towards however was 'the man,' so to speak. He always spoke about how money ran the world, and once he had it all, then he would be satisfied. When he started buying me expensive gifts, I always tried to get him to return them as I thought he was taking on extra jobs and he was already spending long hours in the lab. As we started getting closer to the wedding, I noticed he was gone or would take a trip away more and more often. I thought maybe he was having second thoughts, but he said he was just spending some extra time in the lab trying to get a new project done and was collaborating with other labs. I bought his excuses, hook line and sinker and never even questioned his intentions. He always excelled at that..." I continued fiddling with a stray thread on the hospital bed sheets. "...telling you just enough information so that you would drop the topic. Not the truth, but not a lie either."

"Why do you keep talking about this guy in the past tense?" Sam asked, crossing his arms in front of his chest. I was beginning to learn that he was not a patient man.

"Let her finish, son," Robert interjected assertively, causing Sam's posture to stiffen in his chair.

I took another deep breath, knowing I would need it for the slurry of questions that would come rapid fire at me once Sam knew the conclusion to the story.

"I didn't pry into Alex's work as much as I should have, because I had just made a pretty big discovery of my own. I had gotten a grant from the Department of Defense to work on the bacteria Francisella tularensis."

"What the heck is Francisella tularensis?" Sam interrupted, earning himself a glare from Robert, to which he responded by throwing his hands up in surrender. I hoped this meant he wouldn't be interrupting again, as retelling my story was starting to make me feel more physically ill than I already was.

"The reason you haven't heard of F. tularensis, or as it's commonly referred to, Tularemia, is because it is pretty benign. It is rarely contracted and when it is it has a 5% mortality rate. I studied it to see if I could figure out its virulence factor and restrict it as it was pretty stable and safe to work on."

I looked over to see Sam's gaze glazing over in confusion. "I was trying to make the bacteria not as bad of a bacterium?" I tried and saw a glimmer of recognition indicating that my words hit home.

"I figured by learning the virulence factor of this bacteria I could apply the mechanism to other dangerous bacteria, such as Anthrax or botulism. I wanted to help third world countries that had restricted access to clinics by having an aerosol version of a vaccine that could simply be distributed via inhalation, no needles involved."

I braced myself for the rush of emotions that I knew was coming once I released the floodgates. I had pushed the memories deep down inside my consciousness with such pressure that I fossilized them, and now here I was, digging through layers of sediment and time to bring them back to the surface. I focused down at my lap, knowing I

103

wouldn't be able to look Sam in the eyes after this. I balled up the sheets in my fists, trying to gain the strength to finish my tale.

"It wasn't until I overheard a study group talking in the library that I knew something was wrong. I packed up my things and immediately went back to my room, hoping to God, I had misheard them, that I got it wrong and my world was not shattering around me. I turned on the news and it was everywhere. A large group of mercenaries in the Congo had been killed by what looked like a biological weapon. They had identified the bacteria as Tularemia, but since it was naturally occurring, they were investigating whether or not it was an act of bioterrorism. What perplexed the authorities was that the bacteria should not be able to kill at such a high mortality rate and definitely not as quickly. The next words that came out of the reporter's mouth hit me like a punch straight to my gut as they delivered breaking news. It was believed that it had been delivered in an aerosol form as strange air canisters had been found near the site. I immediately went into the bathroom and threw up. As I sat on the cold floor the only thought that ran through my head was that I had shared my research with only one other person. The only other person I trusted to read my work before I submitted it for publication."

"Alex," Sam whispered with an undertone of anger seeping through, and I nodded to confirm his suspicions. "So he stole your work and instead of turning the bacteria down he turned it up to an 11."

"I had never really put it like that, but yes." I smiled sadly.

"Shit Elizabeth. Sam shook his head in disbelief. "What does all of this have to do with what happened tonight?"

"Once I realized what Alex had done, I called the FBI and they assigned me to Robert." Robert squeezed my hand, attempting to comfort me.

104

"I testified, and after a painful and lengthy trial on a global stage, my testimony and the research notes they found when they raided a warehouse Alex had been using as a makeshift lab as well as evidence that he had been working with a shady underground arms dealer, were enough for Alex to be found guilty. My foster family distanced themselves from me, not wanting the scandal to hurt their political careers and ironically was the only good that came out of all this. Just in case Alex or one of his criminal associates wanted some revenge for my testimony and so that no one else of dubious nature would come after me to finish the work Alex had done, Robert put me in witness protection.

"About a year or so later, when none of Alex's criminal associates popped up looking for me to continue his work or come after me, I was released from the witness protection program. Robert and I still felt like it was best if I kept a low profile and kept some anonymity so I continued on with the program in an unofficial capacity and started a new life. I didn't want to be associated with my old life anyway. I went back to school and got a second degree in forensics, wanting to try to atone for the deaths I had caused by doing my part to make sure it *never* happened again. I guess I failed on that front too." I finished, suddenly exhausted, and took my hand from Robert's, lowering my head.

I glanced up to see Sam staring at me, running his hands through his hair. "So, if this Alex guy is the one you met tonight, what's the problem? We know who the scumbag is and we can nail him."

I glimpsed over at Robert, too tired to talk anymore.

"The problem is, son," Robert said, staring Sam straight in the eyes, "Alex died during an escape attempt five years ago."

Sam opened and closed his mouth and then finally spoke. "Okay, well I didn't see that coming."

105

"Neither did I," I said, starting to tremble. "I thought for sure when I was losing consciousness that he was going to kill me for what I did. For betraying him."

"You did nothing wrong," Robert said sternly, almost willing me to believe him. I didn't.

"Your father," I said, turning to Sam "never really believed he was dead like everyone else. Myself included."

"It was winter and, in an attempt, to take over a transport unit he was in, Alex ended up going over a bridge into a frozen lake. They found the vehicle, the bodies of the correctional officers driving the transport, and Alex's jacket with his inmate number on it but no body." Robert added, including the grim details of Alex's assumed death. "I do wish I had been wrong, Elizabeth."

"I never really felt like he was gone either. I've been looking over my shoulder for five years. It seems like we did a pretty good job up until now."

"Until someone screwed it up," Robert growled angrily, glancing at Sam.

It seemed like Sam was about to unload on his father and start a fight, which my budding headache begged me to put a stop to.

'It's not Sam's fault," I said, patting Robert's arm. "They identified me at the lab during the break-in. It was probably the reason why they didn't shoot me in the first place."

"I had almost forgotten about the lab break-in," Robert said speculatively. "We have a lot to talk about, Sam. Come with me to get a coffee. Elizabeth could use some rest. I can fill in the blanks later but for now, let's give her some peace and quiet. I have a few agents stationed outside the door to make sure only the vetted hospital staff go in or out."

106

I was grateful for Robert as I was feeling physically and mentally drained and could use some more sleep. It looked like Sam wanted to continue the conversation, but Robert shot him a look only a man with his authoritative stature could pull off. Sam acquiesced, shooting him a look only a son could give a father, and left the room with a huff. It made me jealous of their relationship. It was fractured, yes, but you could see the love and bond there. That was my last thought before I allowed myself to fall into a deep slumber.

***

I paced in the hospital's cafeteria as my father sat and calmly sipped on his cup of coffee.

"Jesus Dad," I whisper yelled, "Why didn't you tell me you sent a ticking time bomb to my field office?"

"As your Assistant Director, I placed Elizabeth at your office because she is the best forensic scientist that we have on consult." He paused. His calm demeanor was infuriating. It always drove me crazy as a kid. The more angry I got, the more obstinately serene he became. "As your father, I wanted her to be near someone I trusted. I had a hunch something big was going to happen soon and I wanted her to be surrounded by someone I knew would be competent enough to handle the challenge and protect her."

I thought I detected a hint of a compliment in there that I would revisit but I needed answers. Now.

"If Elizabeth created the bacteria that killed all those people, how is she not in jail right now?"

"If she had it her way she would be. Charges were dropped for her testimony, for being a whistleblower, and for the fact that Alex had manipulated her research into something else entirely, proving her innocence. Dr. Beal himself had testified that he had acted alone and that Elizabeth was innocent. I had to make her take the acquittal as she said she felt she needed to be punished for her part in the deaths. I knew she would be too great an asset and it would have been a shame for her to throw her life away rotting in some jail cell, so I convinced her that being out in the world, using her talents for good could be her penance."

"I don't see Elizabeth taking anyone's advice or help. She's the most stubborn person I know." I had only known her a short time, but she wouldn't even take my hand after an explosion and having a gun in her face. She would rather gather the strength to get back up on her own.

"That she is." Robert chuckled, helping himself to more coffee. "She has become a tough woman. I remember when I first met her she was trembling most of the time. She wouldn't make eye contact with anyone and seemed like she was on the verge of tears every second of the day. The betrayal and the anger she felt, she directed it inward instead of lashing out at the world. I'm proud of the woman she's become over these last five years but when I saw her in that hospital bed she looked just like she did then. I pray to God that the small spark she's gotten back hasn't been extinguished for good."

Elizabeth and I didn't always see eye to eye, but she was hella smart, I could see that much, she had good intuition, and was proving to be a strong asset for the team. It was hard to imagine a woman of her caliber being led astray by such a worm of a man. She didn't deserve what happened to her, no one did, but at the end of the day three people were dead and there was an apparent sociopath on the loose.

"So, did Mom know about Elizabeth?"

"Of course she did Son," Robert answered with a smile. "I could never get anything past that woman. She even provided some advice on how to talk to Elizabeth and get her through the more trying times.

Even though she and Elizabeth never met, she cared for Elizabeth deeply. Right Up to the end, your Mother told me to look out for her. She was always selfless like that."

He turned toward me and really stared at me so I would understand the gravity of his words. "It really bothered your Mother that I couldn't tell you the reason behind all the late-night calls and urgent rushing out of the house but she hoped one day you would come to understand."

I was mulling over his words, not really sure how I felt about everything when I felt my phone vibrating in my pocket and took it out to see what was going on.

"Shit, Dominic and Benny have been blowing up my phone." I had about 20 missed calls from the two of them alone. I turned to my father and he nodded, indicating I should answer it.

"What is going on with Elizabeth, is she going to make it?" Benny asked, his voice frantic.

"She's going to be fine. It looks like they just gave her a sedative or something. She's sleeping it off now."

"Well thank tits for that," Benny responded, releasing a deep breath into the phone. "She looked like a corpse when they were taking her away on the stretcher and we were all thinking the worst."

"Benny, what I need to know is what went down after I left the scene." I heard Benny take a pause, indicating he was going to tell me the news I didn't want to hear.

"The scene was clean man. I mean top-notch professionally swept clean. All the footage from the venue's security system was remotely wiped clean. We can't trace the IP from where the footage was wiped from. We couldn't get any IDs from the staff or hotel guests since everyone was wearing masks. We're back to square one."

I didn't like the thought that everything that happened last night and what happened to Elizabeth was all for nothing. It gave me some insight into the case, though.

"If we can't trace the IP address now and we were able to before, we have to assume that everything — from the raid to the suspect in custody, and the sting at the masquerade —was all a setup."

"Um... about that," Benny added, folding in on himself like he was trying to make himself a smaller target. "*Former* in-custody suspect. She was being transported to the county jail for booking and they never made it. I spoke to the Agent who did the handover and all the forms and stuff for the transfer he said was legit. Called county jail and they said they never sent anyone over for transfer. They couldn't even find anything on anyone named Delilah. What is going on man?"

"Shit!" I exclaimed, as I kicked a chair and earned a side-eyed look from my father. "Any tire tracks outside from the getaway vehicles?" There had to be one clue, something I could chase down to nail this sonofabitch.

"There was nothing. It was like they were ghosts. This is like some next-level espionage man. I don't think we've come across an operation of this level before."

"Work with Dominic and pull all the information you can on Dr. Alex Beal. I want everything from his education to what brand of toilet paper he wipes his ass with."

"Alright, are you coming back into the office?" I should have gone straight back to the office but I just didn't feel right to leave Dr. Waller, or should I say Dr. Malory, just yet.

110

"I'm going to go talk to the foremost expert on our suspect." I glanced at my father who was looking away, pretending not to be eavesdropping on my conversation, but I knew better.

"Oh yeah and who's that?" Benny asked, sounding like he was packing up to head back to the office to carry out my orders.

"One Dr. Elizabeth Waller."

CHAPTER 15

I surveyed my hospital room, still perplexed and hoping I was in a horrible nightmare until I pinched herself and saw the IV sticking out of my arm.

"Nurse?" I called out timidly into the intercom.

"Yes, Dr. Waller, what can I do for you?" A no-nonsense sounding nurse responded.

"Is there a gift shop or a store nearby where I could get some essentials and some clothing?" I had no plans of putting on that dress again and as I didn't currently see it in the room I hoped it had been burned. And there was no way I was going to subject my feet to a pair of stiletto heels again. Those things were death traps disguised as footwear. I knew my mind was on the verge of collapse, so I was going to do what one of my therapists had recommended, focus on what you can control, and clothing was something I could handle.

The nurse chastised me that I wasn't cleared to leave yet but removed my IV anyway. She mentioned that an older gentleman had brought a bag of items for me. I smiled fondly as I sorted through the bag. You could tell it was packed by a man, a collection of bottles, pastes, and brushes that didn't form a cohesive hygiene regime, but the sentiment was there, and I appreciated it. In a way, Robert was like a father figure to me, certainly more so than my foster father, and I was grateful that he was in my life.

I scrunched up my nose at a thought that had suddenly invaded my mind. Did that make Sam my brother? I shook that disturbing thought out of my head and began to change. I had just finished pulling my shirt over my head when Sam burst through the door. I hurriedly pulled the shirt down the rest of the way and was about to chastise him when he turned around.

"I didn't see anything!" he practically yelled from the other side of the room. "Not that I'm implying you have anything that someone wouldn't want to see. Shit." I could tell from his body language that he was very uncomfortable and for some reason, I found it comforting. Even the great Special Agent Han could be rattled by a little side boob.

"You curse a lot, you know that?" I was packing up my bags and I thought he would be grateful for the change in topic that didn't concern my state of undress.

"I'm aware." He rubbed the back of his neck with his hands. I noticed he did that quite often. Maybe it was when he wasn't feeling confident in a situation. I'd file that information away, but I knew it would be a futile effort as I would be gone soon.

"Where are you going?" He asked, inquisitorial, grabbing the strap of my bag. I pulled the bag back and continued packing.

"My location has been compromised. Alex knows where I am, and probably wants to kill me, so I need to go. You're a special agent, isn't this witness protection 101?"

"Nothing about you is 101 anything," Sam mumbled as he again pulled my bag away from me, flicking it towards the wall.

"Real mature," I snapped, glaring daggers at him. He grabbed my arm, the uninjured one thankfully, and stopped me from moving any further.

"You are the best chance we have at catching Dr. Beal. You are basically the foremost expert on this guy. I have Benny and Dominic looking into him, but I have a feeling they're not going to come up with much if he's flown under the radar for this long and he has supposedly been dead for the past 5 years. If anyone can give me some sort of a lead to go on, it's you." His grip softened a little.

"Plus," he continued, "you'd have the best FBI team watching your back for protection."

"I can protect myself, thank you very much. I don't think getting blown up, or drugged while in FBI care is the kind of protection I need right now." I sneered, pulling my arm away from him more forcefully than was needed, causing me to get dizzy and lose my balance, but Sam caught me at the last second in a dipped position like we were in the midst of a passionate tango. After awkwardly looking into each other's eyes for a bit longer than was comfortable for either of us, he righted me.

"You alright?"

I steadied myself on the meal cart next to the bed, removing my arm from his grasp. "I'm fine."

He cleared his throat. "So you're going to run away? Like it's not your responsibility to help stop him if you can? Or was all that guilt earlier just for my father's benefit?"

Well that hurt, and was a low blow even for him. I was already feeling a torrent of guilt and anguish as those deaths at the resort were mostly likely in some part my fault, and to have someone like Sam throw it back in my face was almost too much. He noticed his mistake immediately and went to speak when I saw Robert standing in the door frame.

"I think you've done enough for one day, son," he said, patting Sam's shoulder, which was shrugged off in an instant.

"I'm afraid he has a point though, Elizabeth." Et tu, Robert? "I don't believe running is going to solve this problem. You're the best chance we have at catching him. If what happened at the resort in the Adirondacks is any indicator..."

"He's probably only getting started," I whispered, as I sat back down on the hospital bed, feeling quite defeated. I was a woman of logic and it was a logical assessment to make.

"Although my son lacks the finer points of communication, I believe that was what he was getting at. Not only are you the foremost expert on Alex, you're the only one who is familiar with his work."

"You mean my work," I corrected, trying to straighten up and not let the men before me rattle me.

"No, that motherfucker's work. He turned your work into an abomination and twisted it until it was unrecognizable. Looks like the bastard finally built up the backing to try it again. You and I both know this so enough with the self-loathing."

I smiled. At least I knew where Sam got his swearing from and of course, he was right. I wanted— no needed— Alex behind bars more than anyone else, and if I was truly going to atone for my mistakes then this was the best chance I was going to have. I already had three more deaths on my hands and I didn't think I could handle any more.

"Okay Alpha males," I said, bouncing off the hospital bed while maintaining a steady grip on the railing. "What's the plan?" I attempted to project the confidence I was trying my darndest to summon. I knew I would need it if I was going to get through this.

"I'll leave that up to you and Sam, but first you need to go back to your apartment and gather your things," Robert answered, pulling out his phone to make a call to who knows who.

"Alright, where will I be staying then? You have a safe house in the area?"

"The safest place I know." Robert smiled in a way that made me feel instantly concerned. "Sam's apartment."

115

CHAPTER 16

"WHAT!" Sam and I screeched at the same time to Robert's obvious delight.

"This is a hospital, you two should really keep it down." Robert playfully chided.

Sam and I began to mumble out many compelling reasons why it was a horrible idea for me to stay with him, but Robert simply raised his hand, indicating we both needed to shut up.

"Sam's worried about losing his biggest lead on this case and you, Elizabeth, are worried about Alex coming for you. Seems like a win-win to me. Now if you'll excuse me, I'm sure you want to go and grab your things, Elizabeth, and get settled into Sam's place. I'll be in touch." And with that bombshell, Robert disappeared into the hospital hallway.

"Shall we?" Sam gestured toward the door, signaling it was time to go much to my surprise.

"Are you really not going to fight Robert, I mean, your dad on this?"

"Have you ever fought my dad on anything and won?" He grabbed my bag and made his way to the door.

"Touché," I laughed. It felt foreign to me, but not unpleasant, and it was brief, but I could have sworn I saw a slight smile on Sam's face as well.

The drive to my apartment was, in a word, uncomfortable. To pass the time I observed what I could see of Sam's car. It was mostly, and impressively, very tidy. The only litter to be found were a few empty coffee cups which I nudged absentmindedly with my feet.

After the silence became almost unbearable I turned on the radio and was serenaded by I Want It That Way by the Backstreet Boys. I arched my brow at Sam and he quickly changed the channel to a soft Rock station.

"So," Sam started awkwardly with a cough, no doubt trying to avoid any questions about his taste in music. "What can you tell me about Alex?" Ah, so the Inquisition was going to start now apparently. I turned down the music so we could talk without too much background noise.

"What do you want to know?" I answered honestly. Did he want past haunts or any information about my work? If it could help the case I was an open book.

"Why did you get engaged to him?"

Okay well, maybe not *that* open. That was not the first question I expected to come out of his mouth. It was such a personal question and I didn't see how it related to the case at all.

"I mean..." he coughed. "To be engaged to someone you must know them pretty intimately, so what qualities attracted you to him?"

"I don't know what to say that I didn't already tell you at the hospital."" I answered honestly. "We were both orphans, so we had that in common. I guess the regular things that attract any woman to a man. He listened, he was doting, and he complimented me on both my appearance *and* my scientific work which was key. It also helped that he was very attractive and good in bed. I mean he could do this thing..."

"Stop!" Sam exclaimed, and I couldn't stop the giggle that bubbled up. Where the heck did that come from? I hadn't giggled since, ever. Maybe Nina was rubbing off on me.

"You added that last bit to throw me off, didn't you."

"Maybe," I answered in a self satisfied voice.

"Anything *useful* you can enlighten me with?" Sam shifted in his seat and readjusted his hands on the steering wheel. I decided that teasing Sam was one of my new favorite things. I sobered quickly, however, the joy fleeting, realizing that this was a literal life and death situation and I needed to focus on more serious things.

"To be honest, I don't know if I really *knew* Alex. He was devastatingly charming and could manipulate practically anyone to get what he wanted. He was a master at grant writing and getting donations for his research. I always thought I was in on his tricks, but we both know how wrong I was on that front. He is highly intelligent as well. He was the only one who could keep up with me in discussions about my work, even when my professors were struggling to understand my research goals. He is disarming, and people easily gravitate to him. It's not surprising to me that he could potentially set up a criminal network." I paused, not really wanting to remember this aspect of him, but knowing I had to embrace what he really was if I was going to be of any help at all in capturing him.

"He is territorial, and not above using violence to get a point across."

"Okay, what does that mean? Does he get jealous? That's a normal guy thing."

"No, Sam." I took a deep breath remembering what happened all those years ago. "He will completely *destroy* someone if he feels slighted. When we were dating, we went to a local hole-in-the-wall college bar and I went up to the bar to order another round of drinks. A boy who was in one of my classes recognized me, was obviously drunk, and tried to hit on me. I politely tried to rebuff him, telling him I was there with my boyfriend, but he didn't listen. When my drinks were up, and I tried to politely leave to get back to my table, he grabbed my hand, hard, causing me to wince and spill my drink. The next thing I knew the boy was on the ground, his nose bleeding, and Alex was in front of me."

"Okay," Sam said, obviously not impressed. "Guys got a good right hook and defended his lady. Still seems like a normal douchebag guy shit to me. How were you supposed to know that he'd turn into a criminal mastermind?"

"You didn't see the look in his eyes Sam." I shuddered, remembering how it seemed like the flames of hell were dancing in his eyes, seeking vengeance. "I was utterly mortified, and I dreaded seeing the boy in class the following week, but he never showed up. It turned out his offsite housing had burned down. The following day he was accused of cheating, found guilty, and then kicked out of college."

"And you think Alex had something to do with this."

"I'm *sure* Alex had something to do with it. Back then I was blinded by my unconditional love for him, but after the incident, it was like I was seeing him for the first time and I knew, in my gut, that he was capable of terrible, terrible things."

"So, you're saying I should watch my back?" Sam said, teasing me. It appeared that he had a new favorite pastime as well. "I mean, we are going to be living together."

"Oh, like he'd see you as competition." He clutched his chest as if my words had physically injured him and laughed, and so did I, but in the back of my mind I was, just a little, afraid for him.

"If he loved you so fucking much, what makes you think he wants to kill you?" Sam asked, pulling into a parking spot in front of my apartment building.

"I don't think it was love," I answered honestly, unbuckling my seatbelt. I had thought about this more than once in the past years. "I loved him with all my heart. I know that for a fact and I've accepted that, but I think for him it wasn't love. It was more like I was a possession, a toy he didn't want to share with anyone else." A thought entered my mind that was so foul I could feel bile rising in my throat.

"Sam," I asked quietly, afraid of what his answer might be. "What if he's not going to try to kill me... What if he tries to take me?" I could hear the hysteria in my own voice, but I couldn't stop myself. "What if he tries to get me to create something that will kill more people, what if- "

"No," Sam interrupted, parking the car, breaking me out of my downward spiral and turning to face me. "Alex is not getting anywhere near you. I'm going to do my job, you're going to do your job, and together we are going to put this psycho behind bars. Got it?" He stared at me intently, his eyes never leaving mine. "Got it?" he repeated with a little more emphasis this time like he was willing me to believe him, and I wanted to, but in the back of my mind, I knew it was too good to be true.

"I heard you the first time." He glared at me, obviously wanting me to say the words. "I got it, geez." I got out of the car and Sam went to get out as well.

"Oh no, you stay. It's fine, you can stay in the car."

"Like hell I am," Sam said, getting out and slamming the car door. "Did you not listen to anything I just said?"

"Yes, but I didn't think that meant you were going to be with me 24/7. I'm quite capable of packing a bag from my own apartment."

"Let me check it out first. If he knew where you were working and orchestrated the break-in at the FBI and the masquerade I'm sure

120

he could figure out your address."

I hated to admit it, but he had a point. I gestured for him to go ahead and he obliged. I leaned against the car, threw him the keys to the apartment, told him which unit it was, and waited for the all-clear.

"Looks like we are good, you can come up." He called out the window a few minutes later. Subtle. I made my way up and saw Sam giving the place a once over and not looking too impressed.

"How long have you been in this apartment? It looks abandoned with everything in boxes." He surveyed the room pointing out all the things I hadn't bothered to unpack. "Were you planning to make a break before all of this went down?"

"Judgey," I responded, slipping past him to pack up some essentials. I was hoping that my new living arrangements would be short-lived, so I grabbed my laptop, and my Kindle, and packed up most of my clothing into a suitcase. I was going to finish that book I was reading if it killed me. Not even a psychopathic ex-fiancé back from the dead was going to stop me.

"That was fast", he said as I rolled the suitcase into the living room. "I thought women had more, you know, stuff."

"Well, *this* woman has always traveled light. I never knew where my next consult assignment would be and the packing and repacking process wasn't very efficient."

"Duly noted," Sam replied, offering to take my bag, and we went on our way to his apartment which was conveniently only about 15 minutes from mine. Looked like we both liked to live close to our places of work.

Sam's apartment was, in a word, interesting. It was a third-floor walk-up and we were greeted by a few of his neighbors on the way whom he waved back at politely. I'm sure the looks we both received when they noticed he was carrying my luggage would be the gossip of the building for weeks to come and I almost felt sorry for him.

The apartment itself was modest but cozy and welcoming, a complete contrast to its owner. A comfortable-looking yet stylish gray sofa sat in the living room with a sleek TV and entertainment system mounted on the wall with the intention of saving some space. There was a minimalist coffee table, with what appeared to be storage options for magazines or other essentials. Peeking around it seemed to be a one-bedroom, which might pose a problem, but it had a lovely little picture window that I could see myself reading in, and for some reason that was comforting. When things in the real world got to be a bit overwhelming I always found solace in reading and letting my imagination wander.

I was also impressed by how clean it was. In my head, I pictured a bachelor pad with pizza boxes and beer bottles littering the floor and stuff covering every imaginable surface, but instead, it was as clean as a whistle. Considering he hadn't known I would be staying with him until a few hours ago this must be the normal state of his apartment, which left me particularly surprised. I went to put my things down on the couch when Sam stopped me.

"You can take the room. I have an extra set of sheets, so I can put those on for you."

"I can take the couch, really, I don't mind. I'm the one invading your space. Your dad knows you have a one-bedroom, right?"

"Yes, he's aware," Sam answered while looking through a closet and pulling out some pillows, which he tossed onto the couch.

"I'm sure the bastard had a good chuckle over that. It's fine, I fall asleep on the couch most nights anyways."

We settled into our own nightly routines, tiptoeing around each other like we were on a tightrope, and I finally settled into his bed, pulling out my Kindle to read and take my mind off things. I heard the TV click to life in the living room, indicating Sam was winding down for the day as well. In a way, I felt more comfortable than I had been in a while. I didn't know if it was due to Sam's sheets, the thread counts of which must have been higher than any I had ever felt, or if it was the fact that Sam was nearby. I was starting to dare to hope that I might be able to trust him like I trusted his father. I must have been more exhausted than I realized, or the drugs were still working their way out of my system, because I found I was having trouble keeping my eyes open and I drifted, easily for once, into slumber.

CHAPTER 17

It was the same nightmare again, but instead of the chorus of morbid souls that normally screeched around me, revealing Alex's mangled form, a pristine Alex emerged, smirking. I looked down to see my wrists bound and I was unable to move, even blink. I struggled hard, so very hard, but he grew closer and closer. His smile grew wider and wider until it overtook his entire face, morphing his features into some unrecognizable creature. Yet to me, he was somehow still beautiful.

"You didn't think I would let you go, Lizzy." He seemed to project into my mind, speaking without moving his now monstrous mouth. "I'll never let you be free of me."

He got closer and closer until Sam appeared out of nowhere, jumping in between us heroically.

"Pathetic." The thing that was Alex sneered and flicked his hand effortlessly, sending Sam flying into the air. He landed crumpled like a ball of paper, limbs contorted in an impossible way and unmoving. I felt myself trying to scream, to run to Sam, to run away, but he continued to get closer, trapping me in endless torment.

***

I was jolted awake by Elizabeth screaming my name. I grabbed my gun and ran into the bedroom, only to find her eyes closed as she tossed in my bed. I surveyed the room and took a deep breath, realizing there was no present danger. I remembered that my father had texted me that she sometimes had night terrors and that recent events might trigger one, and by the looks of it, this one was a doozy.

"Elizabeth," I attempted to say softly to bring her out of her sleep, but it looked like I'd have to do something more drastic. What was I supposed to do? I wasn't really a gentle human being and the only thing I could think of was to slap her, but I figured that was probably the wrong answer. I sat on the side of the bed and jostled her a bit by her shoulders, hoping that would get her out of it. Her eyes flew open and held more terror than I had seen in grown men who had come home from assignments overseas. She grabbed my face in her hands and began inspecting it.

"Are you okay?" she whispered, still holding my head in her hands and looking around the room frantically like something was going to jump out of the shadows any second.

"I'm pretty sure I should be asking if you're okay." She slowly and tentatively pulled her hands away from my face and pulled the sheets up to the point where only her neck was peeking out.

Her eyes had snapped back to the cool blue gaze they normally held, like steel blinds covering the windows to her soul.

"I'm sorry you had to see that." She sighed, looking at the clock at the side of the bed, and groaned. "And it's basically time to get up for work. I'm officially the worst alarm clock ever."

I couldn't help but let a laugh escape at her attempt at humor. "Did the great Dr. Elizabeth Waller just make a joke?"

"Don't get used to it," She mumbled, attempting to hide the blush creeping into her cheeks.

"Do you think you're up to briefing the team on what you know about Alex and the potential bioweapon threat?" I didn't want to push her, but the faster we got this asshole behind bars, the better it would be for everyone.

"Got to rip the Band-Aid off some time." She hopped out of bed and, just a little bit ashamed of myself, I watched her as she walked towards the bathroom. I had to admit, night terror and all, there were worse sights to wake up to rumpled in my bed.

Elizabeth was finished getting ready before me, which was surprising considering my past experiences were with women who needed quite a decent amount of time before they would dare step out of the house. She had even made a pot of coffee and was sipping on it while watching the news.

"Glad to see you're making yourself right at home," I remarked, putting away the coffee grounds and filters that she had left out on the counter. She swiveled and glanced back at me to see what I was complaining about.

"I was going to pick that up when I was done," She called over her shoulder as she turned her attention back to the local news.

"Right." I didn't like my space being invaded, but it was nice to have some coffee already made. I grabbed a cup and sat down next to her on the couch.

"I didn't see anything about last night on the news at all. What do you guys have going on around here that the FBI presence at a masquerade ball isn't a top news story?" she asked while finishing up her first cup, and then proceeded to get up and refill her cup.

"The venue didn't really want to advertise that they were hosting a potential bioterrorist and we didn't want to get the public panicked, so they've kept quiet."

"That makes sense," She added, sitting back down on the couch. "I checked social media as well and the people that posted seemed to think it was a fire or faulty wiring based on the alarms going off and everyone being evacuated."

I couldn't help but laugh. "You have social media accounts? Isn't that a big no-no in witness protection? "

She turned to me with a look of fake hurt on her face. "Just because I was in hiding didn't mean I buried my head in the sand. It was an account under my assumed last name, Waller, of course, and I never posted any pictures of myself. People find you odd if they can't find you on social media, and I figured the risks were minimal. Plus, it lets me keep an eye out for anything that could pertain to my previous research."

"You don't have to justify it to me. I just think it's funny is all."

"You would," she mumbled into her coffee as we sat in silence, finishing our cups and getting ready to head out.

The drive to the office was strictly business-related, which was fine with me. I loathed small talk and I wasn't great at it either, but I loathed deep silence even more, so I was glad when she brought up the workday ahead. She asked what relevant information would be helpful to the team and said that nothing was off-limits if it helped. By the time we got to the office, we agreed on giving her a few hours to pull some slides together for a presentation and walked into the office to handle our respective duties. We were in the office for no more than five minutes when Nina hurled herself at Elizabeth.

"Elizabeth!" Nina cried, circling her arms around her which most likely was supposed to be a hug, but Elizabeth had her hands straight in the air like she was asking someone not to shoot.

"I was going to go to the hospital," Nina hiccupped, continuing her slurry of words, "but they said I didn't have clearance, and so I couldn't see you, and then I asked Benny, which was a big mistake because Benny is just—"

"Nina," Elizabeth interrupted her awkwardly, lowering her arms

127

and giving her a few pats on her back in what I think was supposed to be a comforting motion. I laughed, and Elizabeth shot me one of her shut up or die looks. I walked away and Nina was still hanging on to her as she tried to make her way down the hallway to her labs. I made my way to the break room, shaking my head at Nina's antics, and ran into Benny and Dominic.

"Is she okay to be here today, man?" Benny asked with genuine concern in his voice, which surprised me.

"She's stronger than she looks. Plus, she's the best lead that we have on Dr. Beal right now so she's putting together a presentation for the group." Dominic nodded in approval, grabbed his coffee, and went about doing whatever the hell that man did. I didn't admit it to anyone, but I was having second guesses about pushing Elizabeth too soon. I couldn't imagine what she was going through. That level of betrayal and then to find out the guy wasn't dead. That would mess up anyone, let alone a civilian.

"Shit," I growled, alarming one of the new guys in the breakroom who wasn't quite used to my outbursts yet. There was one person whose opinion I could use, but I wasn't quite sure it was worth it. I begrudgingly went to my office and pulled out my phone.

"Hello, son." My father answered the phone, dripping with smugness. "What can I do for you?" Then his tone changed to one of concern. "Is everything okay with Elizabeth?"

"What? Yes, she's fine."

"Oh good." He sounded relieved. "It's just not like you to call me out of the blue."

"The question is Elizabeth-related, however."

"Is it really?" He sounded genuinely interested. "How can I help?" As much as I hated asking for help, I knew he would be the best source.

"Elizabeth is back in the office today and is going to give the team an assessment of Dr. Beal." I cleared my throat. "I'm afraid I'm pushing her a little too fast in forcing her to give the presentation and she might, um, break."

I heard my father's belly laugh come through the phone. When he was finished with what I assumed was wiping tears from his eyes, he finally answered me.

"Son, even though it warms my heart to see you actually considering someone else's feelings, I can assure you, you will not break Elizabeth. If she hasn't cracked already she's not about to now. I've known that girl for five years and there's no *forcing* her to do anything. She'll listen to logic and reason. She understood it had to be her in the red dress in that situation as she looked so much like the other women and all the other agents were compromised ."

Well, that was good information to know. We discussed the case in a little more detail and then hung up as I was being called to the conference room for Elizabeth's update. She was already in the conference room when I got there, setting up. If she was nervous, she didn't show it as everyone settled in. I needed to make some opening statements first, so I began the meeting.

"As most of you are aware, the sting operation that took place a little under 48 hours ago was unknowingly a well-laid trap. The operation was not a failure, however, as we now have a lead suspect in our case, Dr. Alex Beal. Alex Beal was presumed dead over five years ago and has now tipped his cards in revealing that he is still alive and was most likely involved in the three deaths at the resort in the Adirondacks. It looks like we are dealing with a form of bioweapon that Dr. Beal has been optimizing for and is ready to put

129

on the black market." I heard some murmurs cascade through the agents as they realized the threat level we were dealing with and waited for them to subside before I continued with the briefing.

"Luckily for us, our new forensic consultant Dr. Waller is familiar with Dr. Beal's previous case and will be providing us some insight into him and the assumed murder weapon used in the Adirondack case and its potential bioterrorism threat. Dr. Waller, the floor is yours."

Elizabeth walked to the center of the room with more confidence than most senior agents providing a report and brought up her first slide.

"I have a few slides and a decent amount of information to go through that might seem technical, so please hold questions until the end." It seemed like she was going to be all business and it made me respect her a bit more.

"Dr. Alex Beal, first and foremost, is a clear and present threat. His intellect, magnetic personality, and ambition are a lethal combination. Having been off the radar for five years, he has had ample time to plan whatever course of action he is now engaging in, and to establish himself as a major player in the bioweapon playing field. He has also had time to assemble a team of highly skilled individuals, evident by the level of subterfuge in getting us to participate in the sting and the break-in of the labs. One of his aptitudes is drawing capable individuals to work with him, in some cases manipulating them to participate in illegal activities with or without their knowledge." She looked away and I knew that was a sore spot for her, but to her credit, she took a deep breath and continued.

"He is highly driven and will sacrifice anything, or anyone, to achieve his goals. It is safe to assume based on this information that the Adirondack incident was a test run, so to speak, or proof of

130

concept for potential buyers. It can also now be assumed at this time that the samples stolen from the labs during the break-in were an attempt to cover up the evidence of the bacteria he was using. Without these samples, I cannot confirm if this theory is correct, but my current hypothesis is that the bacteria used at the resort was F. tularensis. On its own Tularemia is not fatal, but it can be aerosolized, and we can conclude that Alex has increased the rate of infection. An experimental vaccine exists, but it will not be able to kill the bacterium fast enough in the host because its mutated form replicates too quickly. Any questions?"

"No offense, but what makes you the expert on Dr. Alex Beal?" a young agent in the back of the room asked with a bit of attitude. I turned around and shot him a look that relayed my displeasure and was satisfied as he slouched as far down into his seat as possible. Elizabeth graced me with a smile and mouthed a quick thank you before she continued.

"Dr. Beal's work mimics that of my Ph.D. thesis work, which lends me to have a large knowledge base on the subject and how the bacteria might be manipulated."

"Okay so why set up the masquerade event and risk exposure when they could have just laid low, and no offense Doctor, why didn't they just kill you?" another agent I wasn't too familiar with asked from the back of the room. I was curious to see how she was going to tackle this one without exposing her personal connection to Dr. Beal and her former life.

"My current theory" she started a little shakily this time around, "is that they wanted to test the response and capabilities of this Field Office. As to why I wasn't killed, my assumption is that as I am familiar with Dr. Beal's work they might have wanted to secure me as a hostage or a resource but due to the fine work and quick response time of this office they were unable to do so."

Well, I had to admit that was a pretty damn good response. Not exactly a lie but not the whole story. She also threw in some praise for the office which had quite a few of the agents preening. I frowned at how easily she was able to dodge the question though. I hoped Dr. Beal hadn't rubbed off on her too much.

"Any other questions?" Elizabeth asked the room. I gave another sweep look around the room indicating the discussion was over and everyone seemed to catch my drift and refrained from any further questions. I watched as Elizabeth packed up her things from the podium and thought that confidence looked good on her.

***

"I thought I was going to puke. I was so nervous." I responded when Nina asked me how my presentation went. "I think I gave the agents enough so that they are informed and can proceed safely."

"That's great and all,-" Nina added distractedly, staring at my face, "-but did you actually put makeup on today?"

I busied myself back at my desk, putting some distance between us. Did she have telescopic eyes? I hadn't even spent ten minutes on it.

"Was it the tinted moisturizer I gave you? Looks so good and natural, nice work!" Nina said, giving me a thumbs up. I puffed, if I could figure out how to manipulate the vector of infection of a bacterium I was highly capable of using a beauty blender.

"Hey, Nina?" I asked, looking over at her and checking the reagents we had in stock.

"Yes Boss!" I hated it when she called me that. It felt so formal and held a lot of responsibility.

"How would you like to go out for lunch? I just checked my

132

emails and there isn't anything pressing and as they will not be able to calibrate the equipment for a few more days with all the backlog-"

"You're asking me if I want to have lunch together?" She interrupted her eyes swimming looking like she was on the verge of tears.

"Well yes but if you don't want to- "

"No. I mean yes. I mean I definitely want to! I have been waiting for this from the day you started working here. Oh my gosh, it's happening. We are totally bonding!"

What had I done? I was starving and really didn't feel like eating alone which was a relatively new phenomenon for me, but I should have realized this would have been Nina's reaction. I was irrevocably doomed now.

"Let me just get my stuff, this is so cool!" Nina ran off to collect her things. Just at that moment, Sam walked into the lab.

"Where are you going?" Sam said looking suspiciously at Nina and me gathering our things.

"You will not believe it, Sam! Elizabeth and I are, wait for it, going out to lunch! I would totally invite you, but this is kind of a women bonding experience, so you wouldn't get it." Nina was basically bouncing on her heels when she answered Sam.

"You're going offsite for lunch unescorted? Did I hear that correctly?" Sam said ignoring Nina who was basically frolicking around the lab at this time. "Absolutely not."

"Excuse me?" I responded, placing my hands on my hips for an outward display of my displeasure at his attempt to prevent me from going out to eat. I was so close to being hangry at this point, and you won't like me when I'm hangry. Anything getting between me and lunch was going to be in serious trouble.

"You know the threat is imminent at this point," Sam said matter-of-factly. I could feel Nina pouting from somewhere behind me.

"And like I said previously, I can handle it myself." I hoped I was getting the point across, I know I was a bit panicked the other day about being taken but I reminded myself I had trained for this, knew this could be an eventuality. I was ready for Alex. Sam was not backing down from this staring contest and test of wills.

"How about this?" He offered. "There's menus in the breakroom. Order what Nina and you want, my treat, and then meet me on the mats in the gym. I'll show you some self defense moves just in case you may need them." He arched an eyebrow "Unless you don't think you can handle sparring with me?"

"You're on." I responded confidently not breaking contact with Sam for a second "Nina. Find the most expensive restaurant menu from the breakroom and order us some food. Wait. Not just some food. A feast's worth of food."

"So, we still get to do the female bonding?" Nina asked hopefully from the door frame.

"Yes, we do." And after we ate, I thought to myself, I'm going to show Sam just how wrong he was about me.

CHAPTER 18

After eating more Thai food than I should have, I headed toward the lab to grab the stash of workout clothing I kept there just in case I wanted to go to the gym or kickboxing straight after work.

I could tell while we were eating that Nina was slightly disappointed we didn't get to go offsite and do the "female bonding" but that she was still happy with the arrangement. She did most of the talking during lunch which I was fine with as I secretly plotted in my head the best way to take Sam down a few pegs. Sam didn't know what he was getting into.

My therapists had recommended self-defense or yoga as an outlet to help me adjust to my new life and situation after Alex. They thought it would help with my confidence and help ease my tumultuous mind. Yoga seemed too introspective for me and I was not about to explore the deep recesses of my own mind so I went the self-defense route. Little did anyone expect, myself included, I took to it like a fish to water. After I had trained at non-agency gyms and clubs and needed more of a challenge, Robert helped me find some classes the FBI was using to train their agents for an extra challenge. When I put my mind to something I was all in until I perfected it and physical training was no different.

Nina had asked to watch the match to cheer me on but I kindly rebuffered her saying that this was something Sam and I had to work out on our own. I could tell she was upset with the huge pout and dejected look she was giving me but in the end she respected my decision and went back to the lab to take care of a few things I had asked for.

In the locker room I changed, and wrapped my hands in the traditional kickboxing style. I had debated the baggy t-shirt I normally wore when I trained but knew Sam would use that to his advantage as something to grab onto so I went with a tighter crop top and some leggings instead. He felt like the type that would play dirty and I wasn't taking any chances. This was my chance to get him off my back, and release a little pent up aggression if I was being honest. I pulled my hair up into a tight bun, cracked my neck a few times, and headed towards the gym facility they had onsite for training. Sam was already there waiting on the mat stretching wearing the standard issue FBI t-shirt and sweatpants

He stopped mid stretch hearing the heavy metal gym doors clang shut his gaze sweeping over to me with a look of surprise on his face.

"I don't believe that's standard issue gear Dr Waller."

"I don't believe this is a standard sparring session Special Agent Han." I challenged.

"You can still back out if you want," Sam remarked, smirking. "I won't hurt you, too much."

There was no way that was going to happen. I knew he wasn't going to trust me going anywhere on my own without an escort if I didn't prove to him I could hold my own. Plus, it had the bonus of working out some of my frustrations with Alex being alive and all my other baggage by using Sam for some physical exertion. Focus Elizabeth. I cracked my neck once again and got into guard position on the mat which Sam eyed, feigning he was impressed.

"Rules of engagement?" I asked while he evaluated me as his opponent circling like a vulture waiting to pick at my bones.

"I thought we would do traditional sparing and tapping out when you can't handle anymore. Sound good?"

He was confident of himself by the looks of it but my greatest asset when sparring wasn't my speed or strength, it was reading my opponent. Sam was going to underestimate me and go easy believing I had no technique. I could use that miscalculation on his part to my advantage.

"Let's go then." I mimicked with my hand like Bruce Lee telling him to bring it on.

He covered the distance between us quickly signaling he wanted to be done and over with the sparring and went to perform a maneuver meant to sweep my leg and pin me down right out of the gate. Overconfident. As soon as he brought his leg up I immediately moved in to take him off balance as I knew all his weight was on his other leg causing him to catch himself before he fell over. I backed up, resetting and waiting for his next move allowing a smirk to grace my own face. This was going to be fun.

"Nicely done." He smiled standing back up straight, moving back a bit and resetting his defensive stance. "Did you learn that in a self-defense class when you were in college or something?" He teased looking for another opening.

"Nope. Learned that during Mr. Wu's class."

He straightened for a moment, dropping his guard and reassessing me as an opponent. "Mr. Wu, the martial arts instructor who trained my father."

"One in the same."

He laughed. I mean really laughed for the first time since I had met him. It was charming, but I couldn't let it distract me.

"You're full of surprises, aren't you? But you're still going down." He answered mockingly and resumed his defensive stance. We sparred for what felt like an eternity trading blows, one never

137

overtaking the other. The training room echoed with the sounds of our banter as we circled each other, exchanging jabs and feints. I lunged forward, throwing a quick jab that Sam skillfully dodged, a confident grin on his face.

"Nice try," he said, retaliating with a swift combination of punches. I deftly blocked and countered, the rhythm of our movements creating a captivating dance. I was getting fatigued and I could tell I was putting a dent in his stamina as well.

I went on the offensive, moving in to land a left roundhouse which he easily rebuffed. How annoying. He took the opportunity to maneuver himself behind me and put me into a headlock. I grabbed his arm and flung him over my back, He landed on the mat on his back with a satisfying smack.

"That, I learned in self-defense class in college." I stated, standing over him as he grabbed his side and laughed on the mat.

"So, I can see." His smile grew larger as he quickly grabbed my legs and pulled them out from under me so that I landed on my back with a smack. "What move was that?" I asked, trying to hold in my laughter but failing miserably now also on the mat staring at the lights on the ceiling and the halo glow surrounding them and breathing heavily.

"That one?" He said winded laying beside me on the mat. "The Elizabeth ass-kicker."

"I haven't come across that one in my training," I said laughing, enjoying the reprieve of laying on the mat and enjoying the cool temperature it provided. "And I believe the nomenclature is incorrect as my ass is yet to be kicked as I haven't tapped out yet."

I felt something hit my butt and I realized that from his position on the mat, he had managed to literally kick my ass. I gaped over at him and we laughed heartily. I was honestly enjoying this distraction. I didn't realize how much I needed it.

"I stand corrected." I rolled over so that I was on my side, so I could face him "But I haven't tapped out so technically you haven't won."

Sam turned to face me and opened his mouth for an obvious rebuttal when Dominic came bursting through the doors of the training room.

"Sir, there's been another death."

CHAPTER 19

"How many?"

I was immediately sobering up from the reprisal I had allowed myself and jumped up from the mat.

"How many?" I asked again more forcefully. A million thoughts raced through my head. I needed to know how many more deaths I had on my hands. Has a hazmat team been called? Who was trying to secure the scene? Has someone gotten ahold of some vials of vaccine from the DOD? Was it my fault for allowing myself a small sliver of joy into my life?

"One," Dominic answered somberly, looking slightly put off by my sudden outburst and intensity. "And by the looks of it, not a civilian."

"How can you know?" I asked, trying to keep my voice calm and not to display the terror I felt.

"He had a snake tattoo on his wrist exactly like the one you described on one of the perpetrators who broke into the lab," Dominic answered, walking over to offer Sam a hand to get up from the mat.

"Has the scene been secured?" Sam asked entering Lead Special Agent mode. "Has the Bioterrorism Team been called in?"

"Yes, they've swept the scene and pulled samples. The samples were sent for rapid testing at the County Lab we've been rerouting to but considering Dr. Waller's experience I asked them to put aside some samples for her to review when she is able. They were able to take some pictures and footage of the crime scene and the body that we can review until the results come back to say the scene is cleared."

"Thank you, Dominic," I said honestly trying to convey how

140

much I appreciated his forethought to secure me a sample. He graced me with a slight smile that was sort of frightening coming from him but I appreciated the attempt.

"Elizabeth and I will change and then I want to see what we have at the crime scene. I'll want your eyes on this too Elizabeth. Maybe there is something you can gather that would further implicate Alex in all this and get us a lead."

After a quick change and a sobering return to the case at hand, I met back up with Dominic, Benny, and Sam who were beginning to scan through the crime scene photos. Based on the condition of the body I was fairly certain it was the same bacteria as the one that killed the victims at the Adirondack resort. His skin was covered in boils, his eyes red by blood vessels popping, and his hand seemed like it was grasping for his neck to try and get some air indicating he had suffocated to death. It was a horrific sight and I didn't wish it on my worst enemy.

With the positioning of his hands, I could clearly see a snake tattoo on his wrist. Upon seeing it I looked at Sam.

"I see it too." Sam answered somberly. "Well there goes that lead."

Sam continued to flick through the photos and something caught my eye.

"Where is this located? I mean, where did they find the body."

"It was in an abandoned building down at the port. The town is revitalizing the area but hasn't reached that far yet. Luckily for us, no one else was in the area to be exposed. The only reason we found the body was that a loud bang came from the building and some kids playing hooky from school heard it and called the police." Dominic answered not taking his eyes off the photos.

"Those kids were lucky they didn't enter the building and just called the cops," Sam added Dominic nodding somberly in agreement.

"Can you enhance the area of the photo right there?" I asked, pointing to an object on the floor.

"Sure thing Doc," Benny replied with a goofy grin and went to enhance the image. I had tried to persuade him to stop calling me that, but I think it had the opposite effect and it just encouraged him.

"It's what I suspected," I confirmed looking up from the photo to see the rest of the team looking at me for further explanation.

"The sound resulted from an over-pressurization of the canister that is lying on the floor that I asked you to enhance so I could see better. It looks like the deceased was filling up the canister with the Tularemia compound and over pressurized it causing it to explode and expose him to its contents." Something wasn't adding up though. Nothing Alex did was less than perfection.

"What else is on your mind?" Sam asked, noticing I had grown quiet and contemplative.

"This situation doesn't really make sense in terms of how Alex would operate. He would have a highly skilled team working on this knowing that a mistake like that would endanger his whole project bringing unwanted attention his way. He wouldn't have a mercenary, such as what I'm assuming that man is, handling the merchandise, directly."

I grabbed the controller from Benny to further demonstrate my point. "If you look at the equipment he has set up here it's all old, second hand, or stolen most likely, and some of the equipment isn't appropriate for the task I believe he was trying to pull off. Alex would never use subpar equipment as you can see in the canister that looks like it went through some extensive development process. Additionally, the man is not wearing the correct protective equipment at all besides gloves and the space hasn't been sterilized either. In a word, the whole scene is just wrong."

"Do you have any theories as to why?" Sam asked, looking like he was contemplating my words carefully. I had a hunch, but it was only that and I was a scientist, not a detective, so I wasn't sure if it was my place to say anything, but the implications were great if I was right.

"I believe the victim stole the bioweapon, or at least a prototype from Alex. I know there is the whole honor among thieves' code, but I believe this scene is a makeshift lab that he set up to reproduce and sell off Dr. Beal's bioweapon on his own or with another party. The PPE is close to but not exactly what is needed to handle the bacterium indicating he's been around Dr. Beal's work but not fully. This is corroborated by the fact that he was one of the suspects that broke into the lab at the Albany Field Office. The problem happened when he tried to replicate the release mechanism in the form of the canister. He most likely got a faulty canister and underestimated its ability to withstand the PSI and it literally blew up in his face. I think this is the lead you've been looking for Sam to tie Alex to the bioweapon and the deaths."

"And how exactly is that? It's all speculation at this point." Sam answered, staring at the picture to see if there was something he was missing.

"Look at the canister again when the image is magnified. Look at what is etched into the side of it. Property of Dr. Alex Beal." Alex was such a narcissist that I wasn't surprised that he literally put his name on his own creations. That was one heck of a calling card.

"Holy shit!" Benny yelped, causing the rest of us to jump startled.

143

"Good work," Sam mentioned, quickly patting me on my shoulder as he positioned himself to get closer to the monitor displaying the crime scene photos. A sense of pride and accomplishment I hadn't felt in a while swept over me and a smile mysteriously appeared on my face. I felt my phone vibrate in my pocket, finding it odd due to the fact that only a few people had my number, but noticing it was one of the extensions for the Field Office I answered anyway.

"Dr. Waller speaking. May I ask who's calling?"

"Dr. Waller, that's the name you're going with now. Can't say I'm a fan of it, Lizzy." A smug voice came through the phone causing a vice grip on my heart and causing me to momentarily forget to breathe.

"Elizabeth, are you, all right? You look like you've seen a ghost." Benny said from where he sat in the room. I hadn't seen a ghost but I was indeed speaking with one. Finally regaining my ability to move I gestured to the phone rapidly snapping my fingers.

"Alex," I said pointedly and more calmly than I thought I would be able to muster, and hearing the name caught all the attention of the men in the room, Benny running out into the hallway to do I have no idea what, Dominic opening his phone to call who knows, and Sam staring at me and miming to keep him talking as he spoke with Dominic in hushed tones. Yeah, like that was going to be easy when I wasn't sure I could remain standing on my own. I saw Dominic give Sam his phone, Sam gesturing to it as if he would be listening in. I didn't know if that made me feel better or worse.

"That's all you have to say to me after all this time?" Alex crooned in the voice he used when he was being playful. "Haven't you thought of me all these years? I've thought about you every day, especially at night."

144

"I thought you were dead," I responded, trying to keep the quiver out of my voice.

"Liar." He stated matter-of-factly. "I remember how your voice gets that slight inflection at the end when you're lying. Still hurts my feelings though."

"Why? Why are you calling me now?" I was trying to stay away from our personal relationship but hearing his voice was such a shock to my system that I hadn't been mentally prepared for it. I had to refocus and get him to try to say something useful or give away his location. I just had to remind myself he wasn't the Alex I had known. He wasn't the man I was planning on spending the rest of my life with. This *thing* I was on the phone with was a monster and meant nothing to me.

"That's the first question you ask? Lizzy, I'm impressed. You've grown so much since we've been apart." He sighed like he had lamented our years apart. He was acting like we were college sweethearts separated after we graduated and not like he had faked his death after committing murder. I recognized what he was trying to do. He was trying to manipulate me. I had to keep my focus. Maybe if I could keep him on the phone long enough they would be able to track his location. That's what I was doing, for the team, keeping him on the line. I wasn't continuing to get him to talk just so I could hear his voice again after five long years as I had often longed to. I wasn't, was I?

"Fine, I'll answer your question." He continued after a pause that felt like an eternity saving me from my internal musings. "I could never say no to you. I figured since you found my *former* associate and would inevitably link it back to me eventually there was no reason to keep hidden in the shadows. I have missed you my Lizzy."

"It's Elizabeth," I responded coolly. "And you literally put your initials on your handiwork Alex so it was quite easy to link it back to

145

you." I would not let him get under my skin. I would not let him unravel all the work I had done to get myself where I was today. I built myself back up brick by brick after he tore me all the way down. I glanced over at Sam who was staring at me intently. Was I messing this up? Did he not have any faith that I could turn this call into something useful? For some reason, those thoughts struck me deeper than the man currently on the line that destroyed my life.

"You'll always be Lizzy to me and tons of people have the same initials," Alex answered smoothly like he was trying to pick me up at a bar. "Plus I'm a dead man, remember? A ghost from your past." He was attempting to make me question myself but that was the old Elizabeth. He wasn't going to get to pull that shit with me this time. Not when people's lives were on the line.

"You can tell your new *friend* over there to stop wasting his time. They won't be able to trace the number." Sam looked over at me and when Benny came in to whisper in his ear I saw him kick a chair meaning Alex must have been right. Maybe I could reason with him, just maybe I could convince him to turn himself in. It was worth a try while I still had him on the line.

"Alex," I said, trying to use my softest voice, seeing all the men in the room turn to me, arching their eyebrows. It wasn't a voice I would have ever used around them. I hadn't tried to use my 'feminine wiles' before but I figured it couldn't hurt. "Why don't you come in? I'll find you the best lawyer and we can put an end to all this before it gets out of hand. We could talk, just you and me, you were right. As always. I have missed you terribly." I was hoping by appealing to his ego, maybe we could get somewhere. I heard him laugh on the other end of the line and I frowned.

"Seduction and coercion, my dear, were never your strong suit." Alex laughed, the sound in contrast to the severity of the conversation "but I must say I did appreciate the attempt and would gladly offer

146

myself as a willing target for your affections in the future."

Crap. Well, it was worth a shot. All the other ways to get him to provide us with something, anything, were going nowhere. I could see Sam staring at me intently and he didn't look too pleased with me. For what reason I could only speculate. I was doing the best I could. I wasn't a professionally trained FBI agent and was just going along by the seat of my pants for goodness sake.

"I will however- ", he continued "-not be turning myself in, but I appreciate the offer. I died 5 years ago, remember? A corpse can't turn itself in. I did have a question for you though. If you answer it and answer it honestly, I'll give you and your FBI friends a little hint."

I stared at Sam and he nodded as if I should take the offer. I don't think he understood what I was tangling with here. Alex was a master manipulator so whatever he was going to ask of me was surely going to crack what little resolve I was trying to maintain. I guess I would be taking one for the team, not that Sam seemed to care.

"Alright," I answered, steeling myself for what was to come. "What's your question?"

His laughter lilted through the phone causing me to feel a wave of emotions. I had always longed to make him laugh so I could hear it. It was melodic, and reassuring, and he only graced me with it when we were alone, and I prided myself on being the only one who could elicit the sound.

"My question is this, why not come to me before reaching out to the authorities when you figured I had modified your research and released it all those years ago? Did you stop to think just once that maybe you could join me in my endeavors? That you could have stayed by my side as my wife and partner?"

I stood frozen staring at the wall. It had never occurred to me that an arrangement like that was even an option. That all these past years I could have spent with him doing the research I longed to do with infinite funding all the while enjoying each other's company. I could have had the love of my life and my love of science unabashed and willingly if I had spoken with him. I always thought that if I had told him I knew what he was up to he would have killed me. I ran all the scenarios of speaking to him first and it ended with me in a body bag. I hadn't thought that he would have wanted *me*. I thought he only wanted my research, but could he have possibly had the same intense feelings for me that I had for him?

I felt someone gently touch my arm and saw Sam looking at me gesturing his head to the phone reminding me that I hadn't provided an answer yet. Well, at least I knew where I stood with Sam. He couldn't care less about my storm of emotions and what I was going through. He just wanted his lead. Another man using me to get what he wanted. I grew slightly enraged at this revelation.

"You didn't even think of that route did you Lizzy." I heard Alex sigh on the other end of the phone reminding me that I was on a phone call.

"I-" I stammered trying to speak, my voice getting quiet as this was suddenly a very intimate conversation I was having with multiple people trying to listen in. "-I didn't. I thought maybe you would kill me if I knew what you were doing, to be honest. You know I wouldn't be able to aid you in helping hurt innocent people. You know I'm not that kind of person."

Alex scoffed "You wound me dearest. I could never kill you, especially over something like that. The people I deal with are by no means innocent. I'm doing the world a service really."

"Those people at the Adirondack Resort were all innocent people."

148

"Your attempt to get information out of me is adorable I must admit but I'm afraid my lips are sealed on that topic. As much as I enjoy speaking with you after all these years, I'm quite a busy man and have some meetings to attend to."

"Wait!" I said a little louder and more desperately than I intended. "I answered your question honestly so what is our hint?"

"Ah yes, a promise is a promise. I am a man of my word after all." Alex responded matter-of-factly. "Here's your hot tip. The man you found at the warehouse did indeed work for me but was apparently moonlighting for another party. I took care of the loose ends, so to speak. You're welcome agents as I know you must be greedily listening in at this point. It must be quite emasculating to know someone did your job for you."

I peeked over to see Sam seething in a way I didn't think was possible. It looked like steam would come pouring out of his ears at any moment.

"You adjusted the canister so that it would malfunction intentionally." Realization hit me all at once.

"Clever girl. I am boundlessly impressed by your intelligence. The party that hired him has been taken care of as well, again, you're welcome. We can't have anyone pointing a gun in your beautiful face. Plus, you know how much I hate when people touch things that are mine." I had a feeling his last statement wasn't directed at me but at someone else. I studied Sam, who still had his hand on my arm. He quickly removed it like he suddenly realized it was still there.

"Till next time my Lizzy." And with that, the phone line went dead leaving us all to process what had just occurred.

"Okay!" Nina exclaimed, barging into the breakroom. "After that delicious lunch, I decided we needed a dessert feast fit for the queens

149

we are." She took in the room looking at the somber and angry faces. "What did I miss?"

Sam grabbed his cell phone and stormed out of the room. Nina again took a look around the room in confusion.

"No but seriously?" She said putting the sickeningly sweet-smelling confections down on the table. "What did I miss?"

CHAPTER 20

After my phone call with Alex, the agents scattered leaving me alone with Nina and her so-called feast.

"Woah, that's some really heavy emotional stuff." Nina managed to get out between bites of her pastry as I updated her on the call. I left out all the classified bits but even that left enough information that she had an idea of what was going on. She had listened intently as I relayed the events that unfolded gasping and awing like it was some afternoon soap opera. At the current moment, she was really shoveling in her sweets and I had a hard time reconciling how she maintained her figure. I think I had only managed to take a few pity bites of an eclair, my appetite having left me.

"Are you okay? In the head I mean?"

I snorted, not being able to help myself. Nina was a unique creature that was for sure and, much to my dismay, she was rapidly growing on me.

"Do you mean is my mental health okay?"

"Yeah. That's what I said. I mean, he dropped like a huge bomb on you. I saw his photo in one of the reports and he is super hunky. If he said to me 'hey baby come to rule the underground black market with me' I would seriously, I mean *seriously*, consider it."

"It is a bit tempting isn't it," I answered honestly.

She nodded her head as her mouth was again full. I had never taken the time to think what would have happened if I hadn't figured out what Alex was doing and turned him in. Would we have gotten married if I had continued to live in blissful ignorance? Would he have eventually told me about his criminal enterprise when I was so deeply and irrevocably in love with him that I wouldn't have even cared? Would we have had children and lived in a nice home? Would I finally have the family I had always dreamed about?

"Hello. Earth to Elizabeth." Nina said while waving a hand in my face. "You're doing that thing where your face gets all scrunchy and you stare off. Whatcha thinking about?"

"Things that can never be." I sadly smiled while Nina convinced me to drown my emotions in sugar and carbs and for once I obliged her.

***

I stood in his office pacing a hole into the linoleum while on the phone with my father.

"She needs to be removed from the case. Immediately." I knew I was basically yelling at this point, but I was so angry I couldn't help it. For some reason that bastard just got under my skin. I didn't know if it was his smugness or the way he spoke to Elizabeth but something about that man made me want to punch his lights out.

"I would have to disagree, son. It seems to me this whole situation just proves that she will be the key in getting Alex to slip up."

"So, you want to use her as bait?" I asked my father accusingly. "It's too risky. She's got a major conflict of interest."

"Do you have any other suggestions on how we can get to Dr. Beal?"

"No." I relented honestly. From what I could tell from my brief time with Elizabeth she had a pretty strong moral compass but in my time in the FBI, I've seen people do some pretty fucked up things in the name of love. "You didn't see her body language when she was on the phone with him. You could easily see he was affecting her and taunting us all at the same time."

"You better watch yourself, boy." He laughed, "You're starting to sound a little jealous."

Jealous? Sam Han did not get jealous. Certainly not of a biological weapon making terrorist. I was merely pointing out a potential issue with Elizabeth being on the team. Nothing more, nothing less. My father must be losing his investigative touch if that is all that he could come up with.

"I do agree with one of your points, however." He continued not allowing me a rebuttal to his previous remark. "It is risky keeping her out in the open and not relocating her to a safe house. I want you to personally keep an eye on her for her safety and for the success of this case. Continue to drive her to and from the office and don't let her out of your sight."

"Well, at least we agree on something for once," I responded, slightly concerned that we had agreed on something.

"Miracles do happen my boy." He laughed and then hung up.

The rest of the day flew by. Elizabeth holed herself up in her lab preparing for receipt of the samples taken from the crime scene. She said some science mumbo jumbo about needing the samples to incubate overnight or something. I continued to scan the photo of the crime scene but as Alex had indicated, he had securely tightened up any loose ends.

"Damn it," I said out loud right as Benny walked in.

"I didn't even tell you what I had to report yet." Benny quipped sitting down in the chair across from my desk.

"So," I asked impatiently. "What did you find?"

"As Alex indicated, we weren't able to trace his call. He must have some sophisticated toys."

"And?" I was already annoyed that the call basically got us nowhere when I was hoping we would get at least a slight lead.

"Well." Benny continued looking way too pleased with himself. It was the same look he had when he tried out a new pickup line that inevitably failed. "Do you remember when he said I don't like people touching things that were his?"

"Get to the point, Benny. I can feel a migraine forming as we speak."

"I thought that was oddly specific and I saw you were touching Elizabeth's arm. How was it by the way? Her skin looks super soft."

"Focus Benny." I didn't need a reminder about my actions. It was merely an instinct to try and comfort her, but I was seeing that it probably looked unprofessional.

"Geeze leave a brother hanging. Anyway, I thought it seemed like he was talking about you through the subtext and went to check the security cameras we had in the room cause even though the guy obviously has a hard-on for Elizabeth how did he know that you were touching her, or even in the same room for that matter? I asked IT to look into it and according to the tech folks our security feed had been hacked."

"So, what you're saying is that he was watching us the whole phone call."

"Exactly," Benny answered looking very proud of himself. "And before you asked, no, we can't trace it to a physical location as they stopped looking at the feed after the phone call."

154

"Would they know that we checked to see if they interfered with the security feed?"

"I can double-check with the IT group, but I don't think so. Are you thinking what I'm thinking?"

"We need to figure out a situation where someone can touch Elizabeth's again. I humbly volunteer." Benny added hopefully.

"What? No." How Benny wasn't in the HR office all day I would never know. "I'm thinking that if we know they can hack our feed then we can be ready for it and use it to our advantage."

"Bingo," Benny said, lounging back into his chair "Exactly what I was going to say."

It looks like my father was right again. Elizabeth was going to be the cause of Alex slipping up and I would be there ready to put his ass back in jail where he belonged.

 The car ride back to my place was awkward, to say the least. Elizabeth kept to herself looking through her phone or staring out the window. It was a short ride, but it felt like an eternity. I wasn't very good at reassuring someone, but I figured I could give it a try.

"So." I said adjusting my hands on the steering wheel "Today was interesting huh?"

It started out soft at first, I thought she was crying and then I noticed she got louder, and it turned out to be laughter. I glanced over when we were stopped at a red light to see her trying to hide her laugh behind her hands and a smile gracing her face. I hadn't really seen her smile until now. She had of course done the friendly 'nice to meet you' smile on her first few days but it felt robotic and like she was playing the role of the courteous new employee and it held no real emotion behind it. This smile, however, shone like the sun coming

155

over the horizon on the break of dawn. It was breathtaking, and I was trying to memorize it while figuring out how to elicit the response again in the future.

"Interesting is an understatement," she said when her laughter subsided. "First, I kicked your butt on the mat, then the guy who almost killed me blew himself up, and then Alex's call. It was definitely something more than interesting."

"Excuse me." I corrected "I do believe I kicked your butt."

She looked over at me with a side-eye indicating she wasn't buying that I had won for a second, so I redacted my statement.

"Okay, fine, it was a tie. You agree?"

"I concur with your assessment. For now. Rematch?" She asked hopefully looking like she had some frustration she needed to work out. If she wanted to use me as a punching bag there were worse ways to train and she did have some skills, not that I would admit that to her.

"Oh, most definitely." I parked the car but before we got out we had a huge elephant in the room we had to address, and the asshole's name was Alex. "Do you want to talk about your phone call?" I could see her tense up her hand on the handle to get out of the car, but she paused.

"Not really." She said frowning and I mentally kicked myself for running her good mood however fleeting it was. "To be honest, I want a hot shower, a cup of tea, and a good book to escape into. Is that a normal response to something like this?" She seemed to be honestly asking for my opinion.

"Considering your whole situation is not what I would consider conventional, I think that sounds like a good way to cope."

"Okay well then I call dibs on the shower first." And with that, she bounded up the stairs and into my apartment.

While she was in the shower I got a text from Benny saying that they had some new information on the case and that I should come in as soon as possible. Elizabeth was in the shower and I didn't want to deal with the ramifications of opening the door while she was in there, so I left a note telling her that I had some undercovers parked outside the apartment for her protection and made my way back to the office making sure the door was locked behind me.

Once I got in the office everything seemed calm and just like usual making me very curious as to what information we now had on the case was so important that I had to come in right away. I expected to have Benny launch into the case once I entered the office, but no one even sent me a parting glance. I was going to have to actually hunt someone down and I could feel my irritation rising.

"So, what's this earth-shattering break in the case that you guys had that I had to drag my ass all the way back into the office when I had just managed to get home. You couldn't have told me before I left?" I asked Benny and Dominic when I managed to find them. I was met with confused looks when they both contemplated each other for a response.

"Are you feeling okay boss?" Benny asked, attempting to put his hand on my forehead to feel for a fever. I was not amused. I was tired and didn't want to deal with this shit today. I was already feeling unsettled about leaving Elizabeth alone in the apartment after what went down today.

"Cut the shit guys, what's the news? Are you just stalling because someone fucked up?"

"No, we didn't call you. We haven't gotten any additional information since Elizabeth and you left. Where is she by the way? I thought you were supposed to be with her?" Dominic answered this time and he was not one to mince words or joke around.

"Shit," I said aloud as I bolted back towards the main entrance. "Call the squad car watching my place and tell them to be alert."

"But you had the squad car recalled about 10 minutes ago? That's why we were surprised to see you back here and without Elizabeth in tow."

I heard someone shout to me as I raced down the hallway pushing me to get to the exit even faster. This was not a coincidence that I got called away from the apartment and the squad car was recalled. When I got to the main exit there was a group of people that had formed around the door trying their badges attempting to exit going so far as to try and pry the door open as it was locked shut.

"What the hell is happening here?"

"The security system has locked us out sir and closed all the exits including the fire exits." Someone answered from the throngs of people now crowding around the exit trying to leave for the day.

"I want a team getting us back into our security system and getting these doors open now!" I yelled to the group that had surrounded the door and saw some people peel off to carry out my orders. Dominic and Benny had finally caught up to me and were taking in the scene in front of them. Now was not the time for gawking. How the hell could someone get remote control of our security? We were the fucking FBI for God's sake!

"Dominic" I ordered "Call local PD and get a unit to my apartment now! Benny work with IT systems and get us back into our security system!"

I saw Benny move more briskly than I had seen in a while grab

158

the phone from the receptionist desk and put it to his ear. He looked over at me and shook his head indicating the line was dead. Shit. I took out my cell phone and tried calling Elizabeth to tell her to get somewhere safe and found I had no reception. Dominic tried his cell phone but slowly put it away shaking his head indicating he didn't have reception either. They were also blocking our cell signals? Double shit. Elizabeth was at my apartment, alone, with no backup. She was a sitting duck and I couldn't do a damn thing. I scanned around the space and saw a steel chair sitting in the lobby. I smiled, finally, something I could use.

CHAPTER 21

I stood refreshed from my shower in front of the stove as I waited for the kettle to boil.

"I needed that," I said to the tea kettle, stretching my arms into the air as I waited to hear it whistle. I was honestly surprised that Sam even had a kettle let alone a nice selection of teas to choose from. I read the note he left me saying that he was running to the office to get an update about a lead and that he stationed some guys outside to keep an eye out. I was impressed at the thoughtfulness of leaving the note in the first place. I was beginning to find that he was full of surprises, mostly infuriating traits but some revelations were not so bad, like his collection of books and magazines I perused earlier.

I was starting to warm up to Sam, like the rest of the team at the Albany Field Office, and I found I was a tiny bit gloomy about the thought of leaving once the assignment was over. Alas, that was the nature of my work. After Alex was apprehended it would be a complete media circus and having gone through one before and barely making it out with my sanity intact I was not in any hurry to relive it or have Sam and the team wrapped up in it. Come to think of it, Nina would probably enjoy it far more than she should. No, I would disappear quietly, as was my normal routine, and take an assignment elsewhere and move on with my life. I heard my phone vibrate and saw I had a text from Sam.

"Interesting," I said to the now singsong kettle indicating my water was ready and reading the message. "Sam is inviting me out to dinner."

Was he trying to do something nice for me? Again, Sam was full of surprises. Maybe he just felt guilty for putting me in an uncomfortable position or because he was already out of the house and thought it would be good to grab a bite to eat. I wasn't delusional.

160

I knew I was basically being used as Alex bait at this point, but I didn't mind if it meant he was caught. Whatever the reason, I Googled the restaurant and it had all great reviews. He was even sending a car so that I could meet him there. The car was probably to keep an eye on me, but the sentiment, again, was nice.

I quickly dried my hair trying to find something nice to wear. A summer dress seemed the most appropriate and didn't make it look like I had put too much thought into the outfit. I hadn't packed too much with me to take to Sam's place so my choices were suboptimal. I grimly determined that a pair of heeled sandals would complete the outfit and consented to wear them even though I had sworn off heels after the masquerade. The next step was to go and put on some makeup. I dropped the eyeliner when I was finished looking at my handiwork and was instantly angry with myself.

"This isn't a date Elizabeth so why are you trying so hard?" I scolded my image in the mirror.

As I inspected the work I had completed on my face I cringed. It was not a colleagues dinner look, but absolutely a date at a nice restaurant look. A woman doesn't don a smokey eye for a casual dinner with a coworker. It was more effort than I had put into my appearance for, well, a long long time. I wasn't counting the disastrous Masquerade as that was basically an undercover costume. This was something else entirely. I was basically volunteering to glam myself up. What the heck was I doing? I heard a car beep outside and checked out the window of the apartment to see a car idling. It was too late to take all the makeup off and start over, so I resigned myself to going as I was. I grabbed my purse, and made my way downstairs.

I was about to enter the car when I remembered my current situation and that I should show a little discretion due to my criminal ex-fiancé being on the loose. I also noticed that I didn't see any of the undercover folks that were supposed to be watching the place outside but maybe that was the point. If they were obvious about it they probably were not doing a good job. I knocked on the driver's side window and the tinted windows slowly rolled down revealing the nondescript driver inside.

"Good evening." I asked the driver "Excuse me but who is this car for and who sent it?"

"Car is for you Dr. Elizabeth Waller, Agent Han sent me." He answered robotically like I was wasting his time.

"Sorry," I said, feeling kind of ridiculous for asking. "Can't be too careful."

The driver seemingly ignoring my response simply began to roll up the car window. I took that as my cue and entered the car.

The drive to the restaurant was filled with silence as I fiddled with my outfit. Soon enough though the car stopped, and I hopped out finding myself in a brightly lit plaza. Before I could thank the driver, he was already pulling away. I faced the restaurant and suddenly unexpectedly grew nervous. This was just a business meeting to be sure so there was nothing to be anxious about. Right? Plus, this was Sam who found me barely tolerable on a good day. There wouldn't be any multiverse in which he would want to be anything other than coworkers with the likes of me. I mean, if I was being frank, becoming friends would be pushing it at this point.

The only sound to comfort me out of my current spiraling thoughts was the slow clack of my sandals as I made my way toward the restaurant's entrance. The restaurant front was reminiscent of a Bistro and the blue exterior made it stand out from the other storefronts flanking it. There were multiple tables outside that were all unoccupied which I found odd as it was a warm June night. The slight breeze made the prospect of sitting outside and people watching quite appealing. Walking past the deserted tables I made my way into

162

the restaurant and was greeted by a rustic but impressive lobby with a bar to one side and plenty of seating if one was waiting for a table. The lighting was low and moody tinged with the promise of a romantic evening and I found I was growing uncomfortable with Sam's selection of venue. Perhaps he didn't know the mood of the place and simply glanced at the menu when picking the restaurant. I couldn't see the main dining area from the lobby and no one was at the hostess podium or the bar, so I waited patiently. It seemed like the place was dead at the moment.

I peeked at my phone to see what time it was. I was beginning to think they were in between services as it was an off time for a meal, not quite lunch, and not quite dinner. After waiting around to see if anyone returned to their posts or for Sam to show up, I decided to venture back around the lobby to what I imagined would be the main dining room. As soon as I rounded the corner I stopped dead in my tracks kicking myself for not following my instincts when I felt something was off. Sitting there, sipping on a glass of red wine like he had not a care in the world was my worst nightmares made into a physical form.

It was Alex, in the flesh.

He saw me and smiled that smile of his that used to make me feel like he was so happy to see me and only me. It was so intimate and personal that it made my skin crawl. I backed away slowly, not taking my eyes off of him, and spun around to run towards the lobby when three men in tactical gear came from God knows where and blocked my route. I could have probably taken one but three was pushing it. Well, there went that exit strategy.

"You wound me," Alex said, feigning that he was hurt. "Come join me, wouldn't you?"

"Do I have a choice?" I asked standing my ground trying to figure out if my purse was heavy enough to be a useful weapon. Alex stood

163

and pulled the chair out from the table that was across from his own. "Apparently not."

I slowly walked over and sat in the seat Alex was offering and surveyed the space around me trying to find another available exit. The side door was blocked by another one of Alex's goons. The kitchen seemed to have a few lurking around as well. I was looking past Alex trying to form another strategy and caught him frowning at me.

"I thought you would be happy to see me." He said as he leaned forward across the table trying to reach my hands. I quickly moved them to my lap. "Ouch. We used to always hold hands when we went out to nice restaurants."

"That was before I realized those meals were bought with blood money."

"Touché." He sighed leaning back into his own chair. "How have you been Lizzy? You look beautiful as always."

"Really?" I laughed. "You really want to do this. You killed people using my work, faked your own death, then effectively kidnapped me, what, twice now and you want to play catch-up like we're estranged lovers? I'm not playing games with you, Alex."

"Who said I was playing?" He said with a low serious voice that scared and excited me all at the same time. He sighed, and the tone of his voice snapped back to the leisurely in an instant. "We didn't really get to chat last time."

"Because you drugged me," I answered by crossing my arms across my chest. I understood I was acting obstinate but my higher brain functions were continuing to scan the room trying to figure out how to get out of here in one piece.

164

My options were looking pretty slim at the moment. There was also the added caveat that I didn't know if Sam was here or not. Did Alex orchestrate this whole thing or did he just crash our dinner? Did he have Sam and that was how he was able to text me from his number or did he have some super illegal way of appearing to be a text from another person?

"He's not here" Alex lazily mentioned while taking another sip of his wine like he had just read my mind. "You're Special Agent Friend if that's who you're looking for. I'm terribly insulted that you're not satisfied with my company."

At the moment it seemed like he was toying with me which meant I needed a new plan. I might be able to stall until backup arrived if I could get a message to Sam. Just a slight issue of figuring out how to do that. I scanned the table and my eyes fell on the napkin in front of me. Now, I just needed a distraction.

"Did you trick me into coming here to talk or are we actually going to eat? It's been a long day and I'm quite hungry" I said, taking the cloth napkin off the table, flicking it open, and placing it on my lap.

Alex laughed. "I had almost forgotten how you got when you were hungry." He turned around to call someone over to bring the food. As he was turned I took the opportunity to pull my phone from my purse. I quickly called Sam, muting it, and placed the phone on my lap covering it from view with the cloth napkin taking care not to cover the microphone just in time as Alex turned to face me once more. Soon enough a nervous-looking chef came out with a plated calamari appetizer and placed it in front of Alex and myself. I speared myself a piece on my fork and was about to take a bite because honestly, I wasn't lying when I said I was starving when I paused and brought it closer to inspect it.

"I didn't drug the food if that's what you're wondering." I

165

watched as he leaned over the table, a bit closer than I was prepared for, and he took the bite of food from off my fork, ate it slowly, and sat back down in his seat. God, he smelled good. And I hated him more for it.

I cleared my throat and took a bite for myself. It was heavenly and one of my favorite appetizers which frustratingly enough he seemed to remember. It also tasted pleasantly familiar. Alex seemed to notice my musing and smiled like the cat that caught the canary.

"I acquired the same chef from the restaurant where I proposed to you. Our special place."

I choked on my bite and grabbed the water in front of me to wash it down. No wonder the poor chef looked so nervous.

"You kidnapped that poor man just so you could have dinner with me?" I was horrified and angry at the same time. I knew, morally, that it was not okay to kidnap someone just so you could have a nice fancy dinner but my heart still did that little flippy thing it does when it gets excited. I'd chalk that up to being terrified and hating him for using what had been one of the best nights of my life to manipulate me now.

"Semantics." He answered waving a hand like it meant nothing. "I'm sure you have questions. I'm all ears."

This was my opportunity to pull the conversation back to the case, refocus, and stall until Sam and the team got here.

"How are you bastardizing my work now?" I wasn't even trying to hide the contempt in my voice. I was playing to his ego and I was hoping he would bite. If he was going to use food and pleasant memories, so could I. He used to love telling me all about his work because I had been the only one who could keep up with him intellectually.

"I would call it elevating your work, but we can agree to disagree. I see what you're trying to do but you look so cute when you're determined that I'll oblige you."

He took another bite of his calamari and when he was finished began to speak once more. "I'm assuming you want to get to the good stuff instead of boring you with how I escaped from jail am I correct?

I nodded my head and he frowned. "Alas, I will have to save that story for another day then." He took another sip of his wine and continued.

"Do you remember when we were in grad school my thesis work was on human bacterial gut flora? As you are aware, each person's gut flora has a distinct fingerprint, if you look close enough. I was working on a method of how to profile and obtain samples of an individual's gut flora."

"Yes, I remember. It was groundbreaking work, and you were close to optimizing it prior to the incident." I answered matter-of-factly as I recalled all the times we had been discussing his work.

He smiled as he gazed at me and took another bite of his food. It was like he was waiting for me to catch up in the conversation. His work was really revolutionary for the time. Personalized medicine was a hot topic as much then as it is today. As I thought about it, a slow realization began to creep into my mind.

"Oh my God, no," I exclaimed, dropping my fork to the floor as the realization of what he had been able to do suddenly hit me like a wave. I began to feel queasy at the implications of it so much so that I was almost afraid to speak, but I had to know if it was true.

"You combined my work on manipulating the virulence factor of the bacteria and your work on personalized gut biome therapies to make a bioweapon personalized to a single target that you could

167

employ without even needing to be close enough to touch them."

"No need to be in the same room, heck even the same country actually. Impressed?" He smiled at me, studying my reaction.

"Terrified," I responded honestly. He would only need a swab or a droplet and he could take out anyone he wanted to or was paid to. Was he going to sell this technology to the highest bidder? Were the deaths at the Adirondack Resort an audition for the buyers? My thoughts were raging like a winding river as I glanced at Alex drinking his wine and taking me in. Why was he telling me all this? Did he just want to gloat and show himself as the greater mind and scientist? Why was he risking exposure to being caught by inviting me to talk with him? Then it hit me, and I smiled leaning back in my chair.

"You can't get it to target one subject fully can you," I said more smugly than I had intended to but God it felt good. The three victims at the resort must have all randomly shared one of the markers Alex used. It was lucky more people were not impacted at the resort. If it was a more common marker the results could have been catastrophic.

"Alas," he sighed leaning back into his chair, popping another piece of calamari into his mouth. "The first couple of uses, as you've seen up close and personally, resulted in multiple deaths, like those 2 people you mentioned succumbing along with the target. It has the nasty side effect of bringing-" he paused searching for the right words "unwanted attention. One person stops breathing. It's just a sad circumstance but three random people in one hotel and the Feds get called in. I do have to say, however, that finally seeing you again quite outweighs any unpleasantness I have had to endure."

"You do realize that people aren't your lab rats," I responded hoping my disgust for his actions shone through. "You can't just experiment on them without their consent. That's wrong Alex, very very wrong. They're just innocent people."

168

Alex's eyes seemed to light up with malice. "Innocent you say. No one is really innocent are they Lizzy? That politician was funneling money from his so-called charitable organizations to pay for his mistress and to pay off his gambling debt. That sweet old lady? She stole the winning ticket that won her the trip from her roommate and fellow Bridge player who has Alzheimer's Disease. And that guy that worked the front desk, you don't want to know what lurked in his browser history. No, Lizzy, no one is innocent."

I swallowed as I took in Alex's intensity and the gravity of what he was saying. I need to refocus myself. This wasn't about me. This was about getting justice for those poor people. Whether they were completely blameless or not and making sure no one else suffered the same fate. I needed to start mentally cataloging all this new information so I could relay it to Sam and the team later. Where were they? It had to have been 15 or 20 minutes since I called them under the table and I could feel the phone still hot on my lap. Could they hear the conversation we were having? I hoped they were recording it.

I was starting to feel a bit guilty as awful as it was to admit though, the scientist in me was finding this conversation fascinating. I hadn't had a conversation with a peer at my level in years and I found myself easily falling back into it. Especially someone with such talent as Alex. It hadn't even occurred to me to combine our research. I knew he was using it for nefarious reasons but the potential implications for the medical community were massive.

"You never thought to use the research for helping people instead of harming?" I asked taking a drink of water as the situation was growing more uncomfortable by the minute and I could feel my mouth going dry.

"Honestly, and I know this isn't what you want to hear but, no. What does publishing your findings get you in the research community? Accolades and recognition and maybe, just maybe it will buy you a few more years of research funding for your lab but what after that? There's no money to be made. I know you value knowledge but the rest of the world, my dear, values money. He with the biggest bank account is the one in power and that is where I intend to be."

I knew there was a lot to unpack from that little tirade, but I had to get the conversation pulled back to his work so the team and I could arrest him and get the bioweapon off the streets and out of the hands of buyers.

"I'm assuming you used the hotel's air handling system to introduce the aerosol bacterium as it would be circulated all throughout the hotel to ensure the target was hit."

"Naturally. Nice topic segway by the way" Alex grinned plopping another piece of calamari in his mouth which had the unintended side effect of bringing my attention to his lips. I leaned forward intrigued by the complexity of how he had transformed my work and I wanted to press further on his methods.

"The hotel had 52 rooms occupied when the bioweapon was released and only 3 people were impacted. By all calculations that's an incredibly impressive low deviation. The victims must have all had some very specific yet random genetic mutation in common. Have you tried it on siblings or twins to see how dialed in the gut flora needs to be to affect only one individual?" I gasped, clasping my hand over my mouth horrified at what I had just said. Not only had I just complimented Alex on the killing of three innocent people that he saw as a mere inconvenience, lab rats even to be experimented on, and here I was actually advising him to try it on more people.

Alex's smile grew larger as he leaned over the table bringing his face uncomfortably close to mine. He whispered as if he was sharing a secret forcing me to lean in ever closer.

170

"Have you considered my offer? Would there be any way I could convince you to join me? I am so very close to finding the missing piece to perfect it and having you working with me, side by side, would only hasten the results. We could be partners, and you know how generous a partner I can be." The subtext was hard to miss and I cursed my rebelling body as heat pooled within my stomach.

"Conversely" I offered as a form of rebuttal "you could turn yourself in and perhaps have access to a lab to continue working on a way to capitalize on your work for the betterment of humanity."

He sighed and leaned back indicating that he wasn't going to take my offer and was disappointed that I wouldn't take his.

"No." He started almost as if he had grown bored of our conversation. "You would never willingly work to harm others and I could never force you to even if I whisked you away and chained you to a lab bench. That's an image, however, I'll keep in the back of my mind." He smirked, and my traitorous skin allowed a blush to form as he continued.

"You are far too stubborn for that. It's your nature to heal while mine is to conquer. We're two sides of a coin, yin and yang, light and dark. That's why we work so well together. If you were to join me just think how you could bring me back from the brink of utter destruction, even me out."

I gaped at him slack jawed "Are you seriously threatening me with the lives of innocent people right now if I don't willingly go with you."

He shrugged teasing me with another devilish smile. "You're the one with a pesky conscience, I am not so burdened." He frowned, "Oh don't look so upset."

"Don't look so upset" I sneered at him. "For the past five years, all I did was torture myself! I blamed myself for causing the deaths of those people in the Congo you used as Guinea pigs. I tore myself apart struggling with whether to turn you in or not." I could hear my voice getting louder, but I didn't care. "I have done *nothing* but torture myself all these years so don't fucking tell me to not look upset."

I could feel the tears threatening to burst through my eyes more from anger than anything else as I looked anywhere but Alex's face. I heard his chair scrap as he stood and came and kneeled beside me brushing a tear that managed to escape.

"Don't," I growled as I pushed his hand away. "You don't get to comfort me. You lost that right." He opened his mouth to say something, but the distant sounds of sirens flooded into the room. He stood brushing some imaginary dirt from his knees.

"Regretfully, it looks like our time has come to an end." I couldn't bear to even look at him at this point. I felt him take my hand and pressed a kiss to it. I didn't even look up to see if he was gone.

The next thing I knew Sam was calling my name running over to my chair kneeling in the same spot Alex had been just minutes before. "Elizabeth. Elizabeth, are you alright? Are you hurt anywhere?" I could see him scanning my body and face to see if I was injured in any way. When he was satisfied that I was uninjured he got up and kicked the chair that Alex had been sitting in.

"What is your fucking problem?" He yelled at me looming over where I was sitting. "Do you have a death wish or something? What if he kidnapped you and tried to get you to make more bioweapons or what if he was planning on killing you so there would be no loose ends and no one to unravel his work? Did you even think about that?"

I was trying extremely hard not to rip Sam a new one. I get it. Going missing, especially from his home probably didn't look good for him especially since the Area Director, his father, had given expressed orders to the contrary. I was getting so sick and tired of male egos at this point. This would be so much easier to talk about with Nina, which was saying a lot. I calmly stood and started to make my way to the door which had cleared of agents when I felt someone grab my arm, hard, and saw it was Sam.

"We aren't done here." He said seething more than speaking.

"Oh yes, we are," I replied, ripping my arm from his hand. "And besides. You haven't actually let me do any speaking. You came in here and lectured me. Did you even want to know why I came here? Do you think Alex called and asked me on a date and I said gee whiz I'd love to go out with a mass murderer what time should I be there and what's the dress code?" Sam was quiet and just stared at me indicating I had hit the nail on the head.

"Oh my God that's what you think happened. I knew you didn't think much of me but I didn't fathom that you thought that little of me." I was hurt and vindicated at the same time. How many times have people misjudged me or attempted to put me in a box, label me, and then put me on their shelves? Not anymore, not now, not ever again, not Alex, and as sure as hell not Sam.

"If you want to know, I came here because I got a text from *you* saying that you wanted to meet up for dinner. I thought you were trying to do something nice for a change, but I should have known better. That should have been my first clue. As if you could even care."

Sam and I continued to glare at each other engaging in a battle of wills until Dominic and Benny came over.

"Thank God you're alright Elizabeth we got here as soon as we could," Benny said out of breath. He definitely needed to work out more.

"Calling Sam and leaving the phone on was a wise choice," Dominic added, and I found that getting a compliment from him was a very odd sensation. The boys' arrival didn't soften my mood any however and I just wanted to get out of this restaurant, away from Sam, and most pressing, out of this stupid outfit and makeup.

"Will there be anything else Special Agent Han?" I said not hiding the venom in my voice.

"We'll finish this debrief later, Dr. Waller." That was all the answer I got before he nodded at Dominic and Benny and then walked away to accost another agent about something regarding the scene.

"What the hell is his problem?" I asked Dominic and Benny as I walked to the exit. They looked at each other in confusion, having some sort of conversation using only their eyes, and ended with Dominic nodding in what seemed like approval.

"I'm not sure if this violates bro code or anything-" Benny started out tentatively "but Sam was worried to death about you."

I laughed, not being able to help myself, and waited for Dominic to tell me Benny was wrong when he simply nodded in agreement.

"He threw a chair through a window," Dominic added and then seemingly done with the conversation went to go do whatever it is he does at a crime scene.

"He did what?" I asked Benny for clarification as that did not sound like him in the slightest. He was Mr. Cool as a Cucumber. Not I Throw Chairs through Windows Guy.

"Yeah, man. Sam figured out we'd been played and tried to warn you that you might be in danger, but Alex had locked us all in the building and blocked all the cells and landlines. He basically busted through a window so that he could get outside so that he could drive outside the range of the cell tower blockage and pick up on your call. He figured out what you were trying to do and used it to triangulate your location."

"Oh shit," I said, covering my mouth as Benny smiled at me. Their use of foul language was starting to wear off on me.

"Oh, shit indeed," Benny answered playfully. "I'll be over here if you need me. I'm sure Sam will want to be the one to drive you back to his place so don't go anywhere." I opened my mouth to protest but he cut me off.

"That's also an order from Robert as well who personally apologizes for not being able to be here but says to call him if you need anything."

I sighed and sat down in the nearest chair thinking I could at least alleviate my foot pain. I watched the agents as they buzzed around like bees in a hive and marveled at their comings and goings. I watched as one agent escorted the poor chef Alex had kidnapped out of the restaurant as he was weeping profusely and instantly felt guilty but relieved that he made it out with what appeared to be not a scratch on him. I really needed to stop doing that, I thought, as I removed my heels. I needed to stop allowing the actions of someone else to make me feel guilty. What Alex did was on him, not me, and allowing myself to feel guilt over it was not productive. The same went for Sam. I was not going to allow him to make me feel guilty for putting myself in a situation that I was unaware was perilous. I don't know where this new-found revelation came from, but I was damn proud of it and felt myself straighten in my chair. I guess it takes literally facing your fears to have a revelation of this magnitude.

I also had some additional insight into what Alex was working on and was already trying to formulate ways to detect or deter it. I deflated slightly as I saw Sam wrapping up an ad hoc meeting with his team. I was not looking forward to the undoubtedly uncomfortable drive back to his place.

CHAPTER 22

The drive back was even worse than I had thought it was going to be. Sam was looking straight ahead focused on the road not saying anything. Once in a while, he would field a call through the car's Bluetooth about the case and then the car would return to silence. I felt like I had to say something to clear the air but couldn't come up with anything. And, as I reminded myself, I didn't have to come up with anything. I don't care if he did come to my rescue he didn't have to be such an ass about it. When we finally got up to the apartment I went into the bedroom and waited for Sam to knock on the door or something, but it never happened. Eventually, I couldn't take it anymore and went into the kitchen to make the tea I hadn't been able to drink before.

"Sam, would you like some tea while I'm out here?" I figured offering an olive branch and being the bigger person was a step in smoothing over whatever this chasm of silence meant for our professional relationship. He let out a noncommittal grunt and continued watching some sports show. I waited in silence for the tea to boil in the kettle, so I figured I'd try again.

"I actually have some more insight into the case now if you- "

"You can give your report tomorrow at the Field Office, Dr. Waller." Sam interrupted with an emotionless tone. Well, he didn't have to be a dick about it. Fine, I was done playing nice. If he wanted to keep this strictly professional, which felt absurd because I was currently in his apartment, in my pajamas, sleeping in his bed, that was fine by me. I fixed my tea and made my way back to the room slamming the door. Being a little childish never hurt anyone.

***

176

I heard the door slamming and sighed in relief. At least the awkward situation was over for the night at least. I was being an ass, I knew that, but the fear I had when I figured out Elizabeth was in danger was more than for a colleague and I was having issues reconciling that. It seemed like the moment we started to gain some ground, fucking Beal turned everything on it's head. I hadn't wanted to put someone behind bars as much as I wanted to get him away from society.

Who was I kidding, a large part of me just wanted him away from Elizabeth. This whole case was messing me up in a big way and I needed to focus. Having Elizabeth stay with me was not helping the issue, no matter how much I liked being able to keep an eye on her. I was going to have to be more vigilant in the future about that. I didn't see Alex letting Elizabeth out of his sights anytime soon. Psychopaths think of people as belongings and he definitely still thinks that Elizabeth is his.

My mind went back to the door slamming and I couldn't help but think she should be mad at me. I deserved it. It seemed like she had given up on talking to me for the night, so I turned off the TV and tried to get comfortable on the couch. Tomorrow was going to be a long day.

The next morning went about exactly as I had thought it would. Elizabeth and I stayed out of each other's way, repelling away from each other like polarized magnets as we got ready for the workday, never exchanging a word or even a glance.

The drive to the office was more of the same. I turned the radio on to some talk station and we drove with that being the only conversation to be had. Once I parked the car at the Field Office she jumped out making her way inside before I even undid my seatbelt. I examined the broken window of the field office that had now been secured and boarded up and cringed. I would need to put together a good rationale for that action. Especially since Benny informed me that the sliding doors have a mechanic on the inside that pops them off the track in case of emergencies. It seemed like a good idea at the time and for all we knew Elizabeth could have been in real trouble.

Imagine my surprise when I show up at the scene and she's enjoying a romantic dinner for two with not a scratch on her. If it had not been deemed unprofessional to have thrown a chair there too, then I probably would have. I knew I came down on her a bit hard but the truth of the matter was that I was mad at Beal and not her, but I couldn't help it. I knew I was going to get shit for it from my dad too. It seemed like he had basically adopted her at this point. Did that make Elizabeth my sister? I shuddered at the thought.

When I made it inside Nina had already cornered Elizabeth when she called over to me.

"Sam! Come here." She said, flailing her arms like I wouldn't see her.

"Yes, Nina, what can I do for you?"

"I was just telling Elizabeth how bananas it was here yesterday. Everyone was running around, and all the doors were locked, and my cell phone didn't work. Could you believe that!"

"So, I've been told," Elizabeth answered, arching her eyebrows at me. "It must have been quite an experience."

Elizabeth turned to me, her expression turning serious. "Sam I'd really like to talk to you before the briefing t-"

"Oh, it was," Nina interrupted, clutching her hand to her chest like she was relieving some horrible trauma. "But I heard you were kidnapped and taken to that fancy restaurant downtown so that must have been equally scary. How was the food? By the way, I've always wanted to go there."

"Yes, sitting across from a mass murderer was equally as scary as not having cell service." The playful sarcasm Elizabeth emitted was hard to miss but Nina kept on going anyway completely oblivious. Nina gave me a little wink and I knew what she was doing. She was trying to help Elizabeth lighten up and decompress after last night's events by asking frivolous questions. Her heart was in the right place, but the delivery could use a little work. "And I can't report on the food as Alex kidnapped the chef from our favorite restaurant when we were together."

Nina blinked a few times. "Okay I know he's a bad guy and all but that's kind of hot."

Elizabeth finally laughed, swatting Nina on the arm while scolding her on why it was inappropriate.

"Okay. Okay." Nina added, laughing as well. "No lusting over bad guys. But what about good guys? Sam over here went all He-man and threw a chair through the window so the Agents could come and get you."

Elizabeth and I both choked on our coffees, taking the opportunity to make a quick exit with Nina following close behind asking a slew of follow-up questions. The rest of the afternoon went by quickly and soon enough it was time for Elizabeth's update. I was kicking myself for dismissing her last night but if she really did have some good intel, I would find out soon enough. She took the podium looking more confident than I had seen her look in a while, hiding her exhaustion pretty well and settled in with everyone else.

"Good afternoon everyone." She started straightening up and addressing the room "First off I would like to thank all of you who came to the rescue yesterday. I don't like to play the role of damsel in distress but you all acted valiantly." The room murmured a few small chuckles , and I could tell she was trying to lighten the mood. "On a serious note, I will be taking my personal security more seriously moving forward so as to not put you all in harm's way needlessly. During my time with Alex, I was able to surmise three points that I would like to present to you all."

"One observation I made is that Alex has his own personal security. I saw the same four men the night of the raid at the masquerade and at the restaurant last evening although it does seem like he has added to the ranks. It leads me to believe they are always with him which might make apprehending him a bit trickier as they have been heavily armed. Second, due to his ego and pride, he divulged to me that the bioweapon was indeed based on my past research. New information that I gathered was that he was able to combine his research in gut microbiome mapping with mine to create a bioweapon that can stealthily and efficiently kill a single target due to the customization. Along with this, I was also able to determine that he has not successfully executed this idea at this time as seen in the Adirondack resort case in which he was targeting one person and ended up killing three. I have emailed you all a summary of his work and how he could have potentially used it. I will open up the floor to any questions at this point."

I saw multiple hands go up and Elizabeth decided to call on Dominic probably thinking he would have the most relevant question.

"What's the third item you have for us?"

"It's an item I left out of my previous update that I would be remiss if I didn't include in this one."

I stared daggers at her thinking I knew where she was going with this, but she simply stood a little straighter refusing to wither under my gaze.

"My relationship with Dr. Beal goes beyond the professional. We had a romantic relationship years ago which may be compounding his fixation on me."

180

Quiet murmurs flooded the room as Elizabeth's resolve seemed to grow with every whisper.

"My recommendation based on all current evidence and the information that I just provided is that we should use me as bait." She finished matter-of-factly like it was a logical conclusion.

The room erupted in side conversations and additional questions.

"Everyone quiet!" I yelled to the room giving Elizabeth some time to recover. "What are you proposing, Dr. Waller?"

"It seems to me that the only times we are able to catch Alex slipping in the slightest is when it involves me."

"I get where you're going but what if he does get a hold of you? You are the foremost expert on your body of work and he could use you to perfect the weapon. We'd basically be handing you over."

"That's where I have to disagree." She added smirking like it was her favorite thing in the world to disagree with me. "If we set me out as bait you can get him before I'm even in that position. He's been outsmarting us this whole time and we've been on the defensive, we need to be on the offense. I believe if we just-"

"If you don't have any further information on the events of last night this meeting is over." I knew I was cutting her off, but I didn't want Elizabeth to give any of the other agents any ideas. She opened her mouth to speak and then stopped. She had this look in her eyes like she was calculating something and then stopped.

"That was all. Thank you for your time agents." She collected her things and walked up next to me.

"Your office. One hour." She whispered harshly and then made her way out into the hall and in the direction of her lab. I smirked at her command like she had the authority to give it after delivering such a ridiculous suggestion. Using her as bait had been a massive failure before. We were not doing that again.

I walked past her office and saw her on the phone talking rapidly, tapping on the screen agitatedly with someone as she was looking over some bottles on the shelving. As she saw me walking down the hallway she turned her back and walked away from the glass. Apparently, she didn't want me overhearing her conversation. That was fair play, but it still annoyed the hell out of me.

An hour later, right on time, Elizabeth came into my office.

"I spoke with your father, proposed my idea, and asked him what his thoughts were."

Well, that was a mood killer, especially bringing my dad into the conversation. "Hello. Dr. Waller, how are you? I'm fine, thank you. What did dear old dad have to say? And for the record, I'm pretty sure you've never needed someone to tell you what to do." She appeared thrown off by the compliment but continued with the conversation without a beat.

"Infuriating enough he agreed with you. But, he did concede that my idea had some merit." She huffed as she sat down in the chair across from me. "So, I'm here to see what *your* plan is."

"Your plan wasn't a plan, it was a suicide mission." I corrected her. "And last I checked, I was the Special Agent here and you were the scientist."

"I could pass the Special Agents test with my eyes closed." She answered not one bit of doubt in her voice. I decided to file that away for a later conversation.

"My plan, although not fully fleshed out or the team informed, is to have you monitored 24/7 and wait for Beal to fuck up.

Additionally, we will monitor all channels and use our current undercover agents and informants to see if Beal plans to make a sale." Elizabeth huffed her obvious displeasure at my plan.

"I have two problems with that. One, Alex will not sell a half-realized product. He has too much of a twisted sense of pride to do that. He could, however, have some additional testing planned that he could set into action at any time and put innocent people at risk. We don't know the scale of what he is working on. Two, you just want me to wait around for Alex to try to kidnap me or kill me and be on guard for every minute of every day until God knows when." She leaned forward and stared into my eyes with a level of seriousness that I thought could only be matched by my father.

"Sam. I can't just be passive in this whole matter. I've been looking over my shoulder for longer than I can remember. I want, no, I *need* to be a part of this. I can't stand playing the victim anymore. I need him to be locked away and I need to be part of the solution that accomplishes that. You know I'm the only Achilles heel he has. We need to utilize that and strike *now*. He's close to figuring out how to optimize it. It's only a matter of time before he strikes and we need to stop him now ahead of more people getting hurt!"

"Are you sure you want him behind bars?" I asked seriously, ignoring her subtle pleading. "Are you sure you don't want to join him? You guys seem to get pretty cozy every time you have an encounter." The anger on her face was palpable and rolled off her in scorching waves. I half expected the fire alarms to start blaring.

"Are you really asking me that? You seriously think I would ignore the deaths of those innocent people and welcome Alex back with open arms?" There was a mixture of shock and something like disappointment in her eyes, but I pushed forward.

"Love is a fucked up thing. He appears to be a master of manipulation. What if he convinces you you're both still in love and

183

with blinders on you help him." She actually had the audacity to look disgusted at this point.

"I think my track record proves otherwise. And what do you know about love? I've heard about your reputation. I don't think you understand the concept." She sneered at me with evident spite. Now she was crossing the line.

"Maybe you should try it sometime and loosen up. No, I don't think that would work for you. You're so tightly wound up you'd probably never find anyone to fit the bill."

"Enough." She whispered, staring ahead at me, but I continued anyway.

"Or maybe normal guys don't do it for you. Maybe you need a murdering psychopath to get you off."

"Enough!" She yelled, and I suddenly felt nauseating guilt wash over me.

"Alex may be a murderer, but even he *never* treated me with such disrespect. If your mother was still alive she would be so disappointed in you." She said with venom dripping from her words. I may have crossed the line but she just fucking vaulted across it.

"What did you just say to me!" I practically yelled at her standing from my desk. If she wasn't a woman I would have knocked her on her ass by now.

"I'm done." She said quietly. "I'm done with you, I'm done with this job, I'm done with all of it." With that, she stood up with an eerie robotic calmness and made her way out into the hallway. I followed her out of my office and down the hallway and watched as she went into her lab and grabbed her things. I heard Nina try to greet her, but she just mentioned a few words to her and walked right past her. She

184

speed walked past me, not even sparing a glance in my direction, and made her way to the door. What the hell did she think she was doing now?

"Elizabeth, you can't just leave!" I yelled after her, all the agents quieting and taking in the unexpected show.

"You said it yourself Sam." she stated without emotion turning around briefly "When have I ever needed someone to tell me what to do?"

I watched as she walked outside the Field Office. Where the hell did she think she was going without a detail? She was just being reckless at this point. I knew we had a pretty rough argument, but she was an idiot to take such a risk after the previous night's event. As soon as she walked outside the gates a black sedan pulled up. The door swung open and a hand appeared reaching out to her, bidding her inside.

"Shit. Elizabeth run!" I yelled from the steps of the office and began to run towards her pulling my gun.

I had seen that sedan before and I knew who it belonged to. She gazed at the hand beckoning her to come along, and then focused her attention on me, her eyes turbulent, seeming to be deciding on her next course of action. Her eyes locked into determination, her choice seemingly made. She made her way toward the car and slipped near the wheel well using the wheel to help herself back up and then took the hand extended out towards her easing her into the car not giving me another passing glance. I aimed the gun at the car to fire, but I didn't want to hit Elizabeth. I raced towards the car hoping to get to her before it was too late but by the time I made it to the road I was met with a shower of dirt and stone from the car peeling away.

"Shit!" I repeatedly kicked the curb and ran back into the building Dominic and Benny meeting me halfway.

185

"What happened? Where's Elizabeth?" Benny asked, catching his breath.

"She just got into an unmarked car that I think belongs to Beal."

"Why the hell would she do something like that?" Benny yelled looking down the road like the car would still be in the line of sight.

"I think she's trying to take on Beal on her own." I said putting my gun away and running back towards the office. I needed to get an APB out on that vehicle and for Elizabeth while I figured out how the hell to get her back.

"She's sure got a big pair of lady balls," Benny said, jogging back with Dominic following suit and nodding at Benny's assessment.

"Well, they are going to get her killed." This woman was going to be the death of me and I'm pretty sure was talking multiple years off my lifespan. Benny and Dominic were now staring at me.

"Get going and find her!" They scurried off leaving me to go to my office to make some calls. I sat in my chair running my hands through my hair. I now felt doubly shitty for saying the things I did. I didn't want that to be the last thing that she ever heard from me. I had to focus on getting her back. Then I could apologize. I just hoped we made it to her in time before something horrible happened.

***

Elizabeth sat in the car feeling Alex's gaze rake over her like a predator getting ready to devour its prey.

"As graceful an exit as ever, Lizzy," Alex smirked as I situated myself in the car righting my clothing and moving, so I was as far away from him as humanly possible.

186

"You know I'm not known for being graceful," I replied brushing the dirt off my knees.

"I have to say." Alex continued, amused at my attempt to put space between us, "I'm a bit surprised you decided to run away with me."

"Who says I'm running? I just…" I paused. "I just needed to do something else with my life. I'm tired of feeling under-appreciated, under-utilized, running from who I really am."

"Oh?" Alex said lazily leaning on the console between us in the back seat "And *who* are you really Lizzy."

"You know that better than anyone else sadly enough."

"Indeed, I do." Alex laughed, "But I'd love to hear your own reflection."

"I need to be challenged, to experiment, to learn, to push the boundaries of the scientific community. I'm not meant to sit in a government lab and run routine lab testing while my brain turns to sedimentary rock due to lack of stimulation. I need to be surrounded by like-minded individuals and state-of-the-art technology. I gave all that up as a penance of sorts for all the death that came from my work but I'm tired. I'm just so tired of fighting my nature." I leaned my head against the glass exhausted by my emotional outburst. I had held that in for so long and saying it out loud for the first time felt physically draining.

"I'm very happy you've decided to come with me." Alex took my hand and planted a kiss on it. "Suspicious, but still very glad."

"This doesn't mean I'm agreeing to help you with your work," I said, pulling my hand from his. "If that's your expectation then you might as well kill me."

"My, my you jump to such extremes these days." Alex laughed. "And I understand. We have a lot of catching up to do, but first." He said pulling out what seemed like a metal detector wand "We can't have us being followed now can we?"

He waved the wand over me, looking for bugs or tracking devices I assumed, and then turned his attention to my phone buzzing in my pocket. I handed it over, figuring out that was what he was indicating, and he looked at the phone and frowned.

"Special Agent Han is quite persistent, isn't he? 20 missed calls. That's a bit excessive isn't it?"

"He can go to hell," I answered, crossing my arms and meaning it.

"Lovers quarrel? That Special Agent, Sam, seemed quite upset by your departure." Alex asked inquisitively. He always had been the jealous type right down to the letter.

"No." I laughed at the absurdity of it. "You pretty much wrecked any possibility of me having any substantial healthy relationships after you."

"I'd offer my apologies but hearing that does please me." He purred grinning. He always reminded me of the Cheshire cat from Alice in Wonderland with that mischievous smile. You could never tell if he wanted to help you or eat you alive. He rolled down the window and threw my cell phone out of the still-moving car.

"Hey!" I yelled looking out my own window to see it now lying in pieces scattered over the freeway. Alex laughed.

"Don't worry I'll buy you a new one. Precautions and all."

I could tell I was pouting but I didn't care. I had finally set it up the way I wanted, and Nina had sent some adorable puppy photos,

188

that I would never admit that I enjoyed, that were on there.

"Oh, don't pout now. You know how I hate that."

I was about to say I'll do whatever the hell I want with my face, but I decided against it. We were playing nice right now, him not digging too deep into my motives for leaving the FBI, and I wanted to keep it that way.

"I know this is a bit awkward-" he added pulling something from the cooler "but I'm going to need you to drink this. Full disclosure, there is a sleep-inducing drug in here. I can't have you being able to retrace your steps back to the location we are going to and since you are so intelligent and could most likely figure it out I can't have you conscious. My apologies but it was the only solution I could come up with."

He had the gall to actually look disappointed to drug me. At least I knew what I was getting into this time.

"Is that Coca-Cola?"

"Yes," he smiled. "Your favorite, Coca-Cola in a glass bottle, ice cold."

I would be touched by the thoughtfulness but again he was about to drug me.

"Well then how can I say no." I took the bottle and drank about half until I started to feel sleepy.

I could feel myself slipping into slumber before I heard Alex tell the driver to head back to the lab. I knew I should have been more scared at this point but, for some reason, I felt more comfortable and at peace than I had in a while, like I had purpose. With that thought, I closed my eyes and drifted off.

When I awoke I found that my head was resting on Alex's shoulder who was currently tapping away on a device that seemed similar to an iPad.

"Good morning sunshine." He beamed at me as I shot up forgetting where I was for a moment and instantly feeling dizzy.

"Easy there. The drugs are still wearing off. You were sleeping so soundly that it would have pained me to wake you, so I simply let you doze away." I tried to rub the sleep away from my eyes and looked around, seeing I was still in the car and that we were currently parked in some kind of warehouse.

"Where are we?" I asked, still cloudy from the drugs and temporarily forgetting my current situation. "Never mind, I know you're not going to answer that."

"Come," Alex commanded more than asked as the car door was mysteriously opened by one of his henchmen and offered a hand. We exited the car and I took in my surroundings.

The windows were boarded, and the temperature was regulated. I wouldn't be able to discern if this was still Upstate New York or Chicago let alone the time of day having been unconscious for the journey. As we turned the corner and went deeper into the warehouse words escaped me as the most beautiful lab space that I could have ever imagined came into view. The facilities and equipment were state of the art and looked like it was in no way a fly-by-night operation. Technicians covered in protective equipment bustled in and out of positive pressure clean rooms that lined the walls like bees going from honeycomb to honeycomb. The equipment was gleaming with how new it was and some were pieces I had never even seen before. He had to have been operating from out of this location for a while based on the semi-permanent nature of the setup and personnel.

"Impressed?" Alex asked coyly obviously knowing what my answer would be as it was probably clearly written on my face.

"Very," I answered truthfully. It was a space I could have only dreamed of. It made the FBI labs look like it was made of cardboard and glue sticks. People in lab coats bustled about indicating it was a well-staffed facility. Apparently, crime does pay.

"Where would you like to start? I can see that look in your eye. You want to dig in." Alex said clearly amused.

"Your lab notebooks and notes, if you don't mind. I'd like to get a handle on the mechanism in which you coupled our work before I head to the benchtop."

Alex blinked at me and then smiled. "I'm sorry but I got distracted by your use of coupling where you and I are involved."

I could feel myself blushing. Get it together. "Notes, now, please."

"Ah, that I can easily provide." He surveyed the room, pulled henchman number 45 as I decided to deem him because at this point I was losing count, and watched as he scurried off. A few minutes later a familiar face sauntered over to us whose visage went from seductively gleeful when looking at Alex to spiteful when it finally rested on me.

"Liz, this is my assistant Morgan. Morgan, this is my muse, Lizzy." I could see her face morph into something akin to ugly jealousy.

"Oh, we met at the FBI office where she just happened to set us up for the masquerade. Clever." I had a feeling when she bumped into me before it felt personal, but I couldn't understand why. After seeing the way she ogled Alex I could see it clearly now. Someone wanted

Alex for herself and I was in the way. I'd file that under useful information for another day. I stepped close to Alex allowing him to put his hand around my waist. "Now would you be a dear and run along to get the lab notes I requested." She nearly looked like she was going to strangle me then and there but decided wisely, to let it go. She flashed her nicest smile to Alex, scowled in my direction, and stormed off in the other direction.

"She better be careful or her face is going to stay like that," I murmured as I watched her sulk away.

I could practically feel the gloating emanating from Alex as he chuckled next to me and I jumped away from him remembering my current position.

"I didn't know you were the jealous type?" He continued to chuckle, leading me to what appeared to be an office.

"Well, it's been a while. People grow and things like that." The so-called office was vastly different than I was expecting. It was translucent, looking almost like a science fiction jail cell, and sat smack in the middle of the warehouse. It was locked down like a fortress as well with Alex pulling out a keycard to open it. In the office, two desks sat facing each other setup with dual screens with a keyboard and mouse poised to be utilized. It was similar to the set-up Alex and I had during our graduate student days. He pulled out a chair and I sat down on one side of the desk. He leaned over my shoulder grabbing the mouse smirking as he did, reveling in the effect he had being in such close proximity and began to navigate around the desktop screen.

"All the pertinent information lives in this folder here for your perusal. These computers have no access to the internet nor are they wireless capable."

"Well, that's offensive," I said in mock indignancy.

192

"My have you become full of yourself in my absence." He stated as he opened one of the folders and selected a document. "Unfortunately, good help is hard to find in my particular line of work, and loyalty even harder as you saw with my former associate, so I've limited all the research to these computers."

"What if something happens to these? Where's the backup?" The researcher in me was horrified that all his research was not stored in some capacity. One keystroke and it would be gone for good.

Alex smiled and tapped his temple, his face uncomfortably near mine as he continued to lean over me. "It's all up here. I'm the backup system. Would you like me to pass the information on to you?"

"Well, I think that would be wise but -" Before I could finish speaking Alex's lips were on mine and any coherent thought flew out of my mind. I had almost forgotten how he kissed. He kissed as if he were a dying man and only the taste of your lips were capable of saving him. I squealed in shock which gave him the opportunity to deepen the kiss further. My hands, without command, clasped the side of his face as I got swept away in the dam of emotions he had just broken open. To my surprise, it was him who pulled away leaving my hand suspended and my lips cold missing the warmth of him.

He smiled his wicked smile while I cleared my throat and smoothed out my hair that had somehow become disheveled. "As a man of science, you should know that a kiss is not a way to pass information from one person to another," I mumbled as I focused my gaze downward, suddenly finding my nails very fascinating.

"Well, as a researcher I had to experiment, now, didn't I?" he gloated, standing up and walking behind me. Another individual in a lab coat cleared their throat, walked up to Alex, said something in a voice too low for me to hear, and then glanced back at me.

"Saved by the minion?" I asked, turning back to the computer.

193

"I'm afraid this matter requires my immediate attention. Just wave anyone down if you need anything and it will be taken care of." His eyes briefly glanced at my lips and with a parting smirk for good measure, he left. I let go a breath I didn't realize I had been holding and glanced at the clock on the computer and my thoughts floated back to the FBI Office and those who worked within its walls. Nina should be working on her duties in the lab right about now. I was going to chalk that kiss off as me being a terrific actress and not dwell on it too much.

"Focus. You've got a lot of work ahead of you." I said to myself aloud giving my face a few gentle pats for good measure and dove headfirst into Alex's research.

CHAPTER 23

I stood in a makeshift command center as agents ran to and from as I barked out commands.

"O'Neil, I want a local PD on this now." I barked at an agent as he ran past the phone still in my hand as I waited on hold.

"But you asked me to check on the status of the APB." The poor man shuddered as he stopped dead in his tracks looking like a deer in headlights.

"For Christ's sake, I asked for that hours ago?" My voice was loud and commanding, forcing him to cower even more if that was possible.

"We've got it, Sam." I heard Dominic answer back as he went to talk to O'Neil. I vaguely heard him squeak out a "but he only told me to do it like 15 minutes ago" as Dominic shuffled him off and out of my site shaking his head all the while.

I realized I was being unreasonable, I knew that, but I was still feeling pretty shitty. If I hadn't provoked her she might still be here, both of us taking shots at each other and ending the argument with a round on the mats. From a professional standpoint, I was also a failure at not protecting a witness and I'd already gotten an earful from my father on top of that. From a personal standpoint, I was unfortunately also realizing that my feelings for Elizabeth ran deeper than a working relationship at a time that wasn't ideal.

"Shit," I said aloud, surprising some of the newer staff once again, the more wizen staff going about their business accustomed to my outbursts by now. I couldn't let emotions come into the picture. Not when Elizabeth's life was on the line. I still had no idea if she had completely turned to Alex's side or if she was going into the situation

195

with a half-cocked plan. I knew better though that she would never let herself work by Alex's side and that was the part that had me terrified. If he figured her out she was a dead woman. I heard some commotion going on from outside the office.

"I don't care what the heck he said but I need to talk to him now!" I could tell it was Nina's voice and another officer was barring her from entry as I had said I didn't want to be disturbed. "Unhand me this outfit is from Paris!" I heard her yell as it sounded like an agent was dragging her away. "But it's about Elizabeth!" If I knew Nina and if I wanted to get any peace I recognized I was going to have to talk to her.

"It's okay agent, you can let her pass." The agent let go of her arm and she shot him a dirty look that she could have only picked up from Elizabeth and smoothed her outfit sticking her tongue out at the agent as she rushed towards me.

"Geez you're hard to get a hold of," she stated, looking at the clutter that had begun to fill my office as the search for Elizabeth continued. "It looks like a bomb went off in here."

"Yes, Nina, what is it that you want? You know we are all busy looking for Elizabeth." I didn't mask the aggravation in my voice.

"Well first of all I'm mad at you because I heard your conversation with Elizabeth before she was taken, the whole office did, and nobody talks to my girl that way but-" she flipped her hair and then leaned on the desk with an intensity I didn't know she could possess "we'll hash that out later because I think I know how to find Elizabeth."

Well, that had my full attention and I motioned for her to continue.

"Okay, so, before Elizabeth stormed off, *as she should have*, she made a point to tell me to take stock of the luminescent colorants."

"I don't follow," I stated, obviously confused and a little annoyed that I had gotten my hopes up that Nina had any useful information. She huffed like I was the dumbest person alive.

"I thought it was super weird that she asked me to take inventory on the Luminescent Colorants because we hadn't run any tests in a while that needed them, so we weren't at any risk of running out. Actually, since being here I never had to use them. Why do we even have them? So weird."

"Nina," I growled trying to get her back on track and hopefully lead to somewhere useful.

"Yeah, right, so I wanted to take my mind off Elizabeth being missing and possibly dead or being tortured or something, so I decided to focus on work. I went about my daily responsibilities and then remembered that she wanted me to restock the Luminescent Colorants. So, I went over to the shelf and they were all gone. Specifically, the UV fluorescent pigments. Like every single one."

"I'm still missing the point. Are you coming to tell me that someone is stealing office supplies because I don't have time for petty shit like this at the moment and I'm not sure how it relates to Elizabeth's case-" at which point she cut me off. Another bad habit she must have picked up from Elizabeth.

"You're not listening". Nina growled out in a frustrated manner. "Why would Elizabeth, before she stormed off, perhaps into the hands of the enemy, make a point to tell me to take inventory of a reagent we never use, and then when I do go and look, I find it's completely gone."

I was still utterly confused at the point Nina was trying to make and I could tell she was getting aggravated at my blank stare.

"Ugh, sometimes you field guys can be so dumb." She threw her hands up and spoke very slowly like she was trying to explain something to a two-year-old.

"If you had a super-hot but super evil and smart ex that was trying to kidnap you and you planned on getting caught but knew you would be impossible to find because said ex was like the smartest person on the planet and wanted to leave a trail of breadcrumbs but knew you were probably being watched at every moment wouldn't you leave a trail that was invisible unless you knew where to look?"

The realization hit me like a ton of bricks. "Elizabeth slipped right before she got into the car. She's clumsy but not that clumsy. If she was able to get that color-"

"Luminescent colorants." Nina corrected.

"- if she was able to get *that* on the tires we could follow the tracks to her location. That's genius."

"I know right?" Nina beamed at me. "Elizabeth is seriously the smartest person I know, that's not an evil genius. So, what do we do now?"

"How do we check to see if the tracks are there?" Nina was on a roll so far, so I thought I'd let her continue.

"We just need an excitation source and we can check really quick," Nina said offhandedly like it was a known fact. "We have a small wand in the lab I can grab so we can do a quick check but we're going to probably need a larger one to mount to a car or something to follow it. Oh, and wait until it gets dark to see it more clearly, but a wand should do a spot check. I know a guy on the CSI team. I can get

198

something on a larger scale. He's pretty much in love with me so it should be easy."

Nina handed off the wand and I walked down to the site where the car pulled away. Dominic and Benny were there surveying the scene to see if the initial team missed anything. Benny approached and looked like he was moving to hide behind Dominic.

"I'm sorry man but all we have is a bit of a partial tire print and it came up with nothing. What's that?" Benny said slowly peeking out from behind Dominic. I scanned around and saw what I needed.

"You two grab that tarp over there and give me some shade near this partial." They went and grabbed the tarp making a sort of makeshift tent.

"Um," Benny asked tentatively, holding up his end of the tarp. "Are you feeling okay man? I know it's been a bit much lately dude but if you need to talk about it-"

"Shut it Benny and let me concentrate." I passed the wand over a few sections seeing nothing and then after a minute saw a faint glow going in the direction the sedan took off in. I followed it down, making Dominic and Benny shift with me as I did, earning odd looks from them and found the path leading to the right. I sat down on the ground and laughed.

"Are you having a heat stroke?" Dominic asked without a drop of sarcasm in his voice.

"She left us a fucking breadcrumb trail." I laughed again, causing Dominic and Benny to look at each other with genuine concern for my mental wellbeing.

"Elizabeth. She left us a trail so that we could find her. Nina figured it out. We still have a few hours until the sun sets so let's get a strategy and a team together before it does." I went to walk back into the building and then stopped Benny nearly running into the back of me. I looked around and saw that the camera we had located on the perimeter ended at the gate and wasn't picking up where we were just investigating. There wasn't a camera in my office as well. I could have almost screwed everything up knowing that Alex could still be monitoring our video feeds.

"Did IT ever figure out how to strengthen the firewall on our surveillance feeds?" I turned to Benny asking.

"Well yes and no," Benny answered tentatively as I glared at him indicating I needed further clarification. "They couldn't figure out how he got through the firewall, so they pulled the surveillance off so that it is being backed up on a local server, old school."

"Ok. That could work. It looks like we should be able to work without Alex being tipped off that we are on our way. Pull the team together and get them up to speed. I have a call to make."

I made my way back to my office and closed the door not wanting anyone to overhear. He was due a call not only as Director but as my Father and Elizabeth's friend.

"Son." I heard my father's voice boom on the other end of the line. Every time he said son like that it made me feel like a 10-year-old again about to get scolded and he knew it. "I'm assuming it took you this long to update me on Elizabeth's disappearance due to you working tirelessly to locate her."

"That is correct Sir."

"And how did Elizabeth get herself into this predicament? Don't tell me you let her do something stupid."

"I didn't *let* her do anything. You know how strong-headed she is. She went rogue, jumping into the car of that maniac and driving off to God knows where." It still baffled me why the hell she would do something so reckless not even knowing if we would have picked up on the clues she left in order for us to be able to find her. She was either insane, a genius, or both.

"I think this is the first time I've actually heard you genuinely concerned for someone outside of family. I thought you two were at each other's throats last I checked in." My father questioned a slight smirk in his voice I could practically see coming through the phone.

"Well." I cleared my throat attempting to put into words the relationship between Elizabeth and myself. "Professionally, she is an asset to the team and one that would be a shame if we lost."

My Father's laughter came booming through the line as I rubbed the back of my neck. I wasn't even fooling myself with that line.

"Oh Son, you are a goner." He managed to get out after all the laughter had finally ceased. "So, what's your plan to get our girl back?"

"Elizabeth left us a trail we just uncovered, so we need to pull a tactical team together to raid the location." I informed him ignoring his 'your girl' statement altogether.

"Of course she did." My Father said with a sort of paternal pride. "I'll get you whatever resources you need. Just send the request along and we'll make it happen. Just-" He paused, seeming to choose his words carefully. "Be careful son. This Dr. Beal is as cunning as they come so watch your back."

"Of course," I said and hung up not knowing what to say and lost for words. I think that and the talk we had at the hospital were the most father-and-son conversations we'd had in years. I shivered, hoping this was not a trend. I brushed it off and made my way to find

Dominic and Benny to put the plan together and send requests to headquarters. Every moment Elizabeth spent with that slime bag was making me feel uneasy for reasons I refused to delve into at the moment.

CHAPTER 24

I woke up with a start, forgetting where I was. I found my head resting on a desk, a computer mouse in my hand, and Alex's research on the screen in front of me. As I lifted my head, I saw Alex sitting across from me, one arm leaning on the desk, his chin in his palm gazing at me.

"Is my research that boring to you?" Alex asked with mock hurt in his voice. I looked around finally remembering that the windows were boarded and glanced at the computer clock seeing it was well into the night.

"I'm just not used to pulling an all-nighter anymore," I replied, lifting my arms up and over my head stretching, glimpsing a flicker of something in his eye. I knew what that look was, desire, and I needed to squash it, now.

"What's a girl gotta do to get a cup of coffee or an energy drink around here?" I said playfully, immediately regretting the words as they left my lips. I saw Alex raise his eyebrows at my perceived boldness as he brought his other elbow onto the table, his hand joining the other under his chin.

"Well." He said slowly, deliberately, and seductively. "I have a few ideas in mind."

Nope. I was not a horny little graduate student needing attention from a man, especially this man. I was a grown-ass woman, an intelligent one at that, and I would keep my hormones in check. I was beyond this form of manipulation. At least I hoped I was. Years of therapy helped me discover I needed to trust myself and that I didn't need validation from outside forces.

"Like showing me where the coffee machine is? I am assuming

you are a legitimate supervillain and have provided your underlings with at least a coffee machine or two. Perhaps an espresso machine if they were truly devious."Alex laughed, the sound not as pleasant to my ears as it had once been, getting up from his seat and making his way over to my side of the desk.

"When did you become so sarcastic and cynical?" He inquired offering his hand to aid me in standing up.

I stiffened under his gaze. "You know when." I glared back looking him straight in his eyes.

"Don't blame me." He said closing his hand around mine when I had refused to take it, squeezing a little bit harder than was comfortable. "You should thank me for opening your eyes to the ways of the world back then Lizzy. It lies, it cheats, it deceives, it corrupts. Better your blinders to have been removed by someone who loves you then ripped off by another."

His grip on my hand released slightly and we seemed to snap back into the charming Alex persona again. "And of course, I have a coffee machine. I'm not that unreasonable."

As we walked out of the office and I shook the discomfort out of my abused hand I realized that, for the first time, I had truly *seen* Alex. Not Alex who was charming, cunning, manipulative, and industrious. I saw the true Alex, the one he hides from everyone, including me. I saw it in his tumultuous eyes as clear as day. This was an Alex that wanted to see the world burn down to the ground and it scared the hell out of me and for the first time during my time with him, I was truly frightened.

We made it over to what resembled a makeshift break area fully stocked with snacks and liquid caffeine. At the site of the fresh fruit splayed out on the table, I felt my stomach lurch in protest remembering that I hadn't really eaten all day. I went to grab an apple and pulled my hand back quickly.

"May I?" I asked Alex politely just like I had when we were dating. On that note, where the hell were the reinforcements? Did I make a mistake, again, and put my trust in the wrong person?

Alex smiled and nodded his approval and I grabbed the closest apple biting into it and enjoying the sweetness. I had never noticed when we were dating but thought about it for years afterward. I had always asked Alex permission before I had done something. Including something as simple as grabbing an apple from a bowl of fruit. I cursed at myself for falling back into old habits so easily but by the stupid look of pure unabashed victory that he currently wore on his face, I knew he thought he had won. Fine. Let him think he was winning. I had gotten through a good chunk of his research and had a better idea of what we were dealing with. He was closer to figuring out a means to fine-tune the gut flora targeting but he wasn't quite there yet. Maybe a day or two away which was frightening but further cemented that I made the right decision to let myself be taken. Maybe I could even sabotage an experiment or two to put him further behind allowing the FBI to catch up.

Continuing to enjoy the apple I took the time to take in my surroundings and a new, terrifying realization, began to take its grip on my heart almost causing me to slightly choke on my food. This section looked nothing like the lab area I had originally been brought through. This had all the hallmarks of a manufacturing plant at a pharmaceutical company. People scurried about looking to be filling canisters in massive quantities and loading them onto trucks at a nearby dock.

"What the hell are you doing Alex?" I whispered so that only he could hear me and not alert the other workers. I didn't need to draw any additional attention.

"What does it look like I'm doing my dear Lizzy?" He said innocently the irony was not lost on me.

"It looks like you are producing an aerosol bioweapon in mass quantities. Enough to take out an entire metropolitan area."

"Well, then it looks like that is exactly what I'm doing." He blew off the terrified look on my face and continued as if nothing was happening motioning to the coffee. "That was two lumps of sugar and a creamer, correct?"

"Alex!" I yelled not caring if I was overheard and without taking my precarious situation into account my emotions taking over. "Your research isn't optimized yet. There's no telling if it will take out ten people or a hundred people or even a thousand people. The scale is unfathomable."

"I know." He said stirring the dark liquid and offering it to me. "Isn't it exciting? I just need to do the primary testing, proof of concept so to speak, to get the funding from my generous donors to move forward. I was focusing on one product when I really had two."

I knocked the coffee from his hand in my anger, the dark liquid splashing to the floor. "Alex, this is serious. Innocent people could be killed. The world is not your lab, innocent people are not your guinea pigs."

"Innocent." He ground out through his teeth invading my personal space caging me between his body and the table, that frightening visage from before returning. "You keep saying that word. No one is innocent. Not me, not you, not your FBI friends, and not anyone on this planet. I will take what I want, and I will do as I please and do you know why?"

I tried to step aside and get more space between us but it was futile and for the first time in my life I was unsure if Alex would harm me or not.

206

"Because I can. I am smarter than all of them. I am stronger than all of them. Survival of the fittest Lizzy, and I am about to assert my dominance on this wretched world."

"Alex." I strained a tear escaping without permission from my eye not knowing if it was from fear or from the anger that was welling up inside of me. "I don't understand. What happened to you? You were so kind, so inquisitive, I know the money seduced you from your pursuits but where is this coming from?"

"It was never about the money. What is it that you so eloquently said to me? People change, get over it." He grabbed my hand and began to drag me back to where the office was. I cursed myself for pushing him too hard, "Where you are wrong again Lizzy is that people don't change. This was my nature all along and you just chose to see the things you wanted to see, that I *let* you see. I was hoping my betrayal would open your eyes to the pathetic nature of the world but instead of embracing it, you hid like a coward."

"Stop it," I said, shaking my head not wanting to hear his assessment of me which I knew to be true. I dug in my heels scratching at his hands to get away from him. To get away from the truth that I didn't want to hear fearing that if spoken aloud it would become real.

"No. I don't think I will." He replied, still dragging me back in the direction of his makeshift glass office. I continued to dig and claw at his hand digging in my heels, but he was tougher than I had remembered. "Even after your time in foster care, the fake family that took you in only to abandon you when you needed them, your years of pathetic hiding, you still blind yourself to the world around you. War, disease, poverty, death. The Four Horsemen have galloped right past you and you turn the other way."

"Enough!" I yelled, biting his hand catching him off guard and forcing him to let go of me, freeing me as he scowled, staring at his hand and then back at me, a sick sadistic smile on his face.

"Now you're getting it." He sneered as two men came behind me pulling my hands behind my back to immobilize me. I struggled to get loose, but I was not strong enough and knew I wouldn't get far even if I managed to get loose.

"I can see the hatred in your eyes mixed with your fear." He mocked getting ever closer to my face, unable to retreat. "You were the only one Lizzy who could match my intelligence, challenge me and you will recognize your place is next to me. Maybe not today or tomorrow but when you see how quickly this world will turn on itself when faced with what I plan to unleash, you will understand."

I was wrong. So very *very* wrong. I had thought Alex was misguided, blinded by his own ambition and brilliance and I had miscalculated. He was irrecoverable and undeniably insane. Whatever spell he had cast on me all those years ago and any lingering effect it may have still held on me dissipated like a snuffed-out candle in an instant. I felt lighter, more free, stronger, and more fearless than I had ever felt before. I straightened myself up no longer wanting to be afraid and did the only thing I could think of and spit in his face hitting the mark right on his cheek.

"You are the one who is underestimating here Alex. I will *never be* by your side. I will never want to see the world burn like you do and I will do everything I can until my last breath to stop you." I realized I was being dramatic, but I meant every word I said.

Alex wiped the spit from his cheek, flicking it away as if it was nothing. He stalked closer towards me, unable to escape he quickly closed the distance grabbing my chin in his hand and bringing his face closer to mine.

"Survival of the fittest Lizzy. I'll take what I want." He claimed my lips brutally while I was unable to turn my face away. I could feel what he was pouring into this kiss. It wasn't sweet trying to portray feelings of love and affection. It was primal and demanding of him asserting his dominance. To show my displeasure I bit down on his lip, hard. He pulled away, touching his lip finding crimson on his fingertips indicating I had drawn blood.

"Careful Lizzy." He scorned, his tongue darting out to taste his own blood.

"If you're going to act like an animal I'm going to have to treat you like one. Lock her up in the office and post a few men outside the door for good measure." He commanded without taking his eyes off of me. As they carted me off I could see my new frenemy Morgan smiling at me triumphantly.

"Well, that's the end of you." She gloated tapping on her tablet with obnoxiously long nails obviously reveling in what she had just witnessed.

"Oh, honey," I said with mock sympathy as I was carted past. "Did you miss the part where he basically admitted I was the only one for him? Looks like that's the end for *you*."

I watched as her smile started to fade as realization painfully slowly reached her brain and she whipped her face around now distorted in rage. I couldn't help the laugh that escaped my lips. It was almost too easy. Now I could only hope that she would screw up and I could get myself out of this situation.

We soon made it back to the office and I was pushed inside roughly. I bit my nails, a habit I thought I had lost long ago and glanced at the clock on the computer once again. It was getting late and I had to assume Alex planned to move his tools of destruction in the cover of night and me along with them. If we moved to a secondary location there was no way they were going to find me. I paced trying to think of some way that I could maybe cause a scene or delay the shipments, but Alex had so smartly left me with nothing but a useless computer unable to communicate with anyone outside these walls. The cavalry should surely be coming soon, right? Had I been foolish in putting my faith and trust in others? I shook my head in an attempt to dissipate the negative thoughts. No, I wouldn't think like that. That would mean that Alex was winning, and I couldn't have that. I would bide my time and hope my plan was working.

CHAPTER 25

"It's working!" Nina yelled from the front of the vehicle. She had attached a large UV light to the front of a squad car with zip ties illuminating in the darkness the trail Elizabeth had left us. "I had to promise that CSI guy a dinner and a movie, but Elizabeth is totally worth it." She commented, flipping her hair over her shoulder for emphasis.

"Great work Nina," I said as I walked over to the team that had assembled to carry out the mission.

"Alright listen up folks. Dominic and Benny will be running this main car using the UV to track the trail and the rest of the team will follow. I don't know what we are going to come up against once the trail ends so we need to be prepped for the worse. I want full tactical gear and low-tech communication tools only. This Dr. Beal has some pretty sophisticated technology, so we are going to have to go old school on this one."

I took in the team assembled noticing that we not only had those agents on duty but some volunteers as well who wanted in once they heard Elizabeth was taken. It seems she had made more of an impression on the field office then she had thought.

"Dr. Waller is one of us," I yelled to the crowd preparing to move out. "So, let's get her back and nail that son of a bitch." A ruckus chorus of hell yeah and hollers filled the night air as everyone prepared to roll out. I leaned into the window of the lead car that Dominic and Benny were currently occupying. "Are you all set?" I asked looking down to see the path that was illuminated in front of the car. Benny raised his hand like he was in a classroom and needed a hall pass.

"Yes, Benny."

"So, I'm still not sure why I have to stick my head out the window like a dog. It's really going to hurt my image with the ladies." Benny lamented looking dejected.

"First off, don't worry about your reputation with the ladies, that is a lost cause, second of all, we need you to keep track of where the trail leads and that means sticking your head out the window to get a better vantage point. Any other questions?"

"Well, you don't have to be so mean about it," Benny said dejectedly sulking back into the car.

Nina walked over to Benny and provided a comforting pat on his shoulder through the window.

"They only say mean things to you because you're their friend and think you're cool."

"Really?" Benny answered, turning toward Nina like the puppy dog he was afraid of being compared to.

"Sure." Nina responded giving me a look that said she was not confident in her assessment and walked off, a smiling Benny sinking back into the vehicle.

Dominic took off with me and the rest of the tactical team vehicles following closely behind. The system worked well for the most part only losing the UV trail a few times at busy intersections due to heavy traffic but after some searching, we were able to pick it back up. After about an hour of combined drive time, we ended up in a warehouse district and what appeared to be an abandoned warehouse. The son of a bitch was cocky enough to set up operations right in my backyard. Big mistake. I sent a point team up ahead and waited for their report. On the surface, it looked like one of the warehouses was nothing but abandoned but upon closer inspection it appeared that crates were being loaded onto nondescript moving vans. That couldn't bode well.

"Ok team, here is the situation," I said confidently over the coms "It looks like they have quite an operation going on, so we need to be tactical and hit hard and fast. I need Team Alpha to go and neutralize those moving vans. Use caution as there could be volatile material in there. The Beta Team will be with me entering the building. The surveillance team reported a mixture of civilian looking lab workers and trained mercenaries heavily armed so be prepared for a potential firefight. Minimize casualties and damage to the location. We don't know what they are cooking up in there." I turned to Dominic and Benny who had come back around to my side of the van.

"Anyone have eyes on Elizabeth?"

Dominic shook his head. "Can't get close enough to get a solid visual inside without being detected." We were going to be going in blind and I didn't want Elizabeth to be caught in the cross hairs but the fact that it seemed like they were planning on moving out soon made it clear we needed to act now.

"Alright. Everyone knows that plan. I'm giving the go-ahead. Move Out." I said and watched as the teams moved with precision.

Upon entering the building, the smaller point team saw what looked like an abandoned assembly line that had been used recently. That wasn't a good sign. It meant that they had wrapped up production and that whatever they were producing was now in those trucks outside. We got a bit closer and saw what appeared to be a collection of empty canisters we had previously seen that were held that were filled with the pressurized bioweapon. Elizabeth had led us right into Alex's main operations; it seemed right before it rolled out. I was actually going to have to give her credit for that one. All of a sudden, an alarm began to go wail and people began to scatter.

"Shit, we've been compromised. Secure those trucks and get them out of here and neutralize the hostiles. Let me know as soon as someone has eyes on Elizabeth." I said through the coms.

213

I heard an "over here" echo out in the open space and the sounds of shots being fired.

"Take cover!" I yelled looking to see where the fire was coming from. For paid mercenaries, they were doing a shit job of actually hitting us. I looked over to Dominic who was hunched with me behind a barrel. "Cover me," I said, reloading my gun. "I'm going to go find Elizabeth before the shit really hits the fan."

Dominic nodded and began returning fire to cover my exit. As the mercenaries were so distracted with the team I was able to move over to the right seeing that my team had taken control of the moving vehicles filled with the bioweapons and were relocating them further from the scene. That was one less thing to worry about. I walked a little further and saw a state-of-the-art lab space with people in lab coats hurrying out of the building. I'm assuming they were of the more academic pedigree and didn't have the stomach for violence. Off to the side of the room, I couldn't help but smile at what I was seeing. There was some sort of cube-shaped room made completely of plexiglass and inside, bashing at one of the walls with an office chair was no other than one Dr. Elizabeth Waller.

"I've located Elizabeth," I said over the coms. "She's located in the front right of the building near what looks like labs. Going to extract her now." I heard a response over the line indicating that they had confirmed my message and I went to move in closer; the majority of this section of the warehouse is practically abandoned now. Gun drawn and at the ready, I turned the corner to where Elizabeth was still partially under cover so that she could see me but not draw attention to me. She had stopped her assault on the wall pulling a hair tie off of her wrist and using it to pull her hair back into a makeshift bun and was about to pick up the chair again when she saw me. It was then that she gifted me with one of the most beautiful smiles I had ever seen. She made her way over to what looked like the door and after checking that my surroundings were clear, I safely made my way over.

"Took you long enough." She mocked, yelling through the wall, the beaming smile never leaving her face.

"I don't know. You in a cage is a very tempting offer," I responded back observing the door to see how best to open it.

"Very funny. Now get me out of this thing before Alex or his lackeys come back. They were moving a lot of the bioweapon onto some trucks and I don't know where he plans on releasing them." She said her tone getting more serious.

"Already on it. Got my people moving them out as we speak and rounding up who we can. Now let me take a look at this door." I pulled on the door handle and it didn't budge.

"Well, that is a fire hazard," Elizabeth remarked, realizing the situation just got a little more complicated. "I think there is a pad on the side there. Does it have a pin pad too or just a fob for a key card?"

I took a look at the pad and it seemed like the ones we had for restricted access at the field office. "Keycard. Any other ideas?"

"Couldn't you shoot it or something like the way they do it in the movies?" I gave her a 'really' look, eyebrows raised and she refocused. "Okay well, then can you take the pins out of the door hinges, so we can get the door off?"

"That might work," I responded, holstering my gun and looking around for something to knock the pins out of the hinges.

"Sam," Elizabeth yelled over to me.

"Alex he-" she started her voice getting quieter with her hands now both on the plexiglass wall. "He's-" she spoke slowly and deliberately trying to figure out what to say next and with a trepidation and unsureness that I wasn't used to hearing in her voice and it brought my full attention. "He's not well. Mentally, I mean.

Everything I assumed I was wrong, I was very wrong. I completely missed the mark on his goals and motivations." She stopped searching my face to see understanding when I could only give a look of confusion. She tried again to explain the frustration evident on her face.

"I don't think he's mentally stable. I think he's more dangerous and volatile than we thought he was."

"Sticks and stones Lizzy." I heard a confident voice behind me delivered with such bravado and self-importance that I didn't even need to see the dread in Elizabeth's eyes as she looked at him to know who it was.

"Dr. Beal I'm guessing," I said, turning around slowly not knowing if he had a weapon on him or not. I found him pointing a 45-millimeter right at my temple.

"And you must be the heroic Agent Samuel Han. Here to save the damsel in distress and get the glory?" He motioned to Elizabeth with the gun making me uncomfortable.

I lifted my hands showing I was no threat. "Glad we got the introductions out of the way." I snarked back and indicated over to Elizabeth "and I think we both know she's no damsel in distress."

Alex smiled in such a way that seemed almost evil at its core and I realized what Elizabeth was trying to tell me. Even though he portrayed an image of sophistication and arrogance he was genuinely insane.

"I stand corrected Agent Han" he sneered, obviously not used to being corrected. "I'm enjoying our little chat, but Elizabeth and I have some pressing plans so I'm afraid I'm going to have to say goodbye now." I heard him cock the gun and watched as he took aim.

216

Well, I had a good run. My only regret was that Elizabeth was going to have to witness my brains being splattered all over the plexiglass that currently separated us. I had confidence my team would get her out safe and sound in the end, even if I was not there to see it through. My father would most likely see that she was settled after everything was said and done. She and I never really did get a chance to get to know each other and explore the growing connection we had either. I guess it was two regrets.

"Wait!" I heard Elizabeth yell with what sounded like desperation in her voice as she pounded on the door of her cage pulling me from what I was sure to be my final thoughts with my head intact. "Alex, wait."

She said in a voice that I had never heard her use before. It rang of defeat and sounded very foreign coming from her lips. "You've won." She continued banging her fist against the door a few more times for good measure. "I understand now. You are superior to any man I've ever met. That much is evident. I see how powerless Sam is in front of you and I finally see what you are, and I understand that my place is with you." Alex, at first only stealing glances at Elizabeth while keeping his eyes on me now had her full attention. Whatever she was doing she only had to keep it up. "Let's just go now. Let Sam live with the shame and knowledge that he couldn't beat you and we can watch the world burn, together."

Alex now snapped his full attention back to me and I could tell he had been toying with Elizabeth and me this whole time. He laughed as he repositioned his gun looking like he was about to take aim.

"For a split second there, Lizzy, I think you believed you could fool me." He looked back over at Elizabeth. "How does it feel to know that I am going to end this man's life and there is not a single thing you can do about it? How does it feel to know that in the end all of this I've done, the devastation I'll do, Sam's pending death, all of this" he yelled gesturing to the world around us, "was inevitably due to you?"

217

Instead of seeing Elizabeth slide to the floor against the wall looking heartbreakingly defeated as I expected she grabbed a computer and flung it against the plexiglass, shattering it into pieces.

"You son of a bitch! You have a problem then you fucking come over here and deal with me. Sam has no part in this!"

Well fuck me. Giving it to the asshole *and* swearing like a sailor. I guess I had rubbed off on her more than I thought.

"Don't worry Agent Han." He said gloating just loud enough for me to hear Elizabeth continuing to bang on the plexiglass wall trying to get Beal's attention. "Once I've broken her down, and trust me, I will, I'll rebuild her back up, slowly, piece by piece just the way I want her to be." The thought of him undoing all the work Elizabeth had done to get where she was, the thought of him touching her filled me with a rage I didn't know I could possess, and I stared at him with the rage and the power of a thousand suns.

Beal laughed at my defiance. "Goodbye Agent Han." Before he could pull the trigger, what sounded like an explosion erupted from the other side of the building, the heat of flames hitting Alex and me distracting him just long enough for me to grab my gun and aim to fire. Alex was only thrown off for a minute as he returned fire, as we both dove for cover. I had to take care of him quickly. If the fire was spreading, Elizabeth was a sitting duck stuck in that fucking box.

218

CHAPTER 26

I continued yelling, pounding on the wall to get Alex's attention back on me when I heard what sounded like an explosion. I turned toward the sound and could see flames coming from a room that looked like it held flammable gasses. The fighting must have spilled over and an errant bullet must have nicked something causing a small explosion. I went back to grab the office chair again to see if I could make any dent in the wall when I heard the click of the door being opened. Chair in hand I glanced over to see my doppelganger Morgan holding a keycard to the reader with a smirk on her face. I tentatively put down the chair and walked over stepping out of the room trying to keep one eye on her and one eye on where Alex and Sam had ended up.

"Thanks?" I said tentatively trying to figure out what was going on.

"Don't thank me yet bitch." She replied pulling out a switchblade.

"Really?" I said tired of this jealousy game and backing up not knowing how much experience she had with blades and moving away hands up. "You're going to hurt yourself with that thing. I don't have any beef with you. I don't want Alex. You can have him."

She took a swipe at me and I jumped back but not quick enough feeling the blade slide across my skin. I held my side feeling the fabric of my shirt beginning to become wet. It stung like hell, but I knew it wasn't deep enough to be life-threatening. Morgan was quickly rising to the top of my shit list. I followed her with my eyes as she smiled manically circling like a shark getting even more excited by the scent of flowing blood.

"Once he sees you bleeding out on the floor and realizes that I'm the one who did it, that I'm the superior one, he'll want me." Morgan really needed to seek some professional help. I suppose crazy attracted crazy. She continued to laugh, and I saw her begin to coil like a snake ready to strike again.

"Don't fool yourself." I mocked trying to distract her and get her off her game taking advantage of her insecurities. "Attacking an unarmed person. Pathetic. He's only ever wanted me and always will. You were just warming his bed until he found me again."

She lunged toward me screeching like a banshee brandishing the knife wildly. I got into fighting guard and threw a front kick, landing it right in her stomach and knocking the wind out of her, which caused her to drop the knife and sent her sliding across the floor. Those kickboxing lessons were worth every penny. Holding her stomach, she popped up screaming and came after me again like a fast zombie looking for a meal. I reset and clocked her right in the face with a jab, watching her slump down to the ground out cold. Pain coursed through my hand and I shook it out. I would have to remember that punching things without gloves really hurt.

Leaving her on the ground, I grabbed the knife as pain emanated from my side, the adrenaline having made me forget about my wound, and began to look around feverishly trying to see where Alex and Sam had gone.

***

Beal and I traded shots as the fire continued to consume the building.

"Give it up Beal," I yelled over in the direction his shots had been coming from. "It's over. Your facilities are destroyed, you're running out of bullets, and you've lost." I was responded to by a few bullets straying uncomfortably close.

220

"I don't lose." I heard Beal yell back in my direction, obviously taking the time to regroup. "I'll set up a new facility, make the weapon even better this time, and when I'm ready, I'll come for my Lizzy again."

The thought of that lunatic getting his hands on Elizabeth again began to cloud my judgment for a split second as I fired over in his direction. "Shit," I said aloud as I knew I needed every bullet in the chamber and couldn't be spending them on careless shots based on some knee-jerk reaction. I heard Alex's laughter as it echoed through the space.

"Did I strike a nerve special agent?" I was about to retort back when out of the corner of my eye I saw our escaped woman going after Elizabeth with what appeared to be a knife. I stood to run in her direction but was halted when I felt radiating pain in my shoulder and dove for cover. The little fucker managed to graze me. I focused back over to Elizabeth and saw she now stood over the woman that was attacking her who was now splayed out and on the ground.

A smile formed on my face. "Give her hell Elizabeth!"

I saw her lean down to grab the knife, wincing as clutched her side and pulled her hand away now covered in ruby red blood. Considering the state that Elizabeth and I were both in, I needed to end this soon. By my count, he should only have one or two shots left, and unfortunately, he seemed to be a good shot. I could see that Elizabeth had a line of sight on me and she started in my direction. I made eye contact with her and waved for her to get the hell out of there, but she simply shook her head and continued her course straight to me. She ran past a set of crates Beal emerging and grabbing her as she passed. He pulled her in front of him using her as a shield and edged his way toward the exit of the building keeping his gun trained in my general direction.

"Beal let Elizabeth go," I yelled emerging from my cover, keeping my eyes and my gun on Alex and avoiding eye contact with Elizabeth.

"I don't think I shall." He replied coldly clutching Elizabeth closer to him his arm wrapped around her midsection hiss escaping her lips as he pressed on her wound.

"I know you aren't going to hurt her," I responded calmly, calling on my hostage situation training. He was an asshole, but however twisted he was, I knew he wouldn't hurt Elizabeth.

"And I know you aren't going to take a shot at me at this range because *you* might hurt her." He responded as he inched his way further outside, keeping his back to the burning building. "Seems like we're at an impasse."

I stared at Elizabeth and saw her eyes searching for a plan when I saw something occur to her. I shook my head to indicate whatever she had concocted was a horrible idea but before I could intervene she stabbed Beal in the arm which was caging her in causing him to loosen his grip and allowing her to wriggle out from his grasp. She immediately ran over to me before he could recover from the assault. Backup had now formed behind us, leaving Beal standing alone in front of the burning warehouse.

Beal laughed, pulling the knife from his arm in one sickening swipe and throwing it to the ground with a clatter.

"You always surprise me, Lizzy." Having no other direction to go, Beal began to stagger backwards towards the burning building, his eyes trained on Elizabeth. I saw a realization hit her and she took a few steps toward him.

"Don't Alex." She commanded strongly as he continued backward, never breaking his gaze. "Alex don't please" she begged as Beal continued his trajectory back toward the burning building. "I know what you're thinking, please don't. No one else has to die just please. "

He glanced back to the building and then back to me, my agents beginning to swarm behind me. "I've been to prison. Wasn't a fan." He gazed back over at Elizabeth with a smile so maniacal it sent a shiver down even my spine.

"I'll see you in your dreams, Lizzy." With that, he turned and ran back into the building.

"Alex no!" Elizabeth yelled starting to run toward the building before I grabbed her and pulled her back. "Sam please!" She cried struggling to get out of my arms but before I could say anything a final explosion blew out the windows of what was left of the warehouse. The entire building now erupted in flames, the blow back throwing Elizabeth and myself across the parking lot. Elizabeth and I slowly sat upright staring at the fiery inferno that was now the warehouse. I hopped up to my feet offering Elizabeth a hand to help her up, forgetting the bullet wound in my shoulder instantly causing me to wince as she pulled. She grimaced as well, holding her side, never taking her eyes off of the building. Panic began to creep over her face.

"The canisters!" She yelled looking through the flames of the building frantically. "If they explode it has the potential to disperse the contents which we now know could be catastrophic to the surrounding area and ..."

"Elizabeth." I said in what I hoped was a calming tone but as I didn't use it very often I was not sure if it was any good.

"We need to call the CDC and clear the people out. Do you have, like, a hotline to the mayor or something ..."

223

"Elizabeth." I said again, more sternly this time, causing her to actually turn around and look at me. "We secured all the canisters before the explosion. They were already loaded up on a vehicle."

"Oh." She simply stated her shoulders sagging in relief.

"I have to go check in with the team so that we can start interrogating any suspects to see where else this bioweapon was being produced," I said to Elizabeth as I made my way to the team.

"Don't bother." I heard Elizabeth sigh. "Alex said this was the only production site and all the information on how to produce the weapon was either on the computers that are now probably toast or in his head." I gaped over at her in disbelief.

She shrugged her shoulders obviously seeing my skepticism. "Alex was a crazy, paranoid, psychopath with a twisted view of this world but he was not a lair. Plus, he didn't have any reason to lie." She took one last look back at the building and then back to me.

"They'll check right-" she said in a low voice which was ridiculous based on the blaring fire truck sirens and our proximity to the team. "They'll look for his body or something to make sure he's really gone?"

I could see where her concern was coming from. She'd been told he was dead before and it didn't take.

"Yeah, they'll check." I tried to say comfortingly, something that was out of my normal repertoire. "Now let's get you over to the EMTs. You look like shit."

"I look like shit!" She exclaimed in mock anger a smile gracing the corner of her lips. "You should take a look in the mirror, you look like you're on death's door."

"Well yeah, your boyfriend there shot me." I countered.

224

"Very much an Ex-Boyfriend." She corrected me. "And also, did you see me fight that crazy chick with a knife!" She sounded a little hysterical, but anything was better than the pleading as that bastard had run into the flames.

I chuckled, the movement reminding me that I had in fact been shot "Briefly, you'll have to tell me all the details over dinner."

With that, Elizabeth stopped walking as I continued, and I glanced back at her, a mixture of surprise and happiness on her face.

"Agent Han, are you actually asking me out on a date?" She mocked, eyes squinted with apprehensiveness.

"That depends." I continued something still bothering me. "Are you going to tell me what your plan was?"

"Oh, that." She laughed, the sound melodic and I reveled in being the cause of it for just a moment. "It was pretty simplistic when you think about it."

"Well I'm a simple man so you're going to have to explain it to me."

"All right." She laughed again, and I realized how much I was beginning to like the sound. "But it looks like we'll have to continue the conversation in the ambulance. She indicated with a gesture of her head to the EMTs who were hurrying over to assist us as we were basically leaning on each other at this point. They maneuvered us into the back of the ambulance fussing over our injuries and once they were satisfied we were stable Elizabeth continued with our conversation.

"I realized that Alex had introduced a bug or hijacked the security feeds in the building and was monitoring the field office. I figured I could use that to my advantage to get Alex to come and get me, *but* I had to make it look like I was ready to give up on working for the FBI and go with him with some level of willingness. That's when I formulated a plan and called your father to run it past him."

"So that's who you called when you were in the lab. Nina told me you had used your cell phone multiple times in the lab and it was violating some laboratory rule or something and she was going to give you a, and I quote, stern talking to if you make it out alive."

"I'm in real trouble now." Elizabeth said with a smile gracing her lips.

"Getting back on topic." I continued wanting to know the full picture of what the hell just went down, "How did you talk to my father about your plan without Beal overhearing your end of the conversation if he had the field office under surveillance?"

"Oh, that was easy." She smiled inspecting the IV drip now in her arm. "Morse code. I was tapping on the phone case and the speaker was sensitive enough to pick it up while I talked about book recommendations with him. Your father taught me a while back and I never really had to use it, so I hoped it wasn't too rusty but based on his responses I think he got the message. He tentatively approved of the plan but we both agreed on one thing, not to tell you."

Ouch. That hurts a man's ego. "And why was that if you mind me asking?"

She gave me a look that read 'really' and continued "I needed to fight with you so that it would be believable that I was sufficiently mad enough to drop everything and basically run away with Alex, so I needed it to be authentic and if you were in on it I didn't know how realistic it would look." She had a point as acting was not my strong suit. I thought back to the fight that we had and a wave of guilt washed over me.

"About that-," I replied sheepishly, massaging the back of my neck.

"Don't" she interrupted, looking me in the eyes. "I knew what I was getting into and I know you didn't mean most of what you said and I said some pretty nasty things as well. Let's not talk about it again."

"Works for me," I said, clearing my throat. "I know the second part of your plan, you took the luminescent stuff, and put in the wheel well of the car so it left tracks so that we could follow you there."

"I knew Nina would figure it out." Elizabeth smiled like a proud mother being presented with her child's straight-A report card. "And she did it faster than I had anticipated too. I thought I would have had a bit more time to look over his research but, in the end, it didn't matter." She grew quiet and began to look at the various monitors we were hooked up to.

"Elizabeth." I said in the most soothing voice I was capable of, "You aren't responsible for Alex's death. You didn't cause the entire warehouse to implode." I thought for a second. "Did you?"

"No!" She laughed, breaking the tension in the ambulance. "Incendiary devices are not in my repertoire."

"So, what was the rest of the plan?" I pressed now that I knew she was in a better mood.

"Well" she continued adjusting herself on the cot "There wasn't really much else to it. I figured I could try to find some way to neutralize the bacterium, make it inert, or something but he was already moving it, in large quantities, so that was out. I switched to trying to distract him until you and your team could make it to save the day. Which you all did valiantly I might add." She paused for a minute and then spoke again, her face scrunching in displeasure.

227

"That Morgan was a wild card though."

"That witch with the knife?" I asked, realizing "Delilah" must have been another way to cover her tracks.

"That crazy woman that came at me with a knife. The one who looks just like me. She was the same one that led us to the masquerade trap before she escaped. Apparently, she is obsessed with Alex and thought I was trying to take him away from her. I tried to assure her I wasn't, but words were exchanged, and she became a little unhinged."

"So, you knocked her unconscious," I said with a slight smirk nodding my approval.

"Damn right I did." She replied, beaming a smile of pride. Suddenly she stopped smiling and quickly sat up. "Did she make it out of the explosion? I left her unconscious in the middle of the warehouse."

"I'll call the other agents on the way to the hospital to make sure they collect her and make sure she actually makes it to county jail this time." Leave it to Elizabeth to be worried about the woman who attacked her with a knife. She seemed to relax while lying back on the cot. We made it to the hospital, were unloaded onto gurneys and sped off in different directions before we could say anything more.

CHAPTER 27

"You got fucking lucky missy." Robert chastised as he put a vase of beautiful flowers on the end table. They were sunflowers which were my favorite and they instantly brightened up the room and my spirits.

"It was just some stitches. I didn't even need surgery." I replied jovially, happy to see my surrogate father figure had come to visit. He smiled and took my hand.

"And I'm glad for it. Just promise me you will not do anything like that again." He said in mock sternness.

"You know she can't do that," an annoyed voice said from the hallway.

"What are you doing out of bed?" I chastised from my own hospital bed.

"I wanted you to see how good I looked in a hospital gown," he said sarcastically. "Why do you think I'm here? I heard my father's voice and wanted to see how the investigation of the scene was progressing."

"Does he ever stop working?" I asked Robert jokingly.

"Do you?" he said pointing to the notes I had been jotting down on a pad and paper the nurses so kindly gave me.

"Touché," I answered, pulling the bed sheet up a little higher.

"Well?" Sam said impatiently, taking a seat in one of the armchairs in the room.

"I've just got some preliminary reports so far but due to the warehouse fire we've only just been given the all clear that it's even safe to enter the building."

I gripped the sheets a little closer knowing what would be on the list of things they would be trying to locate. Alex's body. I didn't know if it was the pain medication or the thought of his charred remains, but I instantly became nauseated. I could feel Sam staring at me from across the room.

"Maybe we should discuss this later and not in front of Elizabeth," Sam said tentatively.

"Thanks, Sam. But I need to know these things as well." I said with as much confidence as I could muster in my current state.

"Did you find Morgan?" I could feel bile starting to rise in my throat at the thought of causing her death.

"It looks like she got away. Again." Sam sneered as if her disappearance was a personal insult. "We picked up a surveillance video from a nearby gas station of a disheveled woman matching her description, so we can assume she is still out there. We put out an APB but no leads so far."

I sunk back into the hospital bed. At least that was one less death on my hands. Alex hadn't shared everything with her, which meant she was much less of a threat.

"Where were the bioweapon canisters transported to? The local CDC branches?" I asked switching subjects.

"Yes," Robert answered back on the topic at hand. "I've gotten you clearance and told them you will reach out when you are up to it."

"I have some ideas that I want to run past them about neutralizing a majority of the canisters but perhaps keeping a few to see if an antibody can be developed."

"You think that's wise?" Sam rebuked from his chair. "I mean that stuff is pretty deadly."

"I concur." I could see the smugness pass onto Sam's face before I continued "But, we don't know if Alex spoke of the compound or provided samples to other organizations, so it would behoove us to have an antibody available for just that eventuality."

"And I think it would *behoove* us to just destroy the whole damn lot so that no one else can get their hands on it." Sam retorted, starting to get out of his chair to make his displeasure known.

"I do believe I am the resident expert here on the bacterium used to develop the bioweapon and based on my professional opinion-"

"And I'm not a professional here?" Sam interrupted "It's *my* professional opinion that-"

"Enough!" Robert interrupted belly laughing at our antics. "When did you too start becoming so close?

Sam and I instantly turned beet red and began to talk over each other claiming in multiple ways that he had it all wrong when Nina, Benny, and Dominic entered the room.

"Elizabeth!" Nina cried running over to my bedside and grabbing my hands like I was on my deathbed staring at all the things I was hooked up to. "Oh, my goodness, look at you? Do you need anything? Can I bring you a snack or maybe your laptop from work? Do you need anything from your apartment? Also, I heard you totally beat up some chick and then the building exploded. Where is your apartment by the way?"

"Nina." I interrupted, smiling, unable to hide how touched I was by her concern. "Breathe." I watched as she visibly took in a breath and let it go and she seemed to settle down. "I knew you would figure out my little trail. Nice work." I could see her preen at the praise and then stand a little taller.

"It was super obvious." Her face scrunched up "But I had to promise that guy in the CSI group a date to get some of the equipment, so you totally owe me."

"That I do," I replied laughing instantly regretting it as pain went across my center and I slightly winced in pain.

"Oh no, I'm sorry!" Nina exclaimed, registering the pain on my face. "I'll try not to be so funny."

This made me laugh some more. This time I held my side to reduce the unpleasant feeling. "That would be like asking the sun to not shine Nina," I answered by patting her hand. Her face scrunched in a pout and then returned to normal.

"Okay." She said centering herself. "Tell me about this chick fight." Benny busted past Dominic who had both been quiet up until this point like he was trying to get a better vantage point to listen from.

"Yeah, tell us Elizabeth." Benny enthusiastically asked, pulling out a notepad. "Leave out no detail like hair pulling, or clothing coming off, or if you accidentally made out with her during it."

Everyone in the room glared in Benny's direction. "What! Don't look at me like that. It's for the official report."

"Yeah, sure," Dominic answered, pulling him by his collar like a mother dog would grab her pup and bring him back toward the other end of the room where he proceeded to scowl.

"Alright," Robert commanded the room. "Let's give these guys some space to rest. God knows they deserve it." Everyone was about to shuffle out, Nina acting like it was the last time she was ever going to see me and promising to return with a bunch of things I hadn't asked for when I heard a phone ringing coming from Sam's direction when he pulled out his cell phone.

"Where were you even keeping that?" I asked jovially, taking in his current state which was similar to mine. The category is post-surgery chic realness which is surmounted by an unflattering hospital gown.

"Wouldn't you like to know?" He replied suggestively.

"Gross," Nina whispered quite loudly from across the room. The room went from jovial to serious in seconds as we watched Sam's face become solemn.

"Are you sure?" He asked whoever was on the other line glancing over at me. "Alright. Well, let me know if you find anything else. I'll expect the full report later." With that, he abruptly hung up the phone and took a deep breath as we all looked at him expectantly.

"That was the Agent heading the investigation at the warehouse. It seems-" He paused and looked into my eyes with a mixture of anger and pity. "-that Beal's body has not been recovered."

I knew, in the back of my mind, I knew Alex couldn't be gone that easily. All these years for it to end in such a way was not an Alex move. He thought too highly of himself to willingly go up in flames. He must have had some sort of escape plan for such possibilities. I was naive to think that this was over.

"Okay," Nina said tentatively, the first one to speak after that bombshell bringing me out of my spiraling thoughts. "The heat and intensity of the fire could have burned from 1100 to 1500 degrees

233

centigrade which would be hot enough to reduce his bones to ashes which would get all mixed in with the rubble so it's still a possibility he's dead."

At this point, we had all turned practically mouths agape staring at Nina.

"What?" she cried as she looked around the room. "I know things too. Also, they should look for anything he was wearing that would have been made from metal. It'll be melted but that would be an indicator that he burned to ash as he should have."

"Okay," Benny said in the corner. "Note to self. Never get on Nina's bad side."

"We'll keep looking," Sam said in what I believe was an attempt at comfort. To his credit, it was a sensible conclusion and next steps, but I had been in this position before. Fool me once, shame on you. Fool me twice, shame on me. And I didn't plan on being Alex's fool ever again.

"And even if he is still alive, licking his wounds somewhere, we'll find him."

"Alright, now we really need to let these guys rest. Move out, everyone." Robert ushered everyone out of the room leaving Sam and me alone in the hospital room in silence.

"It's going to be alright Elizabeth," Sam said, coming over to my bedside. I saw him look at my hand, seeming to be thinking of something requiring the mental capacity of complex Algebra before he took my hand in his. He gazed up at me.

"I half thought you would have pulled your hand away."

"It's not a *horrible* sensation. Plus, you did save my life so I'm pretty sure you deserve this much."

"Elizabeth," he said with a serious tone clasping my hand tighter. "You saved yourself, and a lot of other people for that matter, remember that."

"Thank you," I replied quietly. "And." I paused, unsure of how to put it. "You can call me Lizzy if you want."

Sam's laughter filled the room. "You're not going to bite my head off like you did Benny's if I call you Lizzy? I thought you hated that nickname." I fidgeted in bed and suddenly felt very uncomfortable.

"Well." I stammered like a schoolgirl, very unbecoming for someone of my age. "You, you don't have to call me that I'm just reclaiming that nickname is all and-."

"Okay, okay." Sam laughed and then became more thoughtful leaning in closer until our faces were inches apart.

"Lizzy." He whispered like it was a sacred prayer and with that he claimed my lips. It took me by surprise, but I responded in kind, enjoying the feel of his lips on mine. The kiss started off sweet and innocent, almost probing and testing my reaction. When I didn't pull away but in turn leaned in for more the intensity of the kiss increased his hand finding its way into my hair pulling me even closer and deepening the kiss more to my delight. Not to be overpowered I put my left hand on the base of his neck pulling him even closer. I could feel his smirk against my lips as he continued his assault. I reached for him to bring him even closer when he pulled back slightly and hissed.

"Oh, I'm so sorry!" I exclaimed, bringing my hand to my mouth in surprise realizing I had pressed on his bullet wound. As my hands rested there, I felt my lips swollen from his administration and blushed giddily. When was the last time I had felt giddy?

"Don't ever apologize." He said jovially, taking my now downward chin upwards to face him. "Especially for *that*."

I laughed, and we both leaned in for another round when a nurse came bounding into our room.

"Oh, excuse me!" She exclaimed, forcing her eyes shut like she had caught us doing something far worse than we had. "I, um, need to take Dr. Waller's vitals and check on her stitches so I'm afraid you'll have to leave sir."

Sam leaned back and begrudgingly stood up. "I'll leave you to it." He addressed the nurse as he walked past who was a nice blushing shade of rose at this point. "I'll see you later, Lizzy."

"I'll see you later, Sam," I smirked as he left the room.

As the nurse began her ministrations I drifted off into thought. When I found out weeks ago that Alex was still alive I felt like my world was caving in. That I was slowly beginning to suffocate under the weight of the realization. When I had seen him for the first time in years his pull and the yearning to be with him was staggering and filled me with guilt. But today was different. When Sam had said his body couldn't be located I was concerned but a concern lacking dread or foreboding. It was more akin to a feeling of resolution. After my last encounter with him, and for the first time seeing him for who he really was, I found I didn't feel drawn to him, to please him, or to impress him. I didn't feel like I *needed* him anymore. The only person I realized I needed was myself. That was enough. *I* was enough.

I also learned a valuable lesson that not all people let you down. Nina was a little much, but she was intelligent and eager to learn. Benny and Dominic, polar opposites of each other, were both dependable and were a great addition to any team and didn't even blink when they learned who I really was and accepted me without question. And then there was Sam. He was a surprise I wasn't

236

expecting to find again in my lifetime. Most of the time I wanted to strangle him but even that part of him I was finding to be endearing.

The nurse finished, scurrying out of the room, still more embarrassed than I was, and I went on to jot down my outline for the report I would be giving when I got back to the office because I knew it was going to be a doozy.

CHAPTER 28

I sat in my office at the FBI Field Office, a tower of paperwork covering my desk.

I growled glancing up as an Agent apologetically placed another stack of documents on the only corner of the desk that wasn't covered and ran away most likely afraid of my wrath.

Apparently, when an entire warehouse catches on fire during one of your operations it comes with a lot of paperwork not to mention a lot of phone calls from city officials that included some creative cursing. The good news was, that due to the nature of what was being stored there and a criminal who was thought to be dead returning from the grave, the whole operation was kept hush hush and the media circus never showed up. The chaos that had overwhelmed the field office during Alex's reign of terror had dissipated and was no longer whispered in the hallways business as usual continuing on.

The only outward signs that it had occurred were the sling my doctor was forcing me to wear and the avalanche of paper I was now buried under. There was something that was glaringly different between then and now that was perhaps putting me in a foul mood. Elizabeth wasn't around. After getting discharged from the hospital my father skillfully guilted her into taking some time off after her ordeal which she of course fought and miserably lost. We had talked a bit on the phone or by text but not having her in the office felt wrong.

Nina was her cheerful self, but you could see her look over at Elizabeth's empty desk every once in a while and hunch her normally well maintained posture. Even Dominic who was normally pretty stoic seemed irritated. Her impact on the office was larger than I think she knew, not that I was going to admit to that. In a few months, her time here would be over, the women she was covering for would be returning from maternity leave and she would no longer have a reason to be here. Now that Alex was theoretically a nonissue, she could do whatever it was that she wanted.

With the information we found at the warehouse where Elizabeth was being held, we had enough to track Alex's buyers and take down an entire arms dealing ring. There were even talks of medals. Even though she was supposed to be taking a break with her newfound lease on life, I knew the CDC kept pestering her about the bioweapon we confiscated and her work on it. I was pretty sure they would be offering her a position there any time now. Well, if they were smart they would anyway. She was clearly an asset to this office and I wouldn't mind it if she stuck around. Again, not that I would be telling this to her face.

Suddenly, a streak of pink and sparkles shot down the hallway screaming "Elizabeth's back!" I walked down the hall to see Elizabeth smiling surrounded by coworkers engaging in small talk. The pink and sparkle comet that I could now identify as Nina practically bounded on her heels as she fought to stand the closest to Elizabeth.

"Look! I brought donuts!" I heard Elizabeth shout over the ruckus thrusting two boxes of donuts into the mass, them being swept up by the mob as it slowly dissipated as they followed the donuts like lemmings to the breakroom, a look of relief washing over her face.

"Can I hug you now!" Nina cried now bouncing from foot to foot in anticipation.

"Yes, you may." Elizabeth laughed as Nina squeezed the living daylights out of her causing her some visible discomfort.

"Easy Nina or you'll put her back into the hospital," I remarked, and Nina eased up still clinging to her beloved mentor.

Elizabeth turned and smiled seeing that I was there for the first time.

"Hello, Sam." She said in what outwardly might have seemed a professional tone, but I could read the subtext.

"Hello Lizzy," I replied in turn leaning on the wall of the hallway.

"Oh, you guys are using nicknames now?" Nina asked, suggestively still attached to Elizabeth.

"Yes. And that's enough, kindly let it go please." Elizabeth remarked in a rebuking yet kind tone that indicated she wasn't really upset.

"Fine," Nina said, pouting, extracting herself from Elizabeth's side. "Also, the TC20 automated cell counter seemed like it needed to be recalibrated, so I sent it out for maintenance and I've been using a hemocytometer instead. I'm so glad you're back!" She squealed before giving Elizabeth a final squeeze and running off back in the direction of the lab.

"Well, that was quite a welcome," Elizabeth remarked, smoothing out her outfit.

"That it was. Welcome back Dr. Waller, or should I call you Dr. Mallory now?" I remarked walking closer to her.

"I'm keeping Waller. Seems more fitting for the new me. Moving forward with my life and all."

"So-" she continued dodging me as I got close enough to her and began to walk down the hall. "I got a call from the woman whose maternity leave I'm covering. Apparently, besides having a baby she was searching for jobs closer to her home on her leave, just to see what was out there, and her dream job popped up. She applied, and she got the job."

"Oh?" I asked and watched her face twist into a smile "I guess it looks like I'm out a forensic scientist."

240

"It looks that way." She said coyly. "I was wondering if you were accepting applications?"

I stopped in the hallway grabbing her hand to keep her from continuing to walk down the hallway.

"Elizabeth, are you being serious right now?"

"So, we're back to Elizabeth." She laughed. I glared.

"I mean, is this what you want? What about the CDC or traveling as a consultant." I could feel her squeeze my hand.

"The CDC did make me an offer, and a very generous one at that, and I said I would be able to consult on a case-by-case basis, but I turned the full-time position down. And for traveling," her face got serious as she continued, "it felt like more of me running away from my past and I'm not doing that anymore."

"But are you sure-" she cut me off by putting a finger to my lips to get me to stop.

"Like you said. I'm stubborn. You can't make me do anything I don't want to do." She smiled, removing her finger from my lips and my hands from hers. "And now if you excuse me. I have a lab to run." With that, she sauntered down the hallway out of sight. That woman was going to be the death of me, but honestly, there were far worse ways to go.

***

Back at home, I settled in for the night with a steaming cup of tea wafting a calming aroma throughout the living room, and scrolled through my streaming service for a movie to watch. I landed on Die Hard as it seemed appropriate after these last weeks.

241

"Well," I said to myself looking at the fort of boxes that had formed around the room "it looks like I'm going to actually have to unpack this time."

That, however, was a chore for another day. I smiled to myself thinking about my conversation with Sam earlier in the day. I was honestly a little bit scared of how he would react to me wanting to stay around. I knew he had a reputation for playing the field and I thought it might be the same with me but when I saw in his eyes the excitement he had at the prospect of my staying I was relieved. I was going to stay regardless of what his opinion was, but it was nice to know he still wanted me around. The idea of putting down roots actually sounded appealing to me after jumping from place to place. Knowing that when I unpacked those boxes it would potentially be a long time until I would have to pack them up again was like letting go of a breath I didn't realize I was holding. I had already talked to the Apartment Rental Agency and they were happy to extend the lease meaning I didn't have to relocate.

I told Nina that I was staying, which in hindsight was a mistake in that I should have brought earplugs. She screamed so loud I thought she was going to shatter the glass that had just been replaced in the labs. I found I enjoyed mentoring her and that I wanted to see her prosper and knowing that I could be a part of that would be rewarding.

I stared at the tea which still swirled with honey streaking through the dark liquid and my thoughts drifted to Alex. Even though they didn't instill in me anymore the anxiety I used to feel, I still found that even though he had been banished to the recesses of my mind he still found a way to float back in now and again. Even though the official reports claimed he was deceased, I had a nagging suspicion in the back of my mind it wasn't true. Whether I liked it or not we shared a bond I didn't know how to break. Instead of a bungee cord wrapped around my heart which would cause me to be pulled toward him at neck-breaking speeds whenever he tugged on it, now it was more like a loosely tied string which if pulled on would only send the slightest brush.

If Alex was alive, I would be ready, but I resolved not to live every day looking behind me but instead in front of me. I smiled, finishing up the tea and getting ready for bed. Tomorrow would be my first *official* start date as the permanent Forensic Scientist at the Field Office and I had a lot of work to do moving headfirst into uncharted territories and a certain Special Agent and group of friends and colleagues to look forward to.

I drifted off into a peaceful sleep, not hearing the email notification ding on my phone or the screen glow a fluorescent white in the darkness like a harbinger that would turn my newfound life upside down.

Made in the USA
Coppell, TX
21 November 2024

40697108R00138